A FINAL PAIGE

L. ROSE

CHAPTER ONE
PAIGE

"Again," Nate bellowed down at me.

I groaned and rolled to my stomach. Slowly, I clambered to my feet and bared my teeth at him. "You yell at me one more time, I'm going to take your balls from your body."

He snorted, but before he could open his mouth, Thorn said, "I rather like his balls. Maybe take some toes instead, sweetheart."

I shot Thorn the finger, and he chuckled. Until Alex used his power and put him in a bubble. When Thorn started floating up to the roof, his eyes widened. He stumbled around like a fish out of water, cursing up a storm. He pounded at the outer layer, but we all knew nothing would penetrate it. We'd all tried.

My anger disappeared, and I started laughing. But then my feet were knocked out from under me, and I landed with a thump on my back on the floor. Asher stood over me with his hands on his hips.

"Being distracted could get you killed."

"I know," I clipped.

"It could also get someone you love killed," Nate called. I twisted my head to see him standing behind Ezra with his hand around his throat. I knew he wouldn't harm Ezra but seeing it had me screaming at myself under my breath. They'd been teaching me how to protect myself for the last two weeks, and we'd now moved on to trying to show me how to work within a team. To make sure I not only had myself covered but those who would fight alongside me. I thought I'd made progress, but it was obvious I still had a lot of work to do. My body chilled in worry. I fisted my hands and pressed them against my churning stomach. I wouldn't be ready in time.

We were leaving in two weeks.

Two weeks.

It wasn't enough time.

A sense of failure and worry spread through my veins instead of blood. I didn't want to be the weak link. I had to get better.

Slapping the floor as I stood, I ignored Asher's hand he'd held out to help me.

"Love—" he started, but I shook my head.

I ran a hand over my sweaty face. "Don't give me sweet, encouraging words. I don't want them right now."

He nodded. "All right." He dodged left. I slid right and gripped his arm to take him to the ground, but he was too fast. He easily slipped out of my hold and wound his arm around my throat, pressing his front to my back. I grabbed his hand and bent, flipping him over my body. He landed in a crouch, stood, and turned. His movements were a mere blur with every punch and kick as he drove me backward. I deflected each one.

Out of the corner of my eye, I saw Nate approaching Alex, who still held Thorn in a bubble. I ducked under Asher's punch, unsheathed my blade at my ankle, and threw it across the room; it landed just before Nate's toes.

His gaze hit me, but Alex had also noticed Nate now.

Asher tripped me. I fell on my back, rolled, and jumped up.

He stopped and smiled at me. "Better."

It was a good thing I didn't breathe, or I would have been out of breath. Still, my heart was beating so hard in my chest I was surprised it didn't fall out.

It was wonderful to hear his praise, but it wasn't enough yet. Soon we would be walking into the fae territory, and even though we'd asked for permission and it had been given, I didn't like not knowing what would happen. Actually, all of the meetings we'd set up had been agreed upon since they were all willing to meet with the new ghoul queen. Of course they would want to know if I would be a threat to them and theirs. They'd learn I wouldn't be, unless something happened to someone I claimed as mine.

I'd read up on fae between training, yet the information was limited. And those who had been around the fae told me never to trust them. They were conniving, tricky creatures. They could fly, glamour, and talk their way into your home and bed. I'd heard they were the most stunning creatures in existence, and yes, I'd seen pictures in the books I'd studied. Yet, all I could think was that I saw more beauty in my bonded mates.

I wasn't holding out hope in their help. The fae kept to themselves a lot. For all I knew, the new king, who was the son of the former one, wouldn't care what was going on outside of his kingdom. I had asked why we were even going to see them, but Asher assured me they would be an advantage to have on our side. The council were the ones behind the former king's death. Alex was certain the facts my men already had to show the fae, as well as what they could tell us about that night, would be enough for them to not trust the council and hopefully stand with us. Or if not, then to stay out of the fight when it was time for us to go to them.

Only time would tell.

After the fae kingdom, we were moving on to the two missing alphas. The first was from a lion pride consisting of at least five hundred members. The other was a tiger in charge of his streak. Nate had informed me one night while studying that tigers usually didn't group together—they tended to be solitary creatures—but the alpha that had gone missing had been looked up to by many of his kind, which was how he became their leader.

Their groups had also given us permission to enter their territory. However, I had a feeling it could have something to do with wanting to take a good look at the ghoul queen they'd never heard of. Even the fae would want the same, to discover my power and determine if I would be a threat or not.

We had to be careful with how we did things, though, or it could bring us more trouble than just the council.

Lastly, and it was thanks to the woman who'd saved my Asher, we were allowed entry into the deceased master's clan lands to visit the vampires since she'd now taken over as their master. I wasn't looking forward to seeing Cynthia. The interaction Asher had with her concerned me as I could likely kill her if she tried anything. However, Asher told me everything would be fine and Cynthia would listen to what we had to say. It was also likely she'd help us—another thing Asher was sure of. His confidence in her had me wanting to punch her in the face in a fit of jealousy, which was something my men found amusing when they felt and saw how pissed I became every time Asher spoke of her.

Still, I pushed all of that down to worry about when the time came and, instead, got into a fighting stance. I curled my fingers at Asher and said, "Come at me."

He smirked and then disappeared.

Only that time I brought my powers forward. It helped me see his movement better. Just as he stopped behind me, I twisted, grabbed, and dropped him to his back on the floor. Though, I was sure he allowed it because when I straddled his waist, his hands slowly slid up my thighs. The movement paused, and he rolled me to my back, got to his feet, and crouched in front of me. Nate's growl was pointed at the door, so was Ezra's in his shifted form, and as Thorn's feet touched the floor, he withdrew his sword. Alex, with his delicious power, aimed his glowing-white hands at the door.

It was then I heard it—the heavy footfalls of maybe three people. Quickly, I stood just as the doors to the gym burst open and in them stood a puffing Leon and two of his brothers.

"What's wrong?" I demanded, taking a step forward, until Asher's arm swung out to hold me back.

"Yasmin." My sister's name from his lips had my heart taking off in flight and angst twisting my stomach. He went on. "She was outside with Sophie and two of our brothers. They…." He shook his head.

Jake, Leon's younger brother, continued with "We

didn't know the real Sophie was actually inside, since the fake scented the same as the real one. We were all fooled."

Fear grabbed at me. "Then who was Yasmin walking with? Is my sister okay? What happened?"

"We don't know who the imposter was, but the fake Sophie attacked them."

"Where's Yasmin?" I yelled.

Leon's frown said enough, even before he admitted, "We don't know. We have every shifter out searching for her."

I shoved Asher's hand from me and raced from the room. My men followed, as did Leon and his brothers. The guards who'd been outside the gym joined us as well.

"Does Eric know?" Thorn asked.

Leon shook his head. "We kept it quiet. Until...."

"Until we knew more," Jake finished.

"We're sorry we failed you, my queen." Leon's lips thinned. He hated himself, but I couldn't allow it when they would have done everything they could have.

"Your brothers who were with Yasmin?" I asked.

Sorrow crossed his features before he steeled his expression into a blank one. "One didn't make it. The other is with a healer."

We made it outside. Jake pointed at the entryway that led out toward the town behind my castle. I kept moving. "Whoever has done this will pay in flesh and blood," I told him, even knowing it wasn't going to be enough.

Yasmin.

She could be next.

She could die.

I shook my head. I couldn't let that thought settle.

"Thank you, my queen," he said softly.

"Asher?" I called.

He veered left. "Blood, off into the woods."

"That's where our kin were found."

"How do you know Yasmin and Sophie were out here with your brothers in the first place?" I asked, pulling to a stop behind Asher. He lifted his nose and sniffed the area.

"We keep each other informed of all movements. Plus, we questioned a shop owner who they passed. She saw Yasmin and who she thought was young Sophie walk from the castle together with our brothers not far behind. She said she overheard Sophie saying she wanted to show her mom something."

A trick. Yasmin would follow Sophie anywhere, just like most of us. Only we would have sensed the power used to alter the appearance of whoever was behind this. Though perhaps not since two bear shifters, who had good senses, hadn't. I clenched my jaw and glanced around. Two pools of blood marred the leaves, dirt, and grass. Leon's brothers. My heart ached for them.

Nate and Ezra, who had both shifted at some point, took a few bounds forward and growled. They glanced back, then forward, and took off running. We quickly followed. I hadn't even considered how people would react seeing Ezra back as we'd run through the township and even the castle. He hadn't shifted around anyone but us, and in training only. All they knew

was that he was a part of Lucifer's entourage. Lucifer had since left with Virginia and their people, but were coming back when we traveled. It was something to worry about later.

My throat closed as we entered a clearing and I saw Yasmin being held with a knife to her neck by a woman I didn't know.

The woman smiled. "Finally, it took them plenty of time to let you know."

"Who are you and what do you want?" Asher asked.

Nate and Ezra pawed at the ground, snarling from where they stood just in front of me.

"If anyone moves, I will slice her open."

"Answer my mate's questions."

"My queen," a guard called. I glanced to the side as he stepped forward. "Her name is Tenaya. She is Grace's daughter."

Fuck.

Fuckety fuck.

Yasmin stared at me with tears in her eyes. Her lips trembled as she smiled sadly at me. She knew this could be it for her. I shook my head slightly, telling her there was still hope. I had my men, the guards. We could kill this bitch without harming my sister.

Dread filled me to the brim. Even with the strength, the magic around me, they were still a distance away. If Tenaya saw Alex disappear, she would kill Yasmin with a quick swipe.

Please, please do not take my sister away from me, from her family. Please.

Another guard moved close. "She is also the one in battle who took her own life."

Tenaya laughed. "Yes, it was so easy to fool you all with all the blood around. So easy to cover the beating of my heart with a spell."

"What do you want?" I pressed. There had to be something she wanted or... no, no, no. It couldn't just be for revenge. I hadn't even remembered her besides when she pretended to take her own life. I'd been so far away, I didn't recognize her. Now closer, I saw the resemblance to Grace.

Her smile was pure evil. "I see the panic in your eyes. You know why we're here."

"Please don't kill her."

"Then you shouldn't have killed my mother."

"She murdered people for power, sent my mates to Hell, conspired with demons," I called. "Yasmin is an innocent human being."

Her grip tightened on my sister, and Yasmin whimpered. I fisted my hands. I wanted to tear into the woman. Rip, bite, and kill.

Instead, I locked my body down. Tears welled in my eyes. "Please, please don't kill her. She has a husband, children."

Tenaya smiled again. "Oh, I know."

"Why?" I asked on a whisper.

"Because you took my mother," she answered simply.

My eyes connected to Yasmin's. She mouthed, "I love you. Take care of them."

My body shuddered in anguish. "I'll do anything."

"I'm not stupid. We make a bargain, and you'll all kill me in the end—do not move," she yelled. The guards stopped. "All I want is to see your pain, and I have." Quickly, she removed the knife from Yasmin's neck. We all rushed forward. A scream tore out of me when she plunged the knife into Yasmin's chest. Into her heart.

I stumbled. Asher grabbed me. Alex appeared out of nowhere and caught Yasmin as her body sagged. Tenaya stepped back, still grinning, only her eyes widened when Ezra leaped. His mouth surrounded her neck and face. I heard a snap just as Nate joined Ezra, and they shredded her to pieces.

Dropping to my knees beside Alex cradling Yasmin, I reached out and gripped her hand in both of mine. Her hand was loose, no strength evident. A sob caught in my throat. Yasmin gazed up at me as her breath stuttered. Blood spurted from her mouth.

"You t-take care of them," she wheezed.

"No, you'll be here to do it." I shook my head again and again.

"I love you so much…. Not your fault."

I dug my top teeth into my bottom lip. "I love you, but this isn't goodbye. It can't be." Her lips pulled up before she went lax against Alex. "Yasmin," I yelled. "Please, please, Yasmin."

Hands dropped to my shoulders. "She's passed out, love. Just passed out."

I lifted my gaze and looked at Alex and Thorn. When Nate pressed himself between them, I met his gaze. Finally, I glanced at Asher. "Get Eric," I ordered.

"Sweetheart, are you sure—"

"Get Eric, now!" I bellowed. Asher disappeared, and the warm breeze blew over us.

I wouldn't—couldn't lose my sister… but if Eric didn't agree, then I would have to say goodbye, and that thought had me trembling in fear.

Ezra, still in his hellhound form, moved to my side. I

ignored the blood around his mouth and curled an arm over his neck, pulling him close. Thorn went to his knee on my other side, Nate trotted around to my back and pressed in, while Alex laid his hand over mine still clutching Yasmin's.

I wasn't sure their support and comfort would be enough for what was to come, but I appreciated it all the same. They would be the only reason I got through this.

CHAPTER TWO
EZRA

Her pain slipped through her walls and had me shifting back to my human form beside her, needing to comfort and protect her. Her arm stayed around me, and I wrapped mine around her waist. When I shifted, thankfully my clothes stayed on; my father had told me it was something to do with the magic within me. I was just glad as Paige hated if anyone saw any of her mates naked. Just like we would be if another saw her bare.

My heart ached for Paige, but also Yasmin. To see her so still with a dagger sticking out of her chest, it was so fucking terrifying. She was a good sister to my mate, a great mother, and from what I'd seen, wife. She didn't deserve this.

If she died.... I couldn't even consider it, as it would mean Paige would lose a part of herself—like she had when I'd died in my hellhound form, from what I'd been told. I hated... fuck no, despised that I'd put her through that anguish. If I could have gotten back to her, I would have in a heartbeat.

Paige trembled against me. Tears ran down her cheeks, but she ground her teeth together in the hope of holding them back.

The air around us blew harder as Asher stopped at our

side. He carefully took Eric off his shoulder and set him on his feet.

"What's going on?" Eric demanded.

With a clenched jaw, Asher placed his hands on Eric's shoulders and turned him our way. He paled, and a mournful cry fell from his lips as he dropped to the ground and crawled to Paige's other side.

"Yasmin," he choked. His hands fluttered out before pulling back again.

"It's okay to touch her," Alex reassured. "I have her body frozen in place so... nothing moves." He gulped, unsure if he said the right thing, but a reassuring and wobbly small smile from Paige had Alex relaxing a little. One of Eric's hands brushed his wife's hair away from her forehead while he used the other to gently press two fingers against her neck. Over her weak pulse. The pulse that we could all hear slowing even more.

"Eric," Paige started, her voice shaking, "you have to listen to me."

"Yasmin," he whispered, leaning into her, putting his face next to her. "Baby, you can't leave me. You can't leave the kids."

"Eric," Paige tried again.

"Honey, we need you." He laughed humorlessly. "I can't survive without you." He made a pained noise in the back of his throat, then shook his head. "We can get through this. We can." He straightened to his knees as his tears dropped freely. "Tell me she can get through this. Then fucking tell me who did this so I can kill them."

For some insane reason, I wanted to yell, "She has a fucking knife sticking out of her heart, how do you think she'll get through this?" Yet I clamped my lips closed because I knew, along with all of Paige's men, that our mate would have a plan, and by the way she looked up at Asher, I knew exactly what it was.

With Asher's slight nod, Paige moved her gaze back to Eric. "There is only one way."

Eric nodded. "Becoming something more?"

"Yes," Paige whispered.

"What?" he demanded. "A shifter? A Ghoul? A vampire?" He laughed humorlessly. "I've been living here and it's still crazy." He looked back down to Yasmin, his bottom lip trembling. "But I would do anything to have her with me."

"You know everything will change?" Thorn questioned.

"I know."

"Your children—"

He shook his head. "Will want their mom in their life. No matter what she is."

"Yasmin?" Paige whispered.

His watery gaze fell on hers. He reached out and took Paige's hand that rested gently against Yasmin's shoulder. "Will never regret the choice we make for her because she'll want more days with her children."

Paige glanced down at her sister and took a shuddering breath. "She wouldn't want to die," Paige said, more to herself than anyone.

"No, she wouldn't," Eric stated. He sniffed, wiped at his face, and straightened even more. "So, what shall she become?"

"Eric, has she ever said anything to you about what she

would prefer?" Asher asked.

Eric nodded. "Yes."

"A vampire," Paige uttered.

Eric looked at her. "How did you...?" He shook his head. "Never mind. You two know everything about each other, even if you haven't spoken of it. Yes, a vampire."

Jealousy hit me, only it wasn't mine. It was Paige's, yet it was quickly replaced by guilt.

"It doesn't have to be me, love," Asher said softly.

She shook her head. "It does. You're the only one I trust to do this, to help her through this, to guide her properly. I... just... I hate to say it, but I won't be able to be around when you do it."

Understanding dawned through me. She'd already thought of Asher siring Yasmin. She wasn't comfortable, but like the amazing woman she was, she'd put herself, her needs aside for others she cared for.

Tightening my hold around Paige, I said, "Alex, take Yasmin to your room with Asher and Eric. Nate, go to the children and reassure them things are fine. Paige, you'll be with me and Thorn."

Paige nodded. She looked at Eric. "She'll be okay."

"She will be. We can't lose her."

"No, we can't."

"I will do everything in my power to make sure your sister lives, my love," Asher reassured, bending to kiss the top of Paige's head. She tilted back, waiting. Asher pressed his lips against hers.

"I know you will. I love you." She was so free with showing her feelings, it was beautiful. The night I watched her dig her way free from the ground was when I knew she would be my mate. I'd cursed everything I could that I wasn't allowed to show her my true form. I'd been spelled to stay as my hellhound for at least a year as punishment for disobeying my parents. Yet it had also been a blessing as I'd been by her side from the beginning, to teach her, get to know her, and love her deeply.

"As I love you."

Not only could I feel her anguish, her guilt, her love, but I could see it in her tense body, her drawn brows, and in her eyes. I curled her in tighter against me and kissed her temple. Asher's hand landed on my shoulder and gave it a squeeze.

"Take care of our mate," he said.

"With my life," I answered.

"Always," Thorn added.

In a blink, Alex disappeared with Yasmin and Eric. The breeze picked up, and Asher swept away to meet them. Paige drew in a shuddering breath, even when she didn't have to breathe. Nate, still in his wolf form, stood and licked Paige's face.

She nodded. "I know she'll be fine. She's in good hands." Her lips thinned before she whispered again, "She'll be fine."

Nate's body contorted with the change. It was smooth and fast, but painful. Still, the man didn't show that it affected him. His expression stayed neutral. Then he was kneeling beside Paige, pulling her into him.

"You're naked," Paige muttered.

Thorn and I snorted. Fear bombarded her, yet she still managed to care that someone would see her mate naked.

Nate let out a huff. "No one is around. How about you

stop panicking and worrying, which gets you nowhere, and go to the training area to kick Ezra and Thorn's asses?"

I winced. It was harsh, but Nate worked Paige in a way that got her annoyed or pissed enough to be distracted. It was what she needed.

"You're a dick," she mumbled with a sniff.

"Yes."

"At least you're my dick."

He kissed her neck. "That I am."

"Fight or fuck?" Nate asked her. My dick jerked behind my jeans.

Her eyes narrowed on what was left of the witch. "Fight."

I stood and held out my hand. "Then we'll battle." It would be good for all of us. The witch had died too soon, too easily, and I needed to get rid of some of the burning adrenaline inside me. I bounced on the balls of my feet as Paige took my hand, and I pulled her up. Thorn got close while Nate also stood.

"I'll go to the kids," Nate said. He leaned down, pressed his lips to Paige's swiftly, then up to Thorn's. He hesitated when his gaze met mine. I puckered my lips and made kissy faces at him. It was good to see Paige smile, even if it disappeared a second later and her eyes drifted off toward the castle.

While I was distracted by Paige, Nate moved in front of me. With one hand he pinched my cheeks so my lips stayed puckered and kissed me hard and fast. My wide gaze caught his shining wolf one. "You're the only one not claimed. That'll change."

I mumbled through my squeezed cheeks until he released them. "Beast to beast, I'd like to see who wins."

His eyes flashed. His teeth lengthened and a snout appeared. "I'll bend you to my will, hellhound," he growled roughly, his wolf riding his voice.

I rolled my eyes. He snapped his teeth in my face before he called forth the rest of his shift, his body twisting and snapping. Nate landed on all fours in his wolf form and strutted to Paige, pushing his head under her hand. Her eyes shot down to him, and she smiled softly, curling her fingers into his hair. Nate bumped his body into hers before he took off on a run, straight back to the castle, not only to reassure the kids—Paige's niece and nephew—but to be there for them.

Thorn stepped up behind Paige, and just as his hands landed on her waist, a form appeared out of nowhere. It was lucky Thorn and I had fast reflexes, or Alex would have been dead. Thorn stopped short from throwing a dagger at him, and I pulled back on my punch at the last second.

"What's wrong?" Paige demanded, fear evident in her high-pitched tone. She grabbed for Alex, taking his arm. "Shouldn't you be with Yasmin?"

"My powers still hold her suspended." He reassured her and looked at us. "I'm taking Paige to my room, both of you meet us there," Alex stated. He curled his free arm around Paige's waist, and with a bright flash of white light, they disappeared.

Thorn and I shared a look before racing toward Alex's room.

We arrived and turned a corner to find Paige in the face

of a woman I'd never seen before. I chanced a glance at Thorn, and he said softly, "Sakura, vampire."

Guards stood behind the other woman and glared down at her, while Asher and Alex stood at Paige's back. Eric must have been in the bedroom with his wife.

"Please, please, majesty, allow me to be the one," the woman begged, her eyes down to the floor.

"For the last time, I don't know you, and you expect me to trust you? I've never seen you around. How can I trust you have good intentions?"

"What are you asking of our queen, Sakura?" Thorn questioned.

Only it was Asher who spoke. "She wants to be the one to change Yasmin. I heard her approaching and warned Alex. We both came out here before she could barge in. The guards showed soon after she arrived."

"Why do you want this?" I questioned harshly, wanting an answer she'd yet to give Paige. Yasmin was family as far as I was concerned. We had to be cautious of everyone who tried to be a part of our close-knit connection. I didn't know this vampire, and it seemed neither did Asher or Alex. I glanced at Thorn.

He caught my gaze and said to all, "Sakura is a part of our elite force. She has been one who guards your sister and her family on and off." Thorn looked to Alex's bedroom. "Is Eric able to hear?"

Alex shook his head. "No, the room is soundproof."

"We can't leave my sister suspended much longer without risk." Paige then mumbled to herself, "There's always risk." She lifted her eyes to Asher. "We need to finish this. Can you please—"

"No, he can't. You don't understand the connection," Sakura cried, then snapped her lips together. She went to grab Paige. I snatched her suspended hand and spun her, so I had her back to my chest and locked my arms around her tightly.

"Never touch the queen," I snarled.

Sakura shook in my arms. She stank of fear and determination. "Please, please, let me speak."

Paige's brows dipped as she glared down at my hands. "Ezra." I dropped my arms but stayed where I was. Paige nodded and then said to the vampire, "I know I don't know the connection between a fledgling and their master, but Asher does, and he hasn't advised against it. I trust him and his knowledge that it wouldn't be bad by siring my sister."

Sakura shook her head. "Your bonded male would make an excellent sire; I have no doubt. I know their connection would never come between a bonded pair or group. Bonds are stronger than anything, even a master's hold," she said softly, then dipped her head, eyes back to the floor. "However, Yasmin and I have grown... close. I believe she would prefer if it was I who changed her."

Paige's eyes grew wide. "Close? Ah... as in... you mean you're a friend of my sister's?"

"Yes."

"Oh, right," Paige said, laughing a little. I could sense from her how she'd jumped to another conclusion and then thought she'd been silly for it.

"And something else," Sakura confessed even quieter.

"Leave us," Asher ordered roughly. The guards filed down the hallway.

Paige's anger twisted through me; she had her hands fisted at her sides. "Do you mean you've come between Yasmin and Eric?" I now understood her anger. When I'd first been with Paige and stuck in my hellhound form, she often spoke about how special Yasmin and Eric's relationship was. She would hate anything or anyone that had come between her sister's marriage. Our Paige wished many times to have had a connection like theirs with a man.

Now she had it with us all. It honored me to be a part of it, to have her love and be free to give it back.

"No," Sakura said quickly. "It... no, it wasn't like that. It... I do not wish to explain when you should hear this from someone in your family."

Paige turned her head to capture Alex's gaze. "Get Eric out here." She then stared back at Sakura, who still looked to the floor as Alex disappeared into the room.

Paige's anger still simmered. I moved from behind Sakura, knowing Thorn would grab her if she tried anything—though I couldn't imagine her attacking—and moved to Paige's back. I ran my hands from her shoulders, down her back, and stopped at her waist. She leaned into me, sighing, letting the anger lessen enough that it didn't cloud her mind.

My body hummed in contentment and amazement every time I touched her and she accepted it without a thought. I was really hers, connected for eternity. It made me fucking ecstatic, like a child learning something new and thrilling for the first time.

The door opened to Eric demanding, "What's going on? Why are we not helping my wife?" He saw Sakura.

His eyes widened in surprise then welled. "Sakura," he whispered.

The vampire sniffed and dashed for Eric; their arms wrapped around each other in a tight embrace. In a second, I had Paige turned away from them as she screamed and tried to move in my arms to get to them.

"You cheating, motherfucking, stinking asshole. I will *kill you*. Kill you, bring you back, and kill you again," she roared.

"Paige," Eric yelled as he pushed Sakura behind him. Over my shoulder, I caught him stepping closer to Paige until Alex grabbed him by the shoulder, shaking his head.

Eric sighed. "Paige, I would never cheat on my wife, on your sister. She's the love of my life. You know this."

"Take a moment, *mi corazón*," I whispered into her ear, then kissed her neck. "Let's listen to them, and then if we don't like it, I'll help to gut him like a pig."

She drew in an unnecessary breath, shook out her hands, and then straightened. When she nodded, I dropped my hands and moved to her side as she turned to face Eric.

"Explain," she ordered.

He swiped a hand over his face. "Okay, all right. It's not what you think. Well, it is—" Paige made a grab for him. Asher and I held her back when Eric yelled, "*But*, there's a but...." Paige settled. "Jesus, you should know to trust me, Paige."

"I'll trust you when I know why you were hanging off a woman I don't even know like she is... is... something to you."

"To us. To me and your sister. She's something to us."

Paige's head jerked back. She shrugged off our hold and threw a hand out. "Explain that."

Eric threw his own hands up in the air. "Explain you, explain this place, the people, the connection you have with five men. I don't know how anything works, but since spending time with Sakura, Yasmin and I have both... I don't know, grown to like her... a lot."

"You *and* Yasmin?"

"Yes! I wouldn't cheat on my wife."

"Sakura?"

She nodded and lifted her head, her eyes meeting Paige's. "I believe they are my bonded."

Eric's head whipped around. "Wait, what?"

"Say what?" Paige said.

Eric stepped up to Sakura and took her hands. Paige grumbled behind her thinned lips. Eric ignored her. "Do you mean like Paige has with her men?"

"Yes," Sakura said softly, glancing away from Eric. "I didn't want to say anything. Your marriage is important to me. I care for you both enough to let this go since the bond hasn't been completed." She blushed. How was this woman a guard?

"She has only light duties with other members of the force," Thorn explained as if reading my thoughts. I nodded. Knowing Thorn, he would have employed Sakura if she had asked or if her family had pushed her into the duty. The ghoul was hard when he had to be, but soft under it all.

"She wants to be the one to change Yasmin," Paige said.

"You do?" Eric asked.

"Yes, but... even if either of you do not want me as a bonded, then I would still like a chance to sire Yasmin, so then when I do leave, I will know within myself that she is well or in need of help."

"You would do that for them? Leave if they don't want you?" Thorn asked.

She didn't look away from Eric's gaze. "I would do anything for both of them."

We all heard Eric swallow thickly. Paige didn't look away from Eric's thumb caressing Sakura's hand.

"Yasmin would want you to sire her," he told her.

"Eric," Paige warned.

He faced Paige. "She would." It was his turn to blush. "You, ah, look, this is awkward as hell, but we've been spending time with Sakura. We know there's something we feel about her that we can't and won't deny. There's a connection. We haven't said anything because it's still new."

Paige studied him—his firm posture, his determined eyes. Still she asked, "Are you sure Yasmin would want this?"

"Yes." His voice held strong. "Sakura should sire Yasmin."

I could feel the war within her. She wasn't sure what to believe since she knew nothing about Sakura. Shock and fear, as well as sadness, rolled around inside her. Thorn and I both reached out to her at the same time. We brought her back against us, and just our touch seemed to help.

"Okay," Paige said quietly. "Save my sister, please."

Sakura's bottom lip trembled, and she bowed her head. "It would be my honor, my queen."

Alex opened the door to the bedroom again. Eric quickly hugged Paige, plus Thorn and me since we were so close. "Thank you." He kissed her cheek, and I growled out a warning. Eric smiled and then went to Sakura, curling his arm around her waist and leading her into the room.

"You've done the right thing, love," Asher said. "I'll keep an eye on everything with Alex."

She smiled softly. "Thank you." She blew Asher and Alex a kiss, to which Alex returned and Asher dipped his head, and they followed Eric in, shutting the door after them.

Leaning down, I kissed Paige's neck. She trembled. "You haven't practiced fighting against my hellhound side in a long time, mi corazón. How about we see how you fair?"

"Sounds like a good distraction. Also, what does mi corazón mean?"

I smiled softly. "It means 'my heart,' which is what you have always been, in Spanish. Would you prefer it in French? *Mon cœur*, or Russian—"

"No," she whispered quickly, almost shyly. I could hear her heart picking up its pace. She liked my name for her, and I loved that she did. "I like it in Spanish, how you said it first."

"That's how it'll be then," I told her. "Now, should we go?" I asked, starting down the hall with her hand in mine and Thorn at her other side. "I'd also like to see how well the ghoul can do."

Thorn laughed. "I'd beat your ass, furry head."

Biting my bottom lip, I smiled and hummed under my breath.

"I could," Thorn stated.

Glancing down at Paige, I rolled my eyes. She started giggling, then smiled her thanks for entertaining her.

"You'll be on the floor in a second, hound."

"Yes, you're right. Only it'll be with my cock buried in you while I dominate your ghoul." Paige's scent shifted; her arousal sang to me. I loved how turned on she got from watching her men in bed together. I had yet to see what they were like. If they were as good as our mate, then I knew I'd be more than satisfied in bed.

Thorn tripped. "Jesus, you sound like Nate. You've been hanging out with him too much, and you're wrong. It'll be you under me while I allow you to taste our mate's pussy."

Paige moaned. "Now all of *that* is a welcome distraction of what's really going on. I'll race you." She grinned, and then her power filled the area before she sped off down the hall.

Of course we followed.

CHAPTER THREE
THORN

Ezra was brilliant at distracting Paige. He was a worthy mate for our queen. He'd managed to bring a smile to our lips and ease the ache in our chests over Yasmin. Though guilt stabbed at me for smiling when Paige's sister's life was on the line. Maybe it had something to do with how positive I was that she would pull through and be all right.

Paige had just entered the room, and I was closing in. I dove and curled my arms around her waist, taking her to the ground but twisting in the air so I would land on my back with Paige sprawled over me. I heard Paige's cry of surprise, Ezra's laugh, and then a snarl.

In a second, I was up with Paige pushed behind me as a flash of something barreled into Ezra, taking him to the floor.

Paige's power burst out of her. She transformed before my eyes as she moved to the figure over Ezra, gripped it in a roar, picked the figure up, and threw it across the room. I stood there gaping like a newbie fool as she glanced down at Ezra, saw blood on his neck, and lost it. She screamed as she advanced on the blur of motion, as if she could track it easily. Paige raced back toward Ezra, reached out, and the blur stopped enough for her to take hold and throw the form across the room again.

"Stop this, Aggie, or I will kill you," Paige demanded

harshly around her mouth full of teeth. Her eyes glowed brighter than I'd seen them. Her body also seemed altered, taller, wider.

Wait, Aggie?

Paige growled as she tracked Aggie's movements. I could only see a faint trace of her as she zigged and zagged all over the place.

Paige leaped, spun, and crashed Aggie's back into the wall, pinning Aggie to the stone by a hand around her throat. Aggie's green vampire eyes shot daggers at Paige before she looked back to Ezra. Still, Aggie snapped her teeth as she kicked and scratched at Paige, trying to tear free to get back to Ezra. Paige took hold of one of Aggie's hands, but the other was still free and marking Paige.

Finally, my mind woke up, and I wanted to kill myself for being so slow, so slack, allowing the queen, but most of all, my mate, to deal with such a threat.

I moved, taking Aggie's other arm and slamming it against the wall. I moved close and yelled, "Aggie, stop."

She didn't. Her gaze didn't move from Ezra. He slowly got to his feet with his hand on his neck. He would heal, but the wound seemed to be taking its damn time.

"Aggie, enough," boomed from across the room, at the other entrance into the fighting area. "Do not move," the familiar voice added. Aggie froze, her arms and legs dropping. She hung against our hold while she kept staring at Ezra like he was her favorite dessert.

"Paige, I'm fine," Ezra tried, but we both knew Paige wouldn't calm, not with Aggie being a threat to her bonded male. She wouldn't stop until it was safe for Ezra, even if Ezra could take care of himself.

Clyde was at our side instantly. He bowed. "I apologize, my queen. She was unguarded for a moment. We thought she was getting stronger at denying her hunger."

"Why isn't she looking away from Ezra?" Paige demanded darkly, pulling Aggie away from the wall by her neck and thrusting her back against it. "I don't want to hurt you, Aggie. Just look away and get out of here."

She didn't remove her stare or move.

Paige's anger intensified. It burned through me and fed my own.

"She bit him, Clyde," Paige snapped.

"What and who is he, my queen? If I know, then I'll understand why his scent called to her. Why she won't look away after one taste. He came with the devil, said to be Lucifer's own son, and goes by Azrael, and yet you call him Ezra. Like you did your hellhound, but he perished."

Tension filled Paige, and I didn't like it. Clyde was a trusted adviser. He'd sworn his allegiance to her. We could trust him, not only because of that, but because I'd seen him with Aggie, who he'd sired, and also Felnick—a fellow guard who was devoted to Aggie before she was sired by Clyde. He'd treated both of them like they were his treasures. He'd proven himself in many ways in my eyes.

"That's because he is all you've just said," I told him. I felt Paige's eyes on me. We'd slipped up; we knew we would, but at least it was only around Clyde. In public, we were supposed to call Ezra by Azrael. "How did you find out he was Lucifer's son? That wasn't knowledge the queen or Lucifer wanted people to know since the devil knows he's not well-liked, and it could bring more danger to not only Ezra but also to our community. As far as we knew, the people only think of him as Azrael, a replaceable lackey to Lucifer." The devil himself helped spread the knowledge that he wouldn't care if anything happened to Azrael. He was only leaving him behind as punishment and to keep an eye on Paige.

"A concubine of Lucifer's slept with a vampire of mine while they were here. When he told me, I made him swear to tell no other, and as far as I know, he hasn't."

"Then why did you question the queen about it when you already knew?"

"I didn't know Azrael and Ezra were one and the same. I also wanted to see if I had the trust back that I give freely."

"You do, to some extent. My men will always come first," Paige said.

"I can understand that. You hold in your hand someone I will put before anyone else. Even others I have sired."

It was lucky Aggie thought highly of and looked up to Paige. It was unfortunate considering the situation we were in, though.

"Does what he is explain why she won't be distracted from Ezra?" I asked.

"Unfortunately, no." He turned to Ezra and bowed in respect. I had to guess it was because he knew Ezra was related to Lucifer. "If you will, could you please remove yourself so my fledgling may calm down, and then we should be able to find out."

"I won't leave—"

"Ezra... fuck, I mean, Azrael, please. I can't hurt her, and I don't want you harmed either. Please."

His jaw clenched, but I knew he would do anything Paige asked. Just like any of us would.

"I'll send some guards and wait back in your room," he answered grudgingly, then stormed from the room.

I waited for Aggie to start up again, but she just watched him go, staying motionless like her master had ordered. Yet I could see the pain in her eyes, in the way she swallowed again and again.

"Aggie," Clyde called. "Look at me."

Slowly, she pulled her gaze away from the door Ezra had exited from and met Clyde's gaze. "Please release her."

"Clyde," I called, unsure.

"She won't move. Release her."

"I won't risk her going for Azrael," Paige said.

"She won't. I swear it, my queen."

Paige grumbled under her breath as she dropped her hands and took a step back. I removed my own hold and moved to Paige's side.

Aggie stumbled forward. Clyde flashed in and caught her. She let out a sob. "I couldn't stop myself. I couldn't."

"It's all right, darling. It's all right," Clyde reassured, running his hand over her hair.

She lifted her head and looked to Paige. Red-tinged tears stained her cheeks. "I'm so sorry, my queen. So sorry. I didn't want to. I didn't mean to, but the hunger took over. It felt like I had just woken new when I caught his scent. It was the most delicious scent I have ever experienced."

"It's okay.... I mean, it's not. I nearly killed you, Aggie. I never want to do that. You're my friend, and I'm sure if I did, Felnick and Clyde would come after me."

Clyde's jaw clenched. I didn't like seeing it because it meant Paige was right. He would come after her no matter her being queen. I could understand the bond between master and fledgling, but this was something more.

"Are you both bonded?"

Aggie's blush said enough.

"What about Felnick?" Paige asked.

"He is with us as well," Clyde replied.

Paige laughed. "It seems we're setting a trend with more than a couple in a bonded match."

Curling an arm around her waist, I tugged her close and kissed her temple. "I wish we could take credit for it; however, there are many bonded groups with more than two people. Yet we are the first here with a mixed-species group."

"Well, at least we have that." She smiled up at me before looking back at Aggie. "I think it's best if you stay in your quarters until we leave and take Azrael since it seems it's only the newly born who are affected by his scent." She glanced at Clyde, who nodded. "It means we'll have to watch Yasmin closely as well or move her to someplace else with guards."

"What's this about Yasmin?" Aggie asked.

Paige blinked quickly, her body tensing. I moved her in front of me to wrap both arms around her and told them what happened.

Aggie reached out a hand, and Paige took it. Then Aggie said, "I'm sorry this is happening and then I added to your stress."

Paige shook her head. "You couldn't help it."

I nodded. "Exactly. We'll need to find out why he's so

enticing to the newly turned, especially since we're going into vampire territory soon."

Paige looked up to me and said, "We'll need to speak with Azrael and his father." She glanced back to Aggie and Clyde.

"We won't say anything of who he is. We promise," Clyde announced.

Paige nodded. "Thank you."

"However," Clyde said, "if you're not careful with his name around everyone, rumors will be spread, and it's bound to come out."

He was right.

So far, we'd been lucky and only kept him around us. We hadn't even announced he was one of Paige's bonded mates. The whole situation was damn awkward.

Paige must have come to the same conclusion because next she said, "You're right. I'll speak with Lucifer and Ezra about it."

"He's your bonded as well, right?" Aggie asked nervously. "Or else you wouldn't have acted like that if he wasn't."

I caught Paige's smile. "Yes."

"People are already speaking of you two. Putting together their own thoughts. You had to know it would be this way with you in the spotlight."

Paige sighed, something she still did often, even when she didn't have to breathe. "Yes. We were stupid to think questions wouldn't be asked or we wouldn't be watched too closely since all we do is research and train. I'd hoped, since we were leaving soon, that we could blame the trip on how close we got."

"Don't worry. We'll think of something," I told her.

"The truth is always best," Aggie said.

Paige studied her, then nodded. "It's because of Lucifer's concern for his son that we've said nothing."

"Come on," I said, tightening my hold on her for a moment. "We'll go and get this sorted."

"I'm sorry again, my queen," Aggie said softly.

"*Paige*, Aggie," she emphasized. "We're friends, even after this."

Aggie's bottom lip trembled. "Thank you."

I opened Paige's bedroom door and shifted back so Paige could enter. I nodded to the men outside before stepping through and closing the door behind me. Paige already had Ezra in her arms fussing over him.

"Are you okay? Does it hurt? Do you need anything?"

Laughing, Ezra grabbed her hands, stopping her from inspecting his neck. "I'm fine. As you can see and feel, it's healed."

She pushed her forehead into his chest and mumbled, "I was so scared." She gripped his tee and lifted her gaze to his. "She had you on the ground, tearing into your neck. I was so damn terrified. I could have lost you again."

His expression softened. "You won't lose me, mi corazón. Spells no longer work on me with the protection from Alex. I would have removed Aggie, but I didn't want to hurt her."

Paige groaned in frustration. "Next time remove her,

even if it harms her. She'll heal just like you had to. You come first, Ezra. You."

He tucked her long blonde hair behind her ear. "Okay, Paige."

I molded myself to her back and saw her glare up at him. "You're just saying that to make me happy and stop harping."

He smirked. "Who, me? I would never."

"I could kick you right now," she told him.

I grinned at him while he chuckled. "You would never," he said before dipping his head and kissing her lips. Like always, as soon as one of us touched her lips, she was lost in the moment. My body tingled as I watched them hold each other close and deepen the kiss. Christ, it was so damn pleasurable to witness them together. Paige's arousal swamped the room and swirled with Ezra's and mine.

I wanted to get lost in the sensation, to take it further. Unfortunately, we had things to do.

"Sweetheart, Ezra," I said gently, kissing the side of Paige's neck and reaching out to touch Ezra's. They pulled apart, both panting. I gave them a thin-lipped smile. "Sorry. You can finish this soon, but for now, we have to figure out why Aggie was drawn to you."

"You're right," Paige said with a touch of annoyance, though understanding lit her words.

A hand landed on my waist. I glanced down to see Ezra's smooth skin touching me. Looking back up, I took in his smile. "We'll get to the bottom of this, and then you'll bottom for me."

A sharp bark of laughter dropped from my mouth. Christ, he was cocky.

"You wish, little doggy." I shoved his shoulder. "Now call your father and see if he knows why a fledgling would be enticed by your scent from miles away."

Ezra winked, then glanced down at Paige. "He's hot when he's bossy."

Paige laughed. "That he is."

If my heart worked, it would be pumping blood to my cheeks. I knew Ezra was a smart-ass, even when he was in his hellhound form when I'd first met him, but to have the man in front of me, this was different. I liked it. Not that I'd let the man know.

It was amazing how the Fates found the perfect mates for Paige. Not only for her but for all of us. We got along, we each brought something different to the group, and we were all on the same page when it came to sexual needs. Male and female.

Perfect.

I rolled my eyes and pulled my phone from my back pocket. "Enough you two." I handed the cell phone to Ezra. "I presume you know how to get in touch with him."

"I do." He nodded with a smile and pressed some numbers before putting it on speaker for all of us to hear.

"Ghoul, how did you get this number?" Lucifer answered.

"How did you know it was my phone?"

The devil laughed. "I know all."

"Meaning Mom would have found everyone's phone number and given it to him," Ezra explained.

Lucifer huffed. "You spoil my fun, son. How are

things? Do you need me to come kill, maim, slice, or burn anyone?"

"No, we—"

"Is Paige treating you well? She's cute, but that temper of hers—"

"Hello, Lucifer," Paige called.

"Ah, sweet Paige. It's good to hear your voice, my dear." His voice was light. In the few days he'd stuck around, we'd discovered Lucifer had a big sense of humor. He taunted and teased Paige a lot because he knew he could get a rise out of her.

"I'm sure it is," Paige replied deadpan, then coughed out, "Asshole."

Lucifer chuckled. He also enjoyed how Paige didn't care Lucifer was, well, the devil. She said anything she wanted, and he'd respected that.

"We have a situation, wiseass," she added.

"Tell me," he said coolly. Paige explained what happened and about how we felt regarding our people knowing exactly that Azrael was Ezra and also Lucifer's son.

"Fuck," he barked. After a long, drawn-out groan, he said, "We didn't think you had any of their blood in you."

"Who's blood, Dad?" Ezra asked, his voice low and annoyed.

A member of our family calling Satan "Dad" was something I wasn't sure I'd ever get used to.

"Your mother's grandmother was of a mixed breed. She was a seer, a witch, and also... a unicorn shifter."

My eyes widened as shock swept through me. I met Ezra's equally surprised gaze.

Paige asked, "What am I missing?"

"I'm guessing the men are looking at each other in shock?" Lucifer commented.

"Yes."

"It's because, my dear, unicorns—whether purebred or mixed race—have been extinct for centuries. Their blood called to newly turned vampires. It was like a drug for them. They fed and fed until the victim died, and then the vampire usually died soon after as well from ingesting too much unicorn blood."

"Why?"

"Unicorns are as humans have made them out to be, magical. They're made of light and all that is good. Too much of their blood, for ones as dark as vampires, kills them."

Paige's gaze shot to us. "Aggie—"

"I believe she did not take enough to harm her. However, have her master feed her his blood, and since it was a small amount, it should counteract the diluted amount of unicorn blood Azrael has."

"Why wouldn't Ezra's blood call to older vampires since their senses grow with age?"

"For about two weeks, a fledgling's senses are stronger than even the oldest master vampire. Until they have themselves under control and their senses settle, they will be a risk for our son."

Paige glared down at the phone, slightly offended Lucifer felt he needed to warn us. "We'll keep him away from any new vampire."

"Or if we happen upon any, we will protect him with our life," I said.

Ezra's gaze warmed on both of us. "I can also make sure I protect myself more."

"Yes, you will," Paige said.

"I know you're in good hands, son. Which is why I'm not there dragging you back to Hell. Now, as for the other matter, I believe it would be for the best if the truth came out also. I have trust in your family, son. I know they will protect you, and you will do everything you can to make sure they're safe too. However, it would still be wise to have extra protection. I'll be sending Xi to you."

"Dad—"

"No, he is skilled in all areas. As I said, it's not because I think any of you are incapable, but it would ease mine and your mother's heart if you allow us this. Not only for you, son, but for your mates."

There, right then, when Lucifer mentioned Ezra's mates, I knew the devil had won the argument.

"Fine," Ezra bit out.

"Thank you, son. Speak soon and stay safe, or else there'll be hell to pay," he said on a laugh and then hung up. Ezra passed me the phone back, and I put it in my pocket before I hid my smile behind a cough and turned my back to them for a moment. Lucky I had, else I would have attacked the man appearing out of nowhere.

Xi, who Paige described as looking like the male actor Jason Statham—not that I knew who he was—stood with his hands clasped behind his back.

"Xi," I said.

He tipped his chin as Paige turned, and then he said, "Queen, ghoul, and young master."

"Thank you for coming to assist us, Xi," Paige said,

her lips twitching at Xi's robotic tone and serious expression. "And please call us by our names. Paige, Thorn, and Ezra." Paige winced. "I mean—"

"Ezra," Ezra said with a smile and a wink. "Always Ezra."

"As you require." He tipped his chin down again. "If you do not mind, I would like to wander the area to make sure things are safe."

"That's fine," Paige said. "Thank you."

His brows dipped before he bowed and walked out of the room.

Paige spun to Ezra. "Is he always like this?"

"As far as I know. I was never around him much. But I know his family has been working with ours for many decades. He's the best fighter Dad has. Xi would never betray him, and he would do everything in his power to follow through with Dad's orders because Dad saved Xi's and Xi's father's life."

"That's, well, sweet," Paige said.

It was, but knowing Lucifer, there would be a reason why he saved them. Maybe it had something to do with gaining a loyal guard in Xi.

"I suppose," Ezra replied. He ran a hand through his hair, causing it to stick up everywhere. I wanted to reach over and feel how soft it was myself. However, we still had a lot to do.

"Sweetheart, I'm going to Alex's room to let them know we'll need to transfer Yasmin to another wing of the castle and let them know everything that's happened."

"Thank you. I'll speak with Gregory about sending notice out regarding Ezra."

"You don't want to hold court for it?"

She pulled her bottom lip in and bit down on it. A sense of unease shot from her. I wanted to hit myself in the head. Of course she wouldn't want to hold court regarding Ezra, because the last time Ezra had been in that room, he'd died.

"Forget I said anything, sweetheart," I said softly, taking her hand and leaning down to kiss her temple. "Contact Gregory, and I'll be back soon. I'll also come back with news of Yasmin."

"That would be great, thank you." She smiled.

"I also thought we could test something out." I wasn't sure if my idea was a good one, but it could be okay with all of us around.

"What's that?" Ezra asked.

"Having Asher feed from you to see if a master goes crazed as Agg—"

"No!" Paige cried. "I won't risk Ezra's life, and how would you feel if something happened to Ezra? Asher also wouldn't be able to live with himself."

"I think it's worth trying," Ezra said. Paige's gaze swung to him. "We'll be going into vampire territory. I won't risk any of you fighting for me."

"What about their newborns?" Paige demanded.

"We have to confirm with Asher, but I heard they keep them far away from court matters. They won't be within the area because they won't want to start a war over a youngling," Thorn said.

"All we can do is ask Asher," Ezra said. He hugged Paige to his chest, and she wrapped her arms around him.

"You'll all be there. With Thorn and Nate's strength and Alex's power, things will stay in control."

"If Asher doesn't agree, then we keep Ezra away from the vampire territory," I suggested.

"Fine," Paige mumbled into Ezra's chest. Ezra smiled over her head at me. I was glad he was on board with my idea, and I would make sure nothing happened to cause anyone heartache.

CHAPTER FOUR
ALEX

Never in my years had I seen a person be changed over to a vampire. I didn't realize just how hungry they woke. Yasmin, not herself, clung to her husband, feeding on him greedily while Sakura sat behind Yasmin, trying to control the intake.

Sakura lifted her gaze to Asher and me standing at the end of the bed. "She needs more blood." She'd already been through the bagged stuff we'd brought in. We didn't think she'd need Eric, but she had, and yet she still craved more.

"Because she lost so much to begin with," Asher pointed out quietly, answering the unasked question flittering through my mind.

"I could—"

"No," Asher snarled. His quick transformation startled me. His hand snatched out and drew me to stand in front of his body, holding me tightly. "No one has yours."

It wasn't really the time to pop a boner, and yet there it was at his possessive tone. I patted his hand on my stomach. "Okay, big guy. No one feeds from me."

"But me," he bit out around his fangs.

Another pat to his hand, and I said reassuringly, "Yes, that's right. Only you."

Sakura stared at me as if I had grown another head.

Maybe it had something to do with the powerful grumpy vampire at my back I was coddling.

"Guards," I called. The door opened, and two stepped through. I felt bad I didn't know all of Thorn's brethren, but there were many. "Are either of you able to donate blood?" They eyed Asher and paled. I quickly reassured him. "Not him. Yasmin, on the bed."

"I have a mate," one said, stepping back.

"I'm able to."

"Make sure he's replaced outside," I told the other before he left. "What's your name?" I asked.

"Tim. I'm a...." He glanced around.

"A shifter?" I guessed from his smell.

"Yes. A cat."

"A tiger?" I blurted, but then thought it rude, so heat hit my own cheeks.

"No, just a cat." He lifted his chin, indicating he wasn't ashamed.

I nodded. "Asher, can you help switch out Eric?" The man in his wife's arms just moaned loudly. Another blush hit my face because I knew that moan. I'd used that moan when Asher had fed on me and I'd come in my pants a couple of days ago.

Tim walked to the bed with a straight face and stiff posture. "Wrist or neck?" he asked.

"Neck," Asher said roughly. "It's better blood for a newborn." Asher nipped at my neck, causing me to shiver and remember his bite flaming my body, before walking around me as his features morphed back to his human form.

Asher nodded down at Sakura, who pried Yasmin's

teeth from Eric. Yasmin snarled and writhed on the bed. She went to grab for Eric, but Asher moved him quickly over to the couch while Sakura wrapped her legs around Yasmin's arms, and Tim climbed over her, placing his neck in front of Yasmin's face.

"Ready?" Sakura asked.

"Yes," Tim said.

She released Yasmin's head, and Yasmin sank her teeth into Tim's neck. Tim hissed out a breath and a growl but stayed still.

"She's relaxing, not taking in as much," Sakura said. "She'll sleep soon."

I nodded to her and then looked over to Asher to see him helping Eric sit and giving him a bottle of orange juice. A sudden pang of jealousy swept through me. It was ridiculous I felt jealous over Asher taking care of Eric.

Except... he was mine.

I shook my head and clenched my teeth before stalking across the room where I grabbed the glass out of Asher's hand and held it up for Eric instead. I was the only one the men in our group could take care of. Well, except for each other. I didn't want them to show their sweet, caring sides for anyone but Paige and me. Asher's amused gaze locked on my glare.

Yeah, it's okay for him to go all possessive, but I can't feel the same way? Instead, he probably finds me cute and funny. God, I wanted to preen under his gaze. I liked he thought of me that way.

That was messed up. We seriously drove each other crazy, yet we all liked that about one another.

The perfect match.

Eric pushed my hand away. He nodded. "Thanks."

"You'll need to rest," Asher told him.

"I will. She'll...."

"Yasmin will be fine," I said.

We all looked over. Sakura was smiling fondly at Eric. "She's nearly done, and then she'll sleep. Once she wakes, she'll be more herself. Hungry still, but she'll manage it a little more, and we'll have donors ready."

"I can give her more."

Sakura shook her head. "You've given enough. You need to replenish for her. She will want to... um, that is—"

"Once she is in control, she will want to fuck and drink from you many times to regain the connection she had with you," Asher supplied blandly.

Eric coughed, nodded, gave a thumbs-up, and then muttered, "Right, yeah, okay."

The door suddenly opened, and Thorn stepped through. My heart gave a stumble. It happened every time I hadn't seen one of the others in a while, and then when I did, it was as if my heart wanted to reach out to them and climb inside. I'd mentioned that to Paige during a moment of quiet time a couple of days ago, and she'd said she felt the same. We both smiled over it.

I didn't mind if the others didn't feel it. I liked having something shared with Paige. I knew I was... more in touch with my feminine nature than the others. I didn't care. I liked it because not only did it bond me with the guys in a different way, but it matched me to Paige in more ways than they had. Well, that was what I thought, and I was sticking to it.

Thorn's cocky smile had me rolling my eyes. With

them, I enjoyed playing annoyed about how they all knew how my heart acted. They always gave me a look or a smirk or smiled over it, like they did with Paige. Obviously, I wasn't annoyed in the slightest. I simply loved their reaction to it. However, I think they enjoyed it when I acted annoyed.

It was all confusing and yet easy.

Thorn glanced away to the bed, just as Yasmin's eyes fluttered closed and she slumped against Sakura. "Do you have a room far away from this area?"

"Yes," she answered.

"Good. Tim, if you'll excuse us, please."

"Of course, brother." Tim stood from the bed. There wasn't even a wavering to his footing, so I knew Yasmin hadn't taken much from him. He walked from the room quickly.

Once the door shut, Thorn announced, "There's been an issue. It'll explain why Yasmin will have to be far away from here until we leave for our travels."

"What's happened?" Asher demanded.

My mind swirled as Thorn explained everything. It hadn't felt like we'd been in the room long, and so much had occurred. Now Ezra and Thorn wanted to test out Ezra's blood with Asher. It had my gut clenching in fear. If anything happened to either of them, nothing would be the same.

Sakura stood with Yasmin in her arms. "I'll take her to my room. She would hate it if she tried to attack a mate of her sister."

Eric also stood. He swayed a little but stayed on his feet. "I'll help you."

"Actually, Eric, we need you to take over from Nate with your children for a while. We'll need him with us in case…. Just in case."

Eric scrubbed a hand over his face. "Of course. Shit, the kids. They'll need me." He glanced at his wife in Sakura's arms, looking torn with his dipped brows and thinned lips.

"Go. They need you also. I'll send for you when she wakes and after she's fed again. You know she would want you protected as well."

He nodded and made his way over to them. "I know. All right, as soon as she's okay to see me, please have someone come for me."

"I promise," she whispered, looking up at him. He leaned down and kissed Yasmin on the lips quickly, then glanced up and pressed his lips against Sakura's cheek. She closed her eyes. I could tell she was cherishing the touch. I knew I got the same blissed expression on my face every time one of mine touched me.

Eric faced us. "Good luck."

I clenched my jaw. We may just need more than luck. Strength, power, and love would hopefully help us, or I could be jumping to conclusions, and Asher wouldn't be tempted to tear out Ezra's neck because of his unicorn blood. I started praying to anyone who would listen that would be the case.

* * *

"How is she?" Paige asked as soon as we'd entered.

Unconsciously, I made my way to her and took her

hand as Asher pulled her gently back into his body. "She's good," I told her with a smile. "Sakura's moving her to another area, and Eric will be with her later."

The door opened and Nate stepped in. There went my heart. I caught Paige's smile and shared one with her.

Nate slammed the door, faced the room with his hands on his hips, and roughly announced, "We are not fucking doing this."

"Nate—" Thorn tried, taking a step toward him, but Nate's hand shot up.

"No," he clipped. "This is a risk we don't need to take. We'll keep Ezra away from any vampire. Simple as that."

"I assume Eric told you everything?" Asher asked.

"Yes," he hissed.

"How are the kids?" Paige asked. I'd dropped her hand after Nate's first words, ready to go to him, and now she was wringing them in front of her, worried about her niece and nephew.

Nate's eyes softened a little. "They're confused. They know something's going on, but not what. They're smart, though. They know to trust us, trust the people around them. They were happy with Eric home. He composed himself well around them."

She nodded. "Good, great. I'll get down to them, um, soon."

"You agree to this as well?" Nate asked.

Paige shrugged. "I see their point, but of course I'm scared senseless like you are about them both."

"I'm not scared," Nate bit out. He was, but he'd never admit it, else he wouldn't have been fighting us on it.

Ezra moved around us and started Nate's way. Nate

glared at him. "I'll have you all here to help. That's even if something happens in the first place. I have a feeling it won't, though, because mature vampires don't go crazy like the newborns do when scenting me."

"You said it there: we don't know if Asher will be able to contain himself."

Ezra reached out and clasped Nate's jaw. I saw he applied pressure. "This, in a controlled environment, is the best way to go. You know it. Deep down you do."

Nate's jaw clenched, and his nostrils flared. "Fuck," he snapped. "Do it then."

My heart jumped into my throat when Asher stood at Ezra's back. His head dipped into Ezra's neck, and I heard his deep inhale. I took a step closer while Thorn and Paige moved in to surround them. I could work from afar; I didn't want to get in their way in case they had to use their strength to stop him.

"Does he smell different?" Paige asked, her voice tight, her emotions locked down.

"No. Just the same as always," Asher said.

My dick decided it was time to party when Asher licked up Ezra's neck. Ezra hissed out a breath, then gasped when Asher bit into him. Asher groaned, drawing in Ezra's blood. Ezra shuddered, gripping Nate harder.

"Ezra?" Paige said.

"I'm fine. G-Good in fact." He moaned. "Shit, someone touch me."

"Not yet," Thorn replied.

"Asher?" Nate clipped.

Asher's eyes opened, the glow to his eyes brighter than they had been. He stared at Nate but didn't stop drinking.

"Asher," I snapped.

"Someone touch me. Fuck, no one told me this could feel so good," Ezra whined.

"Asher," Thorn growled out.

"Please," Ezra moaned. He dragged Nate's hand down. "Yes, there, just up and down."

"Asher," Paige whispered.

Asher's hand snapped out. He grabbed Paige around the waist and drew her close. He licked at Ezra's neck and then turned his face to slant his mouth over hers. She sagged into him, wrapping her arms around his neck. Paige moved enough for me to see Asher's hand over Nate's as they stroked Ezra's cock under his jeans.

Mine throbbed at the sight. When Ezra rested his head back on Asher's shoulder, his eyes closed, and his lips parted a little as he just took in the pleasure of them touching him. I could barely contain my need. I hadn't realized the height difference. Ezra was just a little taller than me really, while Asher, Nate, and Thorn were all taller. Thinking of Thorn, I looked to him to find his gaze already on me. Slowly, he took the few steps to me. Reaching out, he trailed his fingers down my arm as he circled around me and pressed his front to my back.

"I like seeing you watch them. Witnessing your dick grow hard behind these pants." When he said pants, his gliding hands slid low over my hips and butt, and one hand stopped over my bulge, giving it a squeeze.

Paige broke the kiss, staring up at Asher. He smiled. "His blood is rich, smooth, and delicious, but it doesn't make me want to devour him." Nate snorted. "Well, except in a sexual way."

Paige smiled. She relaxed into Asher more, the panic falling from her body as her desire surged to full speed. My own fear had diminished with Asher's control. He wouldn't have been able to stop if Ezra's blood had called to his vampire.

It meant newborns were the only risk we had when it came to Ezra.

Thorn nipped at my neck, then sucked on my skin, causing me to shiver in delight. I tilted my head to the side for him to have better access, and he didn't disappoint. His tongue trailed up and down it before laying kiss after kiss.

A moan had me opening my eyes and looking across the room. Nate had Paige up in his arms, her legs around his waist while he took her mouth in a brutal, hard kiss, which she returned.

"Alex," Nate barked as he broke the kiss, and I knew what was annoying him. With a click of my fingers, clothes disappeared. All of us were suddenly naked. Nate pressed Paige's back against the wall as he slowly pushed his stiff cock inside of her. I loved how hungry for him she looked. How she bit her bottom lip and her hands threaded into his hair right before she pulled him down for another bruising kiss, like she wanted him inside her at all points she could, pussy and mouth, while their hearts and souls bonded.

She was beautiful. I could stare at her all day long and never feel like it was enough.

A hissed-out breath had my eyes gliding over to Asher and Ezra. However, before I could take in what they were doing, Thorn's hand wrapped around my erection and stroked over and over. My eyes closed. I dropped my head back to his shoulder and ground my ass into Thorn's own hardness.

"I wanted to do this when we were stuck in Hell. I saw you in the shower running your hands over your body, and I wanted to be the one touching you. I wanted to take my time, kiss, bite, and lick every inch. I've been inside you once, Alex. I'm going to need to again."

"Yes" was all I could say.

"Go lay on the bed," he ordered darkly.

To get what I wanted, I did as I was told and lay back. Thorn stood at the end of the bed, running his fisted hand up and down his length as his hooded eyes slid over me slowly.

"Fuck me, you asshole," I heard, causing both Thorn and me to glance over to Ezra and Asher. Ezra had been doing what I did to Thorn, backing his ass up against Asher while Asher drank once more from Ezra. Only after Ezra shouted that, Asher licked his puncture marks closed, picked Ezra up and roughly dropped him onto the bed on his knees.

Asher's eyes glowed. His clawed hands gripped Ezra's hips and jerked him back, rubbing his cock against Ezra, who growled in the back of his throat.

"You want me to fuck you, Ezra?"

"What do you think?"

Asher's hand slapped down on Ezra's butt cheek. "Do you want me to fuck you, Ezra?"

Ezra's gaze lifted from the bed and met mine, his eyes were pure black. Slowly, he turned his head to look over his shoulder and snarled, "Careful, vampire."

"Then answer me, hellhound."

"Yes," Ezra hissed. "Fuck me."

Me, being the helpful person I was, clicked my fingers, and tubes of lube landed on the bed. One near Asher and the other between my own legs as I watched Thorn climb on the bed. His strong, muscular form and smooth skin were meant to be admired, and I was. Like all of them, he was built to fight and to fuck. I squirmed on the bed, knowing I was about to be the one fucked by such a stunning man.

Paige's cry of pleasure sounded around the room just before Nate's low groan, him no doubt coming inside of Paige's sweet warmth. I could hear their kissing, as well as Ezra's growl being cut off by a satisfied, low moan, and I knew Asher was finally pushing into the needy man. But I couldn't look away from Thorn as he ran lube over his erection while gazing down at me like I was his dessert and he was about to devour it.

"Need prep?" Thorn asked, his voice thick and rough.

"No," I whispered. Movement to the side caught my attention. Nate sat in a chair with Paige on his lap, both still wonderfully naked as they watched the show in front of them. My face burned with heat, usually shy about what I said or did or how I looked, but being with Paige and these men, I soon stopped worrying about such things. Though it didn't stop me blushing. Nothing would.

A hand to my cheek pulled my eyes back up to Thorn hovering over me. His thumb ran across my bottom lip. I nipped at it, and his eyes flashed. He sank his thumb into my mouth, and I swirled my tongue around it and spread my legs wider, lifting my hips a little to accommodate Thorn's size as he pressed his tip to my hole and slowly pushed in. Thorn glided his thumb in and out of my mouth, and that thrilling sensation, along with how he filled me, had my gut clenching in delight.

"Christ," Thorn cursed. "You're fucking tight, beautiful, and sweet." He turned his head slightly. "Isn't he, Paige?"

I tilted my head enough to see her but still keep Thorn's thumb in my mouth. She lay back on Nate with her legs spread and Nate's hands between them massaging her clit.

"Yes, so, so beautiful. All my men are."

"I agree," Ezra said on a moan, bringing my gaze from Paige to him. Somehow, he was close, his face inches from mine. Thorn's thumb dropped away from my mouth, and both his hands gripped my thighs as he drilled in and out of me, causing my breath to catch, and then I lost it altogether when Ezra dipped his head and bit at my chest. Lower, he swirled his tongue around my nipple, and I lifted my gaze, drawing in a breath to see Asher behind him, thrusting hard and fast, rocking Ezra's mouth, lips, and tongue across my skin as it trailed up to my neck. My body tingled, and my balls drew up; they all had me on edge.

"How's he feel?" I asked Asher.

"Like home, like you all do, but more, like mine. Like Paige's."

"Yes!" Paige cried. I faced her, seeing her gripping the arms of the chair and grinding her hips down and around on Nate as she climaxed over Nate's fingers inside her. "God, I love you all," she muttered, relaxing back.

"More, vampire," Ezra demanded. Asher leaned over

Ezra and sank his teeth into Ezra's shoulder. Ezra roared. His cum shot out and landed on the bed and me. Ezra saw it. A pleased smile came over him, and he bent his head to take my mouth with his. The kiss surprised me. I soon got carried away with it, and the way Thorn's cock kept touching my prostate each time he pushed himself in.

"Fuck," Thorn yelled. "Fuck." The feel of his cum squirting inside me pushed me over the edge. It was sudden and explosive. I whimpered into Ezra's mouth and felt my release land on my stomach.

Coming back to myself, I panted out my breaths and tried to control my fast-beating heart. I found myself up the bed further with Paige curled into my side and Thorn behind her up on his elbow looking down at us.

"Good?" he asked me with a knowing smirk.

"Yes."

"Does he always do this?" Ezra asked from my other side where he lay on his stomach. He was referring to the purring vampire at his back who was currently taking care of Ezra by running a washcloth over his back and butt.

Nate grunted and held out a glass of orange juice to Ezra. "Yes. Yes, he fucking does, and it's annoying as shit."

I called bull on that. Nate's soft eyes on Asher said another story.

"I will never, never stop loving seeing you all together, loving one another and enjoying each other. Having you all feel what you do about each other, and not just me, makes me feel… it's so hard to describe. It's just amazing," Paige said softly.

"I agree, sweetheart," Thorn said, kissing her hair.

Ezra nodded. "Even though I'm new to this, I'm damn grateful to be a part of our group."

"Our family," Paige said.

"Clan," Asher clipped between purrs.

"Pack," Nate bit out.

Thorn laughed with Paige and me before saying, "I think family is the best way to describe it without getting into an argument."

"Whatever we all are," I started, "we're perfect, and we'll get through anything to keep us all together."

Paige kissed my cheek. "Yes, we will."

CHAPTER FIVE
PAIGE

"You didn't say anything to me," I said gently to Yasmin. We sat on a couch in Sakura's private room. It had been a week since she'd been changed. A long week without seeing her. She hadn't wanted to see me that day either, but we were leaving in a couple of hours, and I couldn't leave without saying goodbye. She looked even better than she had as a human. She no longer had bags under her eyes or eczema spots on her skin; in fact, her skin seemed clear and her hair shiny. She looked perfect, except for the fact she kept swallowing over and over. I hated I was causing her pain.

"Can we argue about this another day?"

I glanced away, tears threatening. "We're leaving. We have to go now to get things done before we meet with the council."

"I should have known. Sorry."

"Don't apologize. Ever. I'm the one who should. I got you in this—"

Her hand flashed out and gripped mine tightly. "Don't you apologize. It is not your fault a crazy witch's daughter wanted revenge. I should have been smarter, and honestly, Eric and I knew staying human wouldn't be an option in the end. Us changing was bound to h-h-happen, um...."

"Should we get Sakura in here?" I asked since she was

eyeing my neck like it was a morning coffee she needed to drink.

"Yes."

The door opened, and Sakura stalked in. She was probably listening on the other side. She went straight to my sister, sat beside her, and held her wrist up. Yasmin bit into it and moaned. Her eyes closed as she took a deep pull of Sakura's blood. I watched as Yasmin leaned into Sakura and the vampire looked at my sister like she was something special while running her free hand down Yasmin's hair. I'd seen them together, with Eric, before he'd left to be with the kids and before I asked Sakura to give us a moment. They'd been... infatuated with one another.

I didn't see any jealousy as Eric lightly kissed Sakura on the lips just after he had Yasmin. Or from Eric when Sakura cradled Yasmin in her arms and kissed her neck just as I entered. Of course, they both froze when they saw me.

It truly was like they'd bonded as I had with my men.

Yasmin licked Sakura's wrist before pulling it down to her lap where she held Sakura's hand.

"I never told you about Sakura and I getting close because you've had so much to deal with on your own."

My heart ached. "I'm still here to listen to you."

She smiled softly. "I know, and I'll still always rant to you, but this was new. At first, I thought I was gaining a friend. Okay, it might have been a friend both Eric and I felt comfortable with hugging and kissing in greeting. But I realized only recently, before the... before what happened, that I felt more for Sakura. I wanted more than what we'd started. It was just *that* morning I spoke with

Eric about it, and he also said he sensed something with Sakura as well."

"And now?"

Yasmin smiled. "Now, I have Eric and I have Sakura… if she'll have both of us."

Sakura grinned shyly. "You both know I will. My life would be dull without either of you."

"The kids?" I asked.

"They'll eventually know because, well, we don't like being apart for long. Also, the children are old enough to know things around here are different than a normal human's ways. Should I feel bad about that? For wanting this to work with Sakura and bring it in front of my children?" She shrugged. "I don't know."

"It's not bad to want happiness. I can already see Sakura brings that for both you and Eric. I'm sure the children will see it and understand. They're smart. They take after their father."

"Hey," Yasmin yelled, and we laughed.

"If things are meant to be, they'll work out," I told her. My stomach twisted. "I'm going to miss you. I'll have Alex pop me back when I can."

"I know you will, and I'll miss you like crazy as well. I wish I could hug you, but I don't trust myself yet, and I'm sure your guard could rip my head off with just a thought."

I glanced back at Xi. He stood statue-still with his arms down, hands clasped in front of him. I snorted. "It could be a possibility." Xi even freaked me out. He was a silent ninja, popping up when I least expected him. Once was while I was in the bath with Ezra. Apparently, he'd called, and when we didn't answer, since we'd been under the water kissing, we came up for air and there he was standing over us. My scream brought the rest of the men into the bathroom. They got a good laugh out of it. I was grateful when Xi left after my men's coaxing, leaving Ezra and me to get back to what we'd been doing.

The announcement went out to my people regarding who Ezra was exactly, what he was to me, and that if anyone wanted to speak of it, to contact myself or Lucifer. I was certain the mention of Lucifer helped keep the haters away. However, I wasn't stupid enough to not believe there could be ones lurking, wanting to best Lucifer or myself. And by doing it, they would harm Ezra, which was why Ezra was never alone. We knew he was strong, he was powerful, and he could protect himself and others against an army, but it was still fresh in my heart and mind how we'd lost him. I was sure it was the same with my other men because two of them went with him everywhere, along with ten other guards. I had my own guard in Xi. I'd been surprised when Xi didn't stick like glue to Ezra. His answer when I asked was "You hold his heart. You are their center. If you die, they will want to. It is you who I protect, child." I could have done without the child part, but he made sense, and I didn't argue with him because I knew he was right—the men would follow me to the grave if I died, and I didn't want that to ever happen.

Pressure suddenly hit my chest. I was about to leave the safety of the castle and walk my men into dangerous situations. Then there was my sister dealing with being a vampire and not being able to see her children in so long. There wasn't only that. I worried about my people, about what could happen in our absence. Virginia had come back to help watch over things and Lucifer promised to pop in and out, of course, wanting to see Virginia, which was reassuring if anyone acted up for Felnick, Clyde, and Aggie.

Although, leaving really didn't sit well inside me.

"I love you," I told Yasmin.

"I love you too. Always."

I shifted my gaze to Sakura. "Thank you for taking care of Yasmin."

She dipped her chin. "You're welcome, my queen."

"Stay safe while I'm away."

Yasmin smiled. "I will."

"I shall make sure your family will be safe, with my life."

I couldn't ask for anything more. I knew Sakura would keep her word. It would be like me promising to take care of my mates with my life.

After leaving their suite, I slowly made my way back to the other side of the castle. Only I took the long way around, out through the market. Most people greeted me with a bow, smile, or a call, which I returned each and every one. Even with the man stuck to my back.

"Can you step back a little?" I asked Xi through gritted teeth. He was doing his job a bit above and beyond, especially since I also had about ten other guards at my back.

"No, I cannot."

I grumbled under my breath, before I was distracted when I saw Michael, Leona, and their little bundle of joy, Zoey, their little horse shifter. I hadn't had a chance to make it to the birth since it was the day Lucifer had shown up and Ezra had come back into my life. However, as soon as I'd heard about Leona giving birth, I was at their room instantly.

"Michael, Leona," I called with a wave.

Both of them smiled brightly upon seeing me. When I was close, they bowed their heads. Thankfully they didn't go into a full bow like they used to. Leona even tried it when I'd come to her room and she'd been breastfeeding. I tried to make them promise not to bow, but they refused, saying it wasn't right. So I got them to compromise to this.

"My queen, do you need anything?" Leona asked, gesturing to the stall they were in front of. It was one with an array of clothing of different types and styles.

"No, thank you. I think Gregory has stuffed my suitcases full to the brim already. Plus, I have Alex, and he can just conjure anything I wish."

"That must be wonderful." Leona smiled.

Michael wrapped his arm around Leona's waist. "You're not thinking of adding a mage to our Equidae, are you?"

Leona blushed and then giggled. They were so darn cute together. Leona shook her head. "You're enough to handle."

Michael grinned. "Good." His gaze shifted to me. "My queen, we'd like to thank you again for gifting us with the stroller for Zoey."

I waved it off and bent over the stroller, cooing at the cuteness who slept soundly inside. "How can we not spoil such sweetness?"

"That's true." Michael beamed. He was a very proud father, and Leona was an amazing, doting mother.

"Please, while we're gone, make sure to keep in the

castle grounds," I said, lifting my gaze from Zoey and then straightening.

Michael nodded. "We will, my queen."

"Thank you. I better be going to see if I need to do anything else before we leave."

They dipped their heads. "Safe travels, my queen. I hope everything works out." Leona smiled.

"As do I, Leona." Or else my men and people were doomed to live a life of pain and hate.

"Are we there yet?" I asked for the billionth time and got the same reaction from Nate, a scowl and a growl as he looked back at me in the rearview mirror. It had me smiling at least. But seriously, I'd been sitting for four hours in a... what Asher called Nissan Nv 3500 4x4, that had been converted to a six-seater so I could have all my men in one vehicle. Nate and Thorn sat up front. I was in the middle seat with Alex and Ezra, and Asher was spread out on the back one sleeping since he hadn't gotten much in the last few days.

I hadn't been the only one worried about leaving the castle. He worked with me on making sure everything would be settled before we left. Another 4x4 was in front of us that held Xi and some guards, and another was behind us with more guards. I was bored out of my mind.

"Try and sleep," Nate clipped.

"I'm not tired."

"I could think of something to do," Ezra said with a

cheeky grin, and then I was up out of my seat and on his lap.

"Set her down and put her seat belt back on," Nate snapped.

"But, Dad," Ezra whined. I laughed behind my hand.

"Now, boy."

"Will you spank me if I don't?"

"I'll do more than spank you if you don't listen," Nate growled out.

"Um… yay," I offered, causing Ezra and Alex to chuckle.

"Ezra," Nate warned.

Ezra sighed. "He's no fun." Still, he kissed my shoulder before putting me back on the seat between him and Alex. Alex reached around me and put my seat belt back on.

"Where is this portal we have to take to the land of fae?" Jesus, that sounded like something someone would say in a book or movie. Not in real life. Then again, my life had been a fantasy since I ended up with five different and so very amazing men.

"It's about another hour away. In Texas."

I screwed up my nose, and Ezra flicked it, smiling. I grabbed his hand and held it on my lap, then took Alex's. "The fae picked Texas to have a portal in? I didn't expect that."

"They have many around the world," Thorn explained. "But the Texan one is closest for us to get to."

"Let me guess, the council has one close to them also, which is how they got someone in and out to kill the former king?"

"It had been activated that same day, yes," Alex said. "But they had a cover for why it was used, of course."

"Of course," I mumbled.

Alex squeezed my hand. "Don't worry. We'll stop their corrupting ways."

"I have faith in you all. I just hate how hard it's going to be."

"Shit," Nate cursed.

I sat straighter and gripped the back of their seats as I searched out the front window. "What? What is it?"

"The car in front of us is braking. There shouldn't be any slowing or stopping until we reach closer to town. This is a straight path."

"Meaning?"

"Something's happening," Thorn said.

"Asher?" Nate called.

"I'm awake."

I jumped at his voice behind us but kept looking out the front window. Waiting, watching to see if anything was about to happen. Nate suddenly braked hard as the car in front of us did, and things from the woods moved out on the road surrounding the vehicles. I had to think "things" because I didn't know what they were since they were all clothed in black from top to bottom. Mesh covered their eyes, making it hard to see if there were normal eyes peeking out.

"Asher?" Nate called.

"Open the top and let me out first."

"No," I cried, undoing my seat belt and turning on the seat.

Asher leaned forward and cradled my face, saying, "You are to follow what we ask to keep everyone safe."

"Then you shouldn't throw yourself into danger. The men can handle this."

"We fight with the men. We fight our battles together. It's the way of a good ruler. We don't hide, love."

Shit, I knew he was right, but it still scared me. Reluctantly, I nodded and flopped back to my butt, leaning into Ezra.

"Send the queen out and you can all keep your lives," someone called from outside the vehicles.

"I'm going out as well," Alex said.

"No," Nate, Thorn, and Asher clipped together.

Ezra snickered. They all glowered at him. His hands shot up. "Hey, don't look at me. I'm sticking by Paige's side like a good boy. Like I was told. I just think it's cute you all get domineering with Alex."

"It's ridiculous," Alex complained. "I have the power to end them all in seconds, yet you all want me to hang back and be the last line of defense with Ezra."

"We've spoken about this," Nate snarled. It was the first I'd heard of it.

"Yes, and I hated it then as well," Alex snapped. "You all treat me like I'm a little boy. I'm not. I'm damn powerful and you all know it."

"Can we talk about this later?" Thorn said. "They're looking ready to attack."

It was true. Some had drawn their bow and arrows, others had swords, and some even had guns. All of them were pointed toward our vehicle.

Nate pressed his finger to let the bulletproof, custom-made sunroof open. I watched him take in a deep breath. "Demons, they reek of sulfur."

"Then I need to be the one to—fucking hell," Ezra finished. I looked to where he was to see Xi standing on the roof of the vehicle in front of us.

"It is you who will live if you leave now. My name is Xi Huang. I am second in command to our lord Lucifer. In the vehicle with the queen you want is Azrael, son to Lucifer—"

"Fuck, should he have announced that?" Thorn asked.

"If you wish to live, then leave." Xi shrugged. "Or don't, and suffer the wrath of my blade and hands."

"We want the queen—"

"So be it," Xi snarled. He threw out his hands, and I heard screams. Demons fell to the ground, convulsing on the dirt path with blades sticking out of their throats.

Asher flashed out of the sunroof, his body too fast to track for most, yet I could see the outline of his hazy form as he raced around the one hundred men—or demons—surrounding us. They didn't know what hit them. All they could do was fall to the ground after their heads had been severed.

I twitched in the seat, gripping the seats in front of me, watching and wanting to get out there myself to help.

"There'll be other chances to fight," Ezra said in my ear.

"I know what Asher means now. We fight together. It shouldn't be only them out there." A few guards had joined the battle. I winced when one fell to the ground with a huge hole in his abdomen.

"We would be as well if I didn't know they could handle it," Nate said, his voice calm yet cold.

"How is that handling it?" I demanded and pointed to the fallen comrade. Only he wasn't there any longer. He was up again, fighting. "What is he?"

"A ghoul," Thorn said, pride held in his tone.

The car rocked. Something had been thrown into it. I climbed over Alex, who was already looking out the window.

However, as soon as Nate growled out, "Paige," I was pulled back against Ezra's chest, and then I saw a demon stand on the outside. He, it, whatever it was, didn't face our way. He was looking at the person who threw him.

Asher, in all his glory, stood on an embankment, his glowing green eyes glaring down at the demon. His fangs and claws were on full display, and I wasn't the only one impressed or turned on by him. I could scent it off all my men. Our response had me smiling.

In the next second, the demon disappeared and Asher stood in its place, holding a head up before he threw it to the ground.

Beside me, Alex's eyes shone purple. He lifted his flat hand up in front of him, and when he closed it, the demon at Asher's back squished into a ball of goop.

Asher spun around then looked at Alex through the window. "Keep doing that from where you are," he said.

"I'm better out there," Alex said through clenched teeth.

"No," Asher clipped.

More demons around Asher turned into goop thanks to

Alex, while they continued to argue. "Just because you've fucked me doesn't mean you can coddle me."

"I can and I will," Asher bit out.

"Oooh, wrong thing to say, man," Ezra sang.

Alex flew up through the sunroof and stood up there, firing sparks of yellow bolts at demons, who melted on the spot.

"Is it wrong I want to give them both head right now?" I asked as I watched Asher tear through more demons while glaring up at Alex.

Ezra and Thorn laughed while Nate snorted. "Not the time, angel."

"Damn," I muttered. "Actually, I'd like to see them both suck each other off—"

A hand covered my mouth as a nose brushed into my hair. "Mi corazón, now isn't the time to speak of it and get us all hard and wanting."

"Fine," I mumbled behind his hand. I pulled it away and sat up. A roar had me twisting back to stare out the front windshield. What I saw I couldn't comprehend, and fear twisted what felt like an invisible knife in my chest. "What is that?"

"A chimera," Thorn said.

I didn't have a clue what that was, but it scared me enough my body shook. "We need to get everyone back in the fucking cars now," I yelled.

Ezra tried to curl his arms around me. "Relax, Paige. It's fine."

"No! Asher, Alex, back in here now!"

"Paige," Nate barked, suddenly in my face. "Relax. That's Xi."

Blinking slowly, I opened my mouth and then closed it.

The beast ate, tore, and bit anything in its path. It looked to have all areas covered around it because it had more than one head. I could see the main head looked like a lion while the one on its back looked like a goat or sheep, but the tail wasn't to be outdone. It ended in a snake's head. It wrapped around a demon and sank its fangs into the body, easily piercing the protective gear they all wore.

I was in awe. My hammering heart settled a little knowing it was Xi and he was on our side, because there was no way in hell I would want to go against him.

"Catch Alex," Nate warned.

Somehow, Ezra gently pushed me out of the way just before Alex fell back through the sunroof, hitting his head on the edge.

"Alex?" I cried when I saw he was unconscious.

"He'll be okay. Beside the egg on his head, which he'll fix," Nate said. "He's just used a lot of juice in a short amount of time."

I nodded. I understood that was a lot of power, yet I still looked him over just in case.

Asher flashed inside the car, into the back seat. His angry gaze didn't sway from Alex while he ground his teeth together. I had a feeling it would be Alex who got a spanking. Nate started the car and slowly drove forward.

Seeing Alex unharmed, I sat back in the seat with his legs on my lap. "We know it's the council sending these hitmen after me, but how did they know where we would be?"

"It could either be someone has ratted us out, or they

guessed our plans and had mercenaries lay in wait just in case," Thorn said.

"I hope it's the latter one," said a tired voice. I swung my gaze to Alex.

I grabbed his hand in mine, so he knew I was there. Ezra squeezed Alex tighter to him and then laid a quick kiss to his head. When his eyes fluttered open and landed on me, I scolded lightly, "You scared me. Again."

He gave me a smile. "Sorry."

"Sorry is not good enough," Asher snarled.

Alex groaned. "Don't start—"

Asher gripped the back of the seat, leaned over, and got in Alex's face. His hard expression sent a shiver of fear through me. "You know what dark spells do to you. They drain you faster than any defensive spell. You put yourself in harm's way. Why?"

Alex's nostrils flared in agitation. "There were too many. I could help, so I helped."

Asher growled in his face. "You knew the formation we would stick to. You knew when you had to step in if something like this happened. You changed it. Why?"

"Because I have the power to help. I just proved it to you."

"You proved you went too far. You passed out. What could have happened if there were some left and you were already on the ground taking a nap? We follow rules for a reason, Alex. You've never gone against my orders before. Why *now*?"

Alex's eyes flashed purple and back again. "Because you could have died." He gripped Asher's shirt in a fist.

"They were coming at your back. I had to protect you. I protect the people I love at all costs."

Asher crushed his mouth to Alex's, and my pussy spasmed. Nate caught my gaze and gave me a knowing smirk. I shot him the finger.

Asher pulled back and ordered, "You will do as you're told. You will yield to me in the field. I know what I'm doing. Trust me, even when we're sleeping together, that I will do *anything* for our clan to keep *everyone* safe to live a long fucking life together."

Alex paled. "I panicked."

"You did."

"I'll listen next time."

"Good." Asher studied his face. "I love you also."

Alex blushed, then nodded. "Okay."

Asher sat back in the seat and crossed his arms over his chest. "We'll need to make sure we're on alert at every stop we make. They may have easily guessed our plan because they know Nate, Alex, and me. Also, if the shoe was on the other foot, they would do the same as we are, gaining trust from people who could stand against them."

"Should we call for more backup?" Thorn asked.

"No. We handled this fine, and we can't go into anyone's territory—that even means the council—with a large number of soldiers or it will look like we've come to battle and not talk. However, I think we may have to adjust when we get to the council since Nate, Alex, and I are already wanted by them."

Alex, from where he still leaned against Ezra, who was giving him a shoulder rub, said, "We know the layout of the council building. I could plant members of our team, or even extras from the castle, within the building dressed as an elite enforcer to try and keep suspicion down and to let us have more people on the inside."

"It's a sound idea," Nate said.

"Yes," Asher agreed. "Let's see first if we can't gain more people to aid our mission from the ones we see."

Nate grunted. "Agreed." He pulled the car up alongside the other. "We're here."

Shit. My stomach bottomed out. Already on this trip we'd been through one battle. Would walking through this portal bring another?

I didn't know, but we had to find out, and I hated that we did.

CHAPTER SIX
PAIGE

We stood in front of a formation of rocks that looked like something out of the old television show *Stargate*. Except the center of it was full of rock, not an empty entryway into nothingness.

"Where's the control panel to get the thing started?" I asked, and everyone looked at me. I shrugged. "You know, you dial in a certain sequence of shapes...." I glanced up at the edges. There weren't any shapes or patterns. "Huh, okay, so is there a magic button to press?"

Thorn pulled out his phone and pressed a few buttons before putting it to his ear while smiling at me. "Yes, Thorn Jones, bonded mate to Paige Alice, ghoul queen, waiting for acceptance into the fae realm." He paused before looking up at something, so I also did. All I saw were more rocks. "Yes. Thank you." He hung up and pocketed it. The men moved, all surrounding me. I had Asher, Xi, and Thorn in front. Alex and Ezra were at my sides and Nate at my back. The other men were scattered from Alex's sides and behind Nate.

Next, there was a flash of bright white light, and Thorn was the first to step into the bubbling glare. I made a noise in the back of my throat and went to grab him. Xi turned and said, "He is fine, Queen." Then he stepped through, as did Asher.

"I'm not sure about this," I told my remaining men.

"Stop being a chicken." Nate laughed, pushing against my back, but I didn't move.

"I hate you, asshole," I snapped. Nate laughed again and applied more pressure.

"Come on, mi corazón. We'll do it together with Alex." They both took a hand and forced me forward.

"What happens if we get lost in the swirling portal and end up being spit out somewhere else?"

Some of the men behind me laughed but were kind enough to cover it with a cough.

Alex smiled. "I'm not sure what portal you've stepped through in the past, but these types are just one step through, and you're there. They can't take you someplace else."

"Right." I nodded. "I knew that. I was just testing you."

"More like delaying while you get yourself together," Nate said, humor evident in his tone. I dropped the guys' hands and whirled on him to give him a piece of my mind, but I was picked up. I buried my head in Nate's chest, wrapped my arms and legs around him, and closed my eyes as I felt him walk forward.

"Open your eyes, angel," Nate said into my hair as he forced my legs down to touch the ground. I unwrapped my arms, opened my eyes, and hit him in the chest.

"Next time I'll kick you in the balls. I would have walked through on my own when I was ready."

He snorted. "We didn't have all day."

A throat cleared. I turned, and my mouth dropped open. I quickly snapped it closed and got myself together by straightening and replacing the glare I'd shared with Nate to a neutral expression.

"King Nelydriel. Elf and ruler of all fae," the equally tall man at the king's side announced. I suddenly felt underdressed. I also should have asked if I needed to bow to a king, or because I was queen, I didn't have to. I didn't know what I was meant to do, but my gut and heart said not to bow, so I listened.

Instead, I took a step forward and said, "Paige Alice, ghoul queen and bonded mate to Asher, Thorn, Nate, Alex, and Ezra."

One of King Nelydriel's dark brows rose; it was totally different from his long white hair, not blond, but pure white. The top half was pinned back, showing off his pointy ears. Heat hit my cheeks because I pictured myself touching his ears while kissing his face.

Oh, fuck no. No! I cut that vision off and clenched my teeth, double-checking my mental shields were up. This couldn't be happening now. He wasn't even using his power for my ghoul side to place a mark on him.

I licked my suddenly dry lips and ignored the way his turquoise eyes shined down along my body as he took all of my short self in. I couldn't help but return the gesture and ran my eyes down his firm, fit body, over his expensive, long-at-the-back and down-to-his-thighs gown-type top, and... oh crap. Were those stockings? I thinned my lips, so I didn't laugh. However, when I got to his cute boots, a sound escaped from me and I quickly brought my gaze back up to his narrowed eyes.

Look bored, Paige. Look bored, and do not get lost in those fucking eyes.

"Paige," Alex whispered. "Something doesn't feel right."

"I thought you would be taller," the king mentioned and sounded snobby while doing it.

"And I thought you would have wings, be three inches tall, and nice."

Someone, from his fifty or so men on his side, barked out a laugh, then quickly shut it off before I could see who it had been. The king's lips twitched while most of his men stiffened and the shorter man with a rounded potbelly beside him gasped. "How dare you compare the great sire to the common folk fairies."

I screwed my nose up. Just fucking great. There was prejudice and probably bigotry there as well.

"Get over it," I told him, and he seemed to choke on his saliva. He stepped forward, but I suddenly had Asher, Thorn, and Xi in front of me. "It's all right, guys," I told them, reaching out to part Thorn and Asher. Thankfully they didn't fight me on it.

"Paige," Alex called. I glanced at him. "Something isn't right."

"What?" I whispered. Unease filled me.

He scrunched up his forehead in confusion. "I don't know."

"Rallis, enough" was clipped. I looked back in time to see that at his king's words, Rallis moved back to his boss's side. The king held out his hand to me. "Welcome to Airrile, Paige Alice. May I show you around before we sit to speak?"

Paige Alice. I sure noticed it wasn't Queen Alice. I took another quick look at Alex, who shrugged. Shit, until he knew what was troubling him, I couldn't be rude and run for the portal.

I glanced at the king's hand and fought the pull to touch him. Though, I noticed it wasn't as strong as what I'd felt with my men, which was good. But then my eyes flicked over his shoulder to a man with long black hair and the pull suddenly intensified. Strange. This didn't make sense. Why did one man's appearance call to me, and yet, it felt as if the other man was the one who held some type of connection to me?

What the hell was going on? Had I finally lost it? Was it this place? Were we even on Earth?

Scolding myself and the runaway thoughts, I forced my eyes back to the king and then placed my hands behind my back and nodded. "Thank you, that would be nice." I fixed a mock smile on my face. I didn't like this guy's attitude since he pretty much ignored my men and looked down on us. I was sure my body was on a high from walking through the portal or something because the king was a stuck-up douche. Unless it was the portal that did something to me. I needed to get this over with and then speak with my men privately about it.

His lips twitched again, and I wanted to punch him in the face because it looked cute on him. So what? His looks were nice, but it didn't mean anything. All I had to do was focus on the stockings and boots because they looked damn ridiculous, and the attraction I felt to his looks would fade.

The king dropped his hand and dipped his chin. "Right this way." He turned and started forward. His people parted for the king, only I wasn't sure if they looked up to him or feared him. As I passed the man with black hair, I shivered and felt like sniffing him, licking him, and even peeing on him. What the fuck?

I pushed it all down, stabbed my fingernails into my palms, and looked out in front of me. That was when I noticed the rest of the area and sucked in a sharp breath.

The warm sun shone down on rolling hills of green pastures and woodlands. A breeze swept over my skin, and I took in the birds singing their songs in the trees near us. The path we were on led us down to a town about the size of New Orleans. The buildings were like something out of a Santa's village that I'd seen in movies, old and beautiful.

I pressed my hands against my stomach while it fluttered even more.

I'd thought my castle and surrounding lands were amazing, but this was picturesque.

"Stunning, isn't it?" the king asked.

I shrugged, blanking my features, and said, "It's okay." He fought a smile, and I heard someone make a sound in the back of their throat, either a scoff, a snort, or a laugh, I wasn't sure, though. What I did know was that it wasn't one of my men. Ignoring it, we walked down the path in silence for a little while, until I asked, "Do you have a name?"

"I do" was all he said. I ground my teeth together.

"You may refer to him only as King Nelydriel," the suck-up said from the king's other side. He spoke in a tone that told me he thought I was so below his master's princess boots I wasn't worth the time of day.

I stopped walking. It took them a few beats to notice. However, the black-haired elf did, and then the others turned to face me. I fisted my hands at my sides, so I didn't punch the king's little minion in the balls. "I think you need to bring your head back out of the king's ass to breathe the fresh air and see with your own eyes that whatever you think about you, about your king, and about your world, doesn't make him or any of you better than my people or me. We all bleed in the same way, and if you keep up the hoity-toity crap, I'll have my hellhound bite your head off." Ezra gave off a growl in the back of his throat. It was too bad it sang to my ears and he looked too handsome for me to think it was threatening in any way. Although it wasn't a show for me and it had the minion taking a step back, which was good.

The king's brow rose again, and I wanted to rip it right off.

"My queen, maybe we should leave," Thorn suggested.

"I think you're right." I turned and started off, fighting the sudden ache in my chest. I caught Alex relaxing before he saw me looking and nodded. He was happy we were going.

"You're leaving?" the king called.

"You've got a view of my butt, which means I'm walking away, so yes, we're leaving."

"No queen should speak or act as you do," the minion called. "It's crass."

I whirled back around. "What's crass is the way you and your king have acted since we've shown up. I would have spoken and acted with respect and manners if I'd been shown it in the first place." I spun back around and started stomping away.

"You came here wanting us to join you against the council. Now you're walking away from that chance?"

I froze because the voice was one I hadn't heard before. It was soft yet deep. I wanted badly to turn around, but I didn't. I dug my nails into my palms once more, and said, "What makes you think that's what we came for since you would be aware that my mate spoke to the king of evidence we have to share regarding his father's death?"

He cleared his throat. "Even though we're in a different dimension, Paige Alice, we still have ears everywhere. We heard they had found out about the new ghoul queen. About how they were coming to your territory to, no doubt, cut you all down. However, you had put them off by stating how you were coming to see them. It was either a stupid or smart move. I haven't figured it out yet."

"Smart. It means my people stay safe." Finally, I turned, my gaze settling on the man with the long black hair standing with his arms crossed over his chest. His battle attire, like all of the guards, looked like it had been made out of hardened gray scales. "Shall we speak in private, *King*, or would you prefer this public show still?" I asked, crossing my own arms over my chest.

Asher hissed. Nate and Ezra growled, readying themselves with arms out for a shift. Thorn and Xi pulled swords free, and Alex called his powers forward as the air around us shimmered. All of them moved to surround me.

I stayed still while the space around us morphed into an empty room the size of my throne room back home. I didn't let the shock register on my face, but I was surprised as hell since I had felt the sun's warmth and the soft breeze from outside, yet none of it had been real.

That wasn't the only thing that changed. The appearance of the man we'd thought had been the king altered into the man with black hair, which meant…. I glanced at the actual king and watched as his black hair disappeared, replaced by the fake king's long white hair and clothes. They had pretended to be one another in appearances.

The guards at his back had their weapons out and trained our way, while his minion smirked, and the fake king grinned like he found this all hilarious. The rightful king dipped his chin down and announced, "My name is Cedrick Nelydriel. I am the true king of Airrile."

My body hummed and my heart raced, but if my mates heard it, they could take it for the shock of what happened. Lastly, as something inside me clicked, making things feel right, my pussy throbbed.

Fuck no. I would fight this mark, this connection. I didn't need another mate, and besides, he had his own lands and people to take care of. I fisted my hands, planted my feet firmly on the floor, and locked myself down.

Nate and Ezra looked at me. I shook my head and showed my determination of not wanting this. Asher reached back and took my hand in his, running his thumb over my skin in reassurance.

I knew they would tell me the Fates had picked this man for me, that he was meant to be in our lives for a reason, but I wouldn't have it. I had my men. I loved my men. There wasn't room for anyone else. Fuck this bond. Fuck my body and heart.

No!

"What is the meaning of these parlor tricks?" Thorn demanded.

"We have had our own problems with the council. People coming under different pretenses, but all were seeking to end my life." He waved a hand to the man now with long black hair. "My brother, Kiered, thought it would be safer if he acted in my place to see if you would also be a threat."

Nate snorted. "You let your brother take the fall if something happened."

Cedrick's jaw ticked. "I didn't *let*." He glared. "I wasn't given the choice. Apparently being the king means my life comes before anyone else's. Something I hate and would change if I didn't have everyone going against me. I also wouldn't allow him to go it alone, which is why I am here pretending to be him as a guard so I can fight my own battles."

"Ha," I let out and pointed at Cedrick. "Sounds familiar. You guys would have me in bubble wrap tied to a bed if I didn't fight for my right."

"I'm sure tied to a bed has some benefits," Kiered said with another grin and a wink.

"Kiered," his brother bit off as my men made some type of noise or growl at the man.

Kiered raised his hands. "Hey, I'm not saying *I* want to tie her to a bed. Relax." I caught his quick glance at Xi. Interesting.

"This is the man you had in your stead?" Thorn questioned.

Cedrick's brows dipped, and he shook his head. "His skills at fighting are beyond most."

"Aww, bro. I love you too," Kiered teased, and I liked him a lot more now that he wasn't pretending to be the toffy king. But did it mean that was how Cedrick was all the time? If that was the case, I was sure my mind, body, and the Fates wouldn't be that cruel and want him to still be in my life. Not that I would allow it.

Kiered stepped forward. "Now, are we able to move this into a room that's more comfortable?"

"I have the meeting room set up, your highness," Rallis said with a bow and a glare my way. I still wanted to stick my finger up at him.

"Please lead the way, Rallis," Cedrick replied, then glanced at me. "After you."

I ground my teeth. I didn't want to walk in front of him. Then again, I also didn't want to have him in front of me either because I knew I wouldn't be able to help myself —I would check him out... unless I had my men do something arousing, then my attention would easily sway to them. The only problem with that was how easily I could get lost in what they were doing and forget everything else around me.

Like now, when my mind wants to run with a thought of them in bed together.

Focus, Paige. Focus goddamn it.

As I straightened my red silk shirt out, Asher, Thorn, and Xi parted. I took the first step forward, then another. My body shivered because I could swear his eyes were on me.

"Holy shit, you're checking out her ass," Kiered whispered. However, he must have forgotten about our advanced hearing. I heard a slap, and then Kiered cursed and some of the men chuckled. I glanced to my men and saw even they held a smirk or a grin over it. I wanted to stamp my foot and tell them to be offended; he was looking at my butt in the first place. I stopped myself from shaking it and let the annoyance go. I was the only one overreacting.

We followed Rallis down a long hallway. Male and female elves scattered out of the way. Honestly, we must have looked a frightful sight. Xi and Asher had blood all over them; I hadn't even thought to get Alex to fix their appearance, not after he had been depleted. Though, I knew he was back in full force, or else he wouldn't have called for his powers in the room earlier.

Leaning into him, I asked, "Was it the glamour that had you on edge?"

He nodded. "I could feel magic, but I didn't know where because it didn't make sense it was coming from everywhere." He glanced at me. "I'll know what to look for now."

I took his hand and squeezed it. Smiling up at him, I told him, "I know you will."

As we went by some windows, I looked out and found the scene they had set in the room was exactly like what I saw out in the real world. It was still beautiful. It had me wanting to go out there and actually see it for real.

A woman walked out of a room in front of us. She sneered, and then her gaze went behind us, which changed her expression into a coy smile and sweet, soft eyes.

No doubt one of the elves behind us was her beau.

We passed by, still following Rallis, when I heard, "My lord, how are you this day?"

My head twisted. I squeezed Alex's hand tightly. I wanted to turn around and smash her face into the door for even speaking to him, but I fought it, and it hurt. My body burned. Ezra and Nate moved closer. They reached out and touched me, a hand to my lower back and one sliding into my other hand. The skin-on-skin contact with my bonded helped cool me.

"Very well, Elizitenth," the king replied.

"May I help with something?" she called.

"Not right now, thank you."

The king was brushing her off calmed me even more. I shook my body out and kept my gaze ahead. We turned a corner, and a group of women scuttled to the side. All of them blushed and giggled, looking at my men and then at the ones or a certain one behind me.

Would slicing their throats open with my claws be too bad, really?

Now I had Asher reaching back, as well as Thorn, to touch me in more ways. One at the hip the other on my arm. I was sure I looked like a fool, but I didn't care, else I would go on a killing spree.

"Is everything all right?" Cedrick asked. He was closer now; goose bumps broke over my skin. My dead skin. How was that even possible?

"Fine," I ground out.

We turned another corner and then down the hall we paused at the double wooden doors while Rallis opened them to another room about the size of the first one we'd been in. Only this one had four large tables, two bars, and a row of long tables off to one wall where food would have probably been set in long meetings.

Rallis moved aside. We entered and went straight for the largest table smack dab in the middle of the room. My men and I spread out on the left side. I sat in the middle. Xi stood at my back with Nate, while Thorn and Asher sat to my right, then Ezra and Alex sat on my left.

Opposite me, Cedrick sat. He was right there in front of me. Right there with his long, perfect hair, his stupid, amazing eyes, and cute, lickable ears.

I could be strong. I could be.

CHAPTER SEVEN
PAIGE

Someone cleared their throat. I jolted a little in my seat and glared over at the man who'd made me lose my train of thought. Cedrick glanced at Asher. At least I hadn't been the only one lost in the stare.

"Shall we start?" Asher asked.

"Of course." Cedrick nodded.

"We came with proof of the council's involvement in the death of your father."

Cedrick's hand shot up. "We already know it was the council."

"How?" Nate demanded.

Cedrick pulled his gaze up to Nate. "It's a thing called interrogation. The people we captured eventually talked."

"So you know it's the council's usual MO?" Alex asked.

"What do you mean, their usual?"

Alex's power filled the room. I gripped the arms on the seat, so I didn't maul him. I didn't even look at him because I knew I would be a goner. At least twenty files dropped with a bang onto the table. He leaned over them and spread some out.

His fingers drummed on the table. "These are files on higher-up members of society who have died suspiciously, been murdered, or disappeared without a trace. They were members of different types of races. Ones who their own people thought highly of. Including the former ghoul queen, your father, and the currently missing alphas of the tiger and lion clans. However, I haven't even mentioned the mage, witch, mermaid, troll, or sphinx. The list goes on, but you get my drift. The one thing they all have in common are the groups the council sent out to investigate."

Motherfuckers. God, I hated the council.

"What does this have to do with us?" Rallis asked from where he stood behind the king. Actually, the only two who sat were the brothers. His other men lined the wall.

"Nothing, if you choose," I said, leaning into the table and resting my elbows on there to clasp my hands in front of me. "It'll keep being nothing if no one stands up to the council. Murders, kidnappings, disappearances will continue happening by their hands if there is nothing or no one to challenge them."

"Why are you the one to challenge them?" Cedrick asked.

I looked to his shoulder. "Because they threatened my people and my land by stating they were coming there. We're not stupid enough to believe they would have come in peace. They would have slaughtered innocent people, and I won't stand for it. I'm going to the council to set my own challenge so one day there will be peace. There will be days filled with minimal occurrences. Days I can look forward to spending with my men and my people, without the threat of them hanging over our heads."

"Will you allow us to take time to think about it?" Kiered asked.

I glanced to Asher as he said, "We leave in two days to travel to speak with the shifters. After that, we're going to a vampire clan whose master was murdered."

"You're hoping they'll step in as backup?" Cedrick asked.

I nodded, staring at his chin. "Yes, and that's all we can do. Hope. If any of you chose not to attend the meeting with the council as... let's say witnesses, then it's fine. We won't hold it against anyone."

Cedrick nodded. "Two days."

"Do you have somewhere in your town we could stay?" Thorn asked.

"It would be an honor to have you as guests here in our palace."

Shit. I didn't think being under the same roof would be good, but at least I had my men to distract me.

Wait... he said castle, right? I wanted to see the outside because I didn't remember one in the scene he'd set in the room earlier. I knew it was him because when he'd used his magic, he'd set off my mark for him. Why else would I want to hump his leg like a madwoman and kill every woman he'd been with or looked at him.

Speaking of... crap, was I really going to have to do this?

Yes, I was. Damn it.

"Thank you," I said, dipping my chin in respect. "There is something you might have to warn your people of though."

"What?" he demanded.

I cleared my throat and shifted in the seat, suddenly uncomfortable. Nate snorted behind me, obviously guessing what I was about to say. I ignored that and Ezra's snicker.

"Look, ah, there's no simple way to say it. I'm a little possessive of my men."

"A little." Ezra laughed.

Alex covered his mouth, and I knew he was smiling wide behind it. At least Thorn and Asher only had a small smirk.

"Okay, I'm very possessive of my men. I don't like it when women or men flirt with them."

"What do you mean by *very* possessive?"

"She's near killed over it. If we hadn't been there, she would have," Asher explained mildly. "We are also possessive of her. Please pass it along as well." Asher lifted his gaze to behind the king and narrowed his eyes. "You've been undressing her since we arrived. If you do not cease, I'll have your blood join with the rest over my clothes."

Cedrick spun around on his seat. "Out," he clipped low to one of his guards, who quickly bowed and left. My stupid body tingled at Cedrick's tone. Kiered chuckled but cut it off when his brother glared at him. Cedrick looked back to two men and ordered, "Let it be known, because if someone doesn't listen, they'll suffer the consequences. Not Paige and her mates."

"You would allow them to come into our lands and spout foolish rules like this?" Rallis questioned snottily. I just knew he needed his balls rearranged on his body.

When his king looked to him, Rallis gulped, paled, and stepped back. "Forgive me for speaking out, my lord."

I didn't trust him. Admittedly, I didn't know him, but

there was something about him that set off alarm bells throughout me. He was so far up the king's good-looking ass it wasn't funny. Yet, he still seemed scared by him. No matter, I'd be keeping an eye on him. I may even have a chat with Cedrick's brother to see if he'd be willing to speak of Rallis and either confirm my mistrust or defend him.

"It's been happening a lot lately, Rallis," Kiered commented while looking at his fingernails. "Is there a reason why?"

"N-No, sir. I just worry for the king is all."

Kiered hummed under his breath. "Anyway, I think we should all freshen up before dinner."

Oh fuck. Did they expect me to eat? What? Normal food? I mean, Alex could bring in a meal for me, which was how the ghouls in the group, including myself, were going to be feeding, but I wouldn't be comfortable eating in front of them.

Ezra's hand slid to my leg. He smiled over at the king. "We'd love dinner, but I'm afraid some of us are on liquid diets."

Kiered chuckled. "But of course. We'll make sure to have something for everyone."

Unease twisted my stomach. I stared down at the table, trying to think of a way to get out of it but couldn't come up with anything.

"Unless you would prefer to retire to your rooms?" Cedrick mentioned. Since I hadn't expected his offer, I lifted my gaze to find him already staring at me. My damn cheeks heated. "I presume something happened on the way here, so you must all be tired."

"We were attacked. So a rest would be good, thank you," I told him.

He nodded. "Kiered will show you to your rooms." He glanced to his brother. "Take them all to the fourth floor."

"Where—"

"Fourth floor," he bit out.

"Of course." He dipped his head then clicked his fingers, and a man stepped close. He spoke in a different language quietly, one I didn't understand, but the guard nodded and raced out of the room.

"Should we be worried about that or what's on the fourth floor?" Thorn asked casually. I was glad he mentioned something because it seemed suspicious.

"Nothing to fear. I'm just removing some others on that floor so you can have it to yourselves."

Kiered looked away when I shifted my gaze to him. What was this about? I wouldn't jeopardize my men if there was a problem.

"Who was on that floor?" I demanded.

"Not of your concern," Cedrick clipped.

"Love," Asher called. "It's fine. I could do with some rest though." Meaning he understood what was said and knew we had nothing to worry about.

"Okay." I nodded, trusting him completely.

"Will you need a room separately?" Cedrick asked suddenly as I stood from my seat.

Nate snorted. "We're fine in the one room."

"Let's just hope the bed's big enough for all of us," Alex murmured, being cheeky for some reason.

"Also, that it's sturdy," Ezra added with a smug smile after.

"Guys," I scolded, not understanding why they were speaking of it in front of the others.

Something snapped. I looked over to see Cedrick dusting something off his hands.

"Right this way," Kiered called from the doorway. His grin was the biggest I'd seen it. I noticed my men were also smirking or smiling over something.

I would get to the bottom of it when we were in the room.

Out in the hall, Kiered started for the stairs. He glanced back and asked, "You're mated to all six of them?"

"Six?"

"Xi isn't a part of the bonded group," Thorn put in.

"Oh, I thought he was." Kiered's gaze slowly ran over Xi in appreciation. Maybe they weren't bigots here. To my utter shock, Xi blushed and looked everywhere but at the man.

"No, he's my guard," I told him. "He was sent from the devil himself because he's the best there is."

"Really," Kiered drew out slowly. Xi's face heated even more, and I caught him miss a step, but he grabbed the railing, righting himself quickly. Interesting, very interesting. I grinned, thinking Xi deserved a little happiness, and I could tell he wasn't disgusted by the thought of Kiered.

"He will need a room to himself right next door to us."

"I'll make it happen," Kiered said. He winked at me.

Ezra groaned. "You guys need to install elevators in this place."

Kiered laughed. "It's in the pipework; however, since we aren't in need of them, it keeps getting pushed back."

"Why aren't you in need of them?" I asked.

Kiered turned on the step at level three. He levitated a foot off the floor and floated up ahead easily, then landed. "See, easier for us."

"That's pretty cool. I forgot you could all do that." We moved to the next set of stairs and started walking up them. "What was also amazing was the glamour in the room earlier. I can see it was a true picture of what's out there." I pointed to a window.

Kiered nodded. "Since the first assassination attempt, we had to move the portal into a secured room in the castle because a couple of times the assassin tried to kill the king on the spot and they'd thought to escape into the woods when they'd realized they were outnumbered. Thankfully, they were hunted and caught."

"How many attempts have there been?" Xi asked.

"About five."

Xi cursed just as we reached the fourth floor.

"You say you keep the glamour up until you know you can trust the person. How did you trust us so quickly?" Nate asked.

Good question.

"Yes, ah, well, we didn't until Cedrick revealed himself to you all."

"Are you saying he knew to trust us?"

Kiered shrugged and led us down the hall. "The guards can start picking a room as we walk down. But you'll be in the second to last room, Paige Alice."

"Just Paige," I told him.

He smiled. "Just Paige."

"Why did your brother trust us, Kiered?" Thorn asked again.

"You'll have to ask him. I'm not sure."

I had a feeling that was a lie. I caught my men looking at each other. Damn it, they were all thinking it had to do with me.

"Although, you telling Rallis to pull his head out of the king's ass was a good indication. No one has spoken so freely before. It's nice."

"Our queen has a habit of speaking freely. Just another reason we love her," Alex said, and I grinned at him, wrapping my arm around his waist. He curled his around my shoulders.

Xi sorted the guards into rooms as we continued down the hall. When we were the last, Kiered called Xi's name, stopping in front of a gold brass door. Honestly, I wasn't a fan of the décor inside. It was over-the-top lavish. It all said "we have money... let me show you." I'd never seen so many paintings in my life.

"This will be your room," Kiered announced and pushed open the door.

"I would like to see the queen's room first, please."

Ezra clutched his chest and gasped. "He said please."

Xi scowled at him. There was lightness in Xi's eyes as he looked at Ezra, which I was sure many would never have been able to spot. My mate loved to give Xi a hell of a time, but it was all in fun. Xi knew it too. It also seemed he was very patient.

"That's really nice of you, but I promise the room won't have any booby traps." Kiered smiled. Xi blinked at him and clasped his hands behind his back. Kiered looked around at us. "Ahh, okay. This way." He chuckled to himself as he mock-whispered to me, "Is he always so serious?"

I nodded. "Always."

Kiered smiled widely before moving off to the next room. I had a feeling he took that as a challenge, and he was going to see if he could break Xi out of his robotic emotions. The only time I'd seen him smile was fighting those demons earlier.

Kiered opened the next door and swung it all the way in before stepping back and sweeping out his hand. "After you, sweet Xi."

Ezra snorted, and I covered my smile with my hand when I noticed a blush on Xi's cheeks as he stepped through ignoring us. I waited in the hall until he came back out and dipped his head. "You may enter."

"Thanks, Xi." I smiled.

"However," he started and turned to Kiered, "I would like to know whose room is on the other side." He pointed to the last door in that hallway.

Kiered coughed and ran a hand at the back of his neck. Were the tips of his ears tinting red? "The king's."

Ezra laughed. "Makes me wonder why he would want us on his floor."

"Yes, I wonder why," Nate said sarcastically.

Well, it had better not have anything to do with me, because I didn't want that. Why would he do that? Did he sense something? Oh shit. Did I share my lust into him? Did he think he was mine now? I wouldn't have him. I wouldn't.

I had my five. Five was more than enough.

Roughly, I heard Xi say something, but I didn't take it in because I was freaking out in my mind. I didn't want my men to think they weren't enough for me. They were. They would always be. Why were the fucking Fates doing this to me?

Wait… the bond hadn't been completed. I could get away from him, from here, and never see him again. Then things would go back to how they were.

Besides, I didn't like white hair. I liked blond, black, brown… not white. I snorted to myself. The way he dressed wasn't a turn-on. Not that I was looking for things to turn me on about him, because I wasn't, and I refused to think about his eyes, ears, and body.

"How's she doing?" someone asked.

"She'll be fine," someone else replied.

Guilt stabbed at me. How greedy could one ghoul be? I had five amazing, perfect mates. They were the absolute best, all challenging me in different ways. All accepting me for who I was. I didn't need another.

And that was final.

I would refuse to complete the bond.

I would dodge Cedrick at all costs.

Blinking, I focused in front of me to see I was sitting on a large bed in an extravagant bedroom. I'd thought mine was big. This was twice its size, with a little kitchenette of its own. Asher stood with Thorn leaning against the wall talking quietly. Alex and Nate lounged on the bed behind me, and Ezra sat between my legs on the floor. Reaching out, I ran my hand through his hair. He turned quickly, getting to his knees.

"Hey," he said.

"Hi, sorry to space out there for a moment."

He took my hands in his and pressed his cheek against them. "It's okay. We understand you've sensed the connection with the king."

I sighed and glanced to my other men. Nate and Alex moved forward on the bed to sit on each side of me. "I've felt the connection, yes. However, I'm refusing to accept it."

"Why, love?" Asher asked, straightening from the wall to come over with Thorn. Both stopped in front of us.

"Because I have five amazing mates already. I don't need or want another." Before he or anyone else could say anything, I shot my hand up. "Please don't say anything. I know you all think this is out of our hands because the Fates picked this choice for me, but the fact is there's a choice to complete the bond, which means it's an out for this connection. I'm taking that out."

"Would Cedrick have a say?" Thorn asked.

"No, yes, well... I don't know." I lifted one hand out from under Ezra's head and ran my fingers through his hair. "You guys didn't know about the connection until Thorn said something. I mean, you felt a little of something, but that was it. If he asks, we'll ignore it, play it off as we don't know what he's talking about. Then we'll leave and I won't have to see him again."

I disregarded my heart since it felt like it was weeping in my chest or ready to explode at the thought of leaving without Cedrick.

"If he decides to join us on our quest?" Alex asked softly.

My stomach fluttered. "I doubt he would. He's king.

He'll have too many other things to take care of here. It looks three times the size of our place. If anything, I think he could send some men, but that's it."

Asher hummed under his breath. I glowered up at him and snapped, "What?"

"Nothing, love."

"Asher." I shook my head. "Actually, I don't want to know. Can we do something else for a moment and then talk business after?"

Asher smiled, showing a bit of fang. "I'm rather parched. Nate, would you—"

"Yes," Nate clipped before Asher could finish.

"Perfect," I said. "Entertain me, my mates."

"Always, my queen," Asher said. As soon as Nate was in front of him, he spun Nate around to have his back to his front. Nate squirmed, bringing on his half form. He snarled as Asher scraped his fangs on his neck. Nate reached behind him, grabbed a handful of clothes, and pulled, flipping Asher over his head.

The fight was on and it brought a smile to my face.

"Alex, they're in too many clothes. Thorn, Ezra, come up on the bed with us." I laughed when Ezra jumped up quickly and bounced flat on the bed.

This was what happiness was made of.

CHAPTER EIGHT
CEDRICK

The women of my land were the most beautiful of all kinds. They had been cherished by many; stories were told of how exquisite they were. Of course, I had indulged in many different women in my time and found them pleasurable. They were tall, legs going on forever. They were soft and thin, with long silky hair and eyes that shone.

Yet, they dulled in comparison to Paige Alice.

Paige Alice, the ghoul queen.

The way my body reacted to her was something I'd never felt. No woman had hardened my cock in seconds after seeing her for the first time. Hell, I had wanted to pull her from her mate's body after she'd come through the portal in his arms and cradle her to me. That was even before seeing her stunning features. She was small. The top of her head only came to my chest. She had curves I wanted to caress, and when her scent drifted over to me, I wanted nothing more than to smell it for the rest of my life.

Had she placed some type of spell on me?

I hadn't heard she was a sorceress.

Shaking my head, I stalked to my windows in my room and looked out. Clenching my jaw because of my stupidity, I exhaled. No, she hadn't put me under a spell, and I knew it. She was meant for me because she was my intended. My bride.

A knock sounded on the door, and it opened before I called out. I knew who it would be. *"Yes, Kiered?"* I asked through our minds. It was a gift all elves had, to be able to speak with each other as long as the person receiving it was open to allow it.

"She's not who I expected."

He could say that again. Aloud, I replied, "Who did you expect?"

"A cold, dead thing that dragged around her body slowly and moaned for brains."

I glared over my shoulder and faced the window again, so he didn't see my smile. "I think you have zombies and ghouls mixed up. However, you're correct. No one could predict what type of woman she would be without seeing it for themselves."

"What type of woman is she, brother?"

"A take-charge, caring, funny, sexy woman."

"Is she... your bride?"

"Yes."

"Is this why you got rid of your women on this floor, to have her close?"

Turning, I sighed and leaned against the windowsill. I ground my teeth together and admitted, *"I can already tell no woman will do but her. However, I won't be taking her as my bride."*

His brows shot up near in his hairline. "Whyever not?"

"We're polar opposites."

He laughed. "I see no difference. You would do

anything for your people, like she does hers. You're both rulers, have a lot hanging over your heads."

"She has *five* men already. Five, Kiered." I shook my head. "I would never leave my people either. It hasn't been long since I became king, and we both know father ran things down when he was ruling. I'm to make a difference."

"You already have, brother. All look up to you in respect and not fear. Father was a sadist; we both know that. He didn't touch us because we were his kin, but it didn't stop him from showing us his real side. I know it kills you that we couldn't save everyone when he was… in a mood. It hurts me also, but you must trust the palace is better off without him. However, we need to show others that coming into our lands and killing one of our own won't go unpunished." He walked closer and then sat beside me against the window. "You know the council has reigned long enough over everyone with their vicious ways. They're like Father in many ways. Are you willing to have them continue on the path of destruction, which could come into our lands again and again?"

"I agree. You know I do. The council will get what's coming to them, and they'll deserve it. Which is why I will assist Paige in their takedown by sending as many men as we can spare with her."

"Our men are legends in their own right. Still…" He knocked his foot against mine. "She'll need your help and protection."

"She has *many* to protect her, and I'm sure the shifters she's to see will be willing to assist to get any information they can on their alphas."

"Are you jealous of her mates?"

I scoffed. "No." A part of me might have been because they got to have who they wanted, and from the looks I saw exchanged, I could tell they shared their bodies as well. It didn't disgust me. In fact, if I was honest, they were all attractive men. All different in their own ways. I could tell the connection they all shared was one of love. They didn't fulfill the bond because it was convenient or because they presumed they would gain more power from the connection. They honestly loved each other.

Not all bonds worked out like that. No one knew how or why the Fates picked as they did. Sometimes it worked, other times it didn't, but I always thought when it didn't work, it was because of the people involved. They didn't put enough into it. One was greedier than the other and expected more out of it.

I shook my head. No matter what it came down to... none of it was for me.

"You are." Kiered laughed. "This is funny coming from a man who sleeps with many women and men in one night, all in the same bed." He sobered when he saw I wasn't finding it amusing. He didn't yet understand why I couldn't have Paige Alice as my bride.

"It never comes down to attraction or sex with a bride connection. Before we can commit, we have to take every-thing into account. Everything, Kiered. If I leave to be with her, who will rule Airrile?" He opened his mouth to answer, but I shot in quickly with "You can't take this on, Kiered. You're skilled in fighting, yes, but in power, I am the only one who will be able to keep our darker brothers on this side. Father's elder powers only passed onto me, brother. I wish we had been equal, but we are not, and it is left up to me to keep peace within our realm."

"The other elders could assist; they've sat back long enough."

"They never assisted with Father because they all thought along the same path as he. Rule with pain, with fear. I won't subject the people to them."

Kiered clenched his jaw and glared at the floor. "She is your bride, brother. Your one and only. Now you've seen her, met her, you will no longer love or be with another because they could never satisfy you in—"

"I know what it means, Kiered," I clipped as I straightened and started pacing the room. "It is a sacrifice I make for our land, our people."

"You're stronger than I could ever be, brother."

Maybe I was. Though I was worried what kind of man would I be when I didn't have my bride to complete me.

"She could move here—"

"She has her own people to take care of."

"They could also come here."

I laughed without humor. "Can you imagine what our people would think of us allowing outsiders to live within our realm forever? Vampires, witches, ghouls, shifters?" I huffed. "Maybe after I've been king for a decade or two, I can make such a change. For now, I'm still gaining the trust of the people, and I won't jeopardize it to satisfy myself."

"Are you sure—"

"Whatever it is you're about to say, yes, I'm sure." I walked toward the bathroom. "Now, can you please see to a meal for them and send it to their room?"

"I think the vampire feeds from a few in the bonded group."

My dick throbbed at the thought of seeing it while he drank from Paige. "Right, then send the rest something." I opened the door and turned back to add, "Shifters eat a lot. I presume hellhounds have the same appetite."

"Did you know he was a hellhound?"

I smirked. "Not until she told Rallis her hellhound would eat him."

Kiered chuckled. "I was sure he shit his undergarments. I can see she eyes Rallis with caution."

I grunted. "She's smart. When you go back with the meal, be sure to have a quiet word to them about him."

He nodded. "I will. Last question. Have you tried to mind speak with her?"

Since she was of another race, but still my bride, I would have been able to mind speak with her still. However, I wasn't willing to try. In doing so, would be another step to completing the link. "No, I haven't and won't."

He offered a sad smile. "Enjoy your cool shower." He winked, then blanched. "That sounded wrong." He went to the door, opened it, and shot out of the room.

Smiling, I enjoyed the new Kiered. Actually, he wasn't new; he was more himself, more out in the open than he had ever been when Father had been around. My brother was loud, liked to tease, was conceited in a funny way, and now didn't care what others thought of him. He preferred men, but had hidden that part of him as Father hadn't approved. If he hadn't pretended to like women, he would have been forced to fuck them in front of people, like our cousin had.

I despised the man.

Hated him with everything I was.

Yet, I hadn't been strong enough to put a stop to him. If only I'd had the elders' power rushing through me back then. I would have slayed him on the spot for his foulness. In reality, it was a good thing he was assassinated in the end.

Thinking of him always soured my mood. Yet, there was another reason turmoil spread through my veins and deadened my heart.

Finding a bride was the most amazing feeling in the realm. It had been; she took my breath away, had my body singing in tune with hers… and I wanted more than anything to claim her.

Denying a bond…. I could already feel the ache from not being near her. I would hurt for a long time, until distance helped dull the pain. However, it would never go.

I just hoped it wouldn't be the same for her.

I prayed she hadn't felt this bond within her and no pain could touch her from this since it would be my decision to not complete it. I could speak to her about it, explain the reasons why. Let her know it had nothing to do with her, but my commitments as king. I had a feeling she would understand, but a small part of me feared she wouldn't and I would see the anguish within her that I had caused. So really, I was being selfish by not saying anything.

Two days.

Only two days I had to pretend she didn't mean the world to me.

I could do it.

I had to.

$$* * *$$

A scream of rage had me transporting myself from the shower to the destination where I felt the anger. I stood in the middle of Paige's room with swords in each hand and gasped at the chaos around me. Her men fought hand to hand against steel and arrow. Paige, dressed in what looked like a little nightie, had a man bent in half on the floor. His feet actually touched his face. It was then I caught another man sneaking closer to Paige, coming up behind her as she demanded answers from the man under her.

In seconds, I stood at her back and brought both swords straight down the middle of the man. Each half fell different ways.

I glanced down to Paige to see her looking up at me with wide eyes. A blush coated her gorgeous face. Her unbound hair wound around her shoulders as if caressing her.

"Alex," she called. "Clothes."

I heard a click and then something pressed against my skin. I looked down to see a black shirt and trousers covered my body. Nakedness didn't bother me, yet it seemed to Paige.

I searched for Alex, who was throwing some type of ball of light toward someone, and nodded when he looked over. He grinned and it caught my breath. Yes, I could see why Paige would be taken with him.

Another opponent moved behind Alex, but before I could say anything, the vampire was there ripping the head off with his bare hands. He then snarled something low at Alex before kissing him hard and flashing off.

I turned back in time to split three more threats in half with ease.

"How does he fucking move with grace like that?" I heard Paige ask. Then heard a grunt before she said, "I'm not talking to you, asshole. Now tell me, who sent you?" A beat later, she cursed, then called, "Thorn!" I didn't have time to look because more advanced. Only then I was taken to the ground and covered by the tiny woman who had her hands over my face.

Suddenly, the room fell silent.

She lifted her head, but not her hands off my face until I dragged them down to my chest. I stared up at her while she looked around the room. "Alex?"

"I'm fine. Not drained at all."

"What have we said about overdoing it?" was barked from Thorn, I thought.

"Relax, they're unconscious, not dead. A simple spell," Alex replied.

"And the spell seconds before that? The fire?" That sounded like the shifter, Nate.

No one got to answer because there was a knock. We all looked over to see Kiered standing there in the opened door with a quivering parlor maid. She shook so much that things on her tray rattled, while Kiered gazed around the room in shock.

"What did I miss?" he asked.

"That is what I would like to know," I snapped.

"Sweetheart, you can hop off the king now," Thorn called.

Paige's gaze snapped down to me, and it was then I realized my hands were on her hips. I gave them a squeeze, feeling that I touched no clothing, but skin. Her nightie must have ridden up. She bit her bottom lip. I wanted to take my cock out, bury it inside her, and watch as she threw her head back on a moan and rode me like my dick was made for her. Which it was. I wanted to run my hands up until they cupped her breasts; then I would bring my mouth up to taste her skin, at her neck first before sliding lower to her erect nipples.

Wait... they were, in fact, currently erect and ready for tasting. Her body reacted to me already.

She shifted back lightly, but I gripped her, so she didn't move lower over my body to find out how hard I was for her.

"Criosd, tha thu mar sin bòidheach," I said, hoping she didn't understand my language, since I had just told her she was beautiful. If she did, I would find another language she didn't understand since I knew over one hundred.

She frowned. "What does that mean?"

Thankfully, I didn't have to answer since Ezra was there lifting her off me with a smirk playing on his lips. He winked down at me, then twirled Paige in his arms and bent her back to kiss her neck. "Now we can get back to what we were doing."

Her eyes closed. She gripped the man tightly even as

he straightened them upright and she smiled up at him like he was the one to create chocolate. Until she blinked and glanced around at the destruction in their room.

"Uh, soon. Right now I want answers." She turned to me as I climbed to my feet. I would have repositioned my hardened dick if she wasn't already looking at me. "Do you know what they are? Are they yours? Did you try to kill us?"

I couldn't help but roll my eyes. "If I wanted you all dead, you already would be."

"Brother, maybe we can adjourn to your room while we have this place cleaned up and the prisoners taken to the dungeon?"

"Fine," I clipped and then stalked from the room. It hurt to think she would suspect I would be involved, which counted for my short, sharp response. However, even after I regretted it, it also could be good to push her away.

"Please excuse my brother. He's under a lot of strain at the moment." I heard Kiered say as I entered the hall from her room.

Someone snorted, another chuckled, before an amused voice said, "I'm sure he is."

My step faltered. Did they know? Did they suspect I was hers and wasn't accepting this bond? My gut clenched, twisted, and then dropped. Would they under-stand if they did know?

It wasn't Paige. I would never reject *her*.

Throwing my door open, I stormed through. I didn't realize the parlor maid had followed until I'd turned back to the door.

"My lord, shall I lay their refreshments in here?"

"Please." I nodded and waved my hand toward the table. "Place them there."

She curtsied and did as I asked. As she took the plates off the tray, the others entered, and I noticed Paige was now dressed in human clothes of jeans and a top. The others also had more clothing on. Kiered kicked the door closed and moved to the table to deposit his own tray. However, the door shot open and hit the wall.

"Merde," the French word dropped from my mouth before I could stop it.

After everyone looked at me, they slowly moved their gaze to the door.

"Thera, now isn't a good time," I told my ex-fiancée, but of course she didn't listen. She gazed around the room as she stepped through the door. Thera and I had been promised to one another when my father was around. She was manipulative, cold, and a bitch. She also didn't understand why I called off the wedding as soon as I heard word my father had died. She still refused to move from the palace, telling me I would come to my senses in the end because it was a politically good move. It was utter shit. I never trusted her father, another elder, so I would rather die than have any part of that man have more say in what went on in the kingdom. Meaning, his daughter would be his own little pawn.

As far as I knew, she had been off visiting her parents. What she was doing back I didn't have a clue, nor why she was staring at the people venomously.

"Darling, you should have told me we had guests. I would have made sure I was home from the start."

Movement had me shifting my gaze to the side to see

Paige's men surround her. Asher even had his arms around her upper arms as he held her to him. What was going on?

Thera stepped closer to me. Kiered stopped her with a hand on her arm. "Thera, such a pleasure to see you. Why are you back?"

"Do I need a reason to return home to my husband? I think not."

Paige made a noise in the back of her throat as she screwed her nose up and narrowed her gaze.

I pulled my eyes from her and said, "Thera, you know the arranged wedding was canceled as soon as my father died." I crossed my arms over my chest. "You will never be my wife, as I've said multiple times. So, explain to me why you come barging into my room without notice."

She laughed. "Oh, darling, you never complained before." She smiled, shrugged off Kiered's hold, and went to come at me.

"Enough," Paige snapped.

Thera froze and eyed Paige since Ezra and Nate moved aside. Asher still held his mate. Thera took a step toward them. Ezra and Nate both growled in the back of their throats. Smartly, Thera stopped. Her nose turned up. "Who are you to speak to me as such?"

Before Paige could say anything, I said coldly, "She is a guest of your king. It is you who is in the wrong by coming in here thinking you have the right, when in fact you don't."

Thera ignored my words and asked again, "Who are you?"

"Thera, you will leave instantly," I ordered.

"I am Paige Alice, ghoul queen. Who is it you think

you are? As far as I can see, you are not wanted or needed in this room and never will be."

Thera gasped dramatically and turned to me. "Will you allow this?"

I had wanted to keep things peaceful, but enough was enough.

"Yes," I told her.

She sneered. "Father was right. You're a weak king." I felt a tap on my mind. She wanted access. She was trying to force it.

"Don't, Thera," Kiered warned, sensing what she was trying to do.

"What's she doing?" Paige demanded.

"Trying to pry open my mind to speak with me. It won't happen, Thera."

She screamed and stamped her foot like a spoiled child. Unfortunately, she turned to Paige, drew a dagger from her sleeve, and threw it at her. Paige cried out when Nate, who moved in front of her, stumbled backward.

Even though he'd caught himself and Thera's aim wasn't good since the blade ended up in his arm, Paige saw red.

Before our eyes, she changed. Her eyes shone red with a black ring around the pupil, and her nails extended into claws. She let out a vicious snarl, and even though Asher still held her, she managed to get out of his hold and race to Thera.

Paige grabbed her by her hair and threw her across the room.

"Love," Asher called.

"Sweetheart," Thorn said.

"Let her go," Ezra mumbled.

None of them assisted her.

Thera got up off the floor with more daggers in her hands. She looked as if nothing had happened to her. Hair, clothes, and appearance all perfect. Whereas Paige looked feral, and I liked it. No, I loved it because she was herself. Her wild, wonderful self, protecting her mate.

"I'll kill you," Thera bit out.

"You can try." Paige smiled.

The room thickened with Thera's power. I stepped closer to Paige, but Alex was there with his hand on my arm, shaking his head. "I have it," he told me on a whisper. "She's safe, magically, and she'll fight her own battles physically."

I eyed him, lost in his glowing purple eyes. His magic swept over me and caused me to shiver. I nodded down at him, since I seemed to be the tallest out of the men. Alex was also the shortest, just above Paige.

Why I compared myself to the men I didn't know. It wasn't like it mattered since I wouldn't be a part of their group.

"As long as she isn't outnumbered," Asher stated.

Nate snorted. "She'd even try to keep us out of it then and take it all on."

Thorn nodded. "She's stubborn."

"In a cute way, especially when she gets angry with us," Ezra added.

Why were they telling me all this?

Thera threw a dagger. Paige dodged it beautifully as she made her way toward the woman. Thera threw the next dagger, and Paige easily moved out of the way. She was on

Thera, a hand wrapped around her neck. She picked Thera up off the floor and held her high.

Elves were strong, but it seemed ghouls were stronger, or at least the queen was.

Thera struggled, choking and gripping Paige's arms.

"Why do you want to harm me? I have done nothing to you."

"H-He s-said I-I h-had to," she got out slowly.

Paige dropped her. Thera landed in a heap. She sat up slowly, rubbing her neck. "What are you doing?" Thera whispered.

"Who said you had to harm me?"

"My father."

"Why?"

"Because the council ordered it—and I will follow through," she yelled, lifting herself up and stabbing Paige in the chest.

We all cried out, until we heard Paige laugh. She leaned into the knife, cupped Thera's face and smiled down at her. "The only way to kill a ghoul is to slice off our heads." Thera paled and then her eyes widened when Paige went on with "You should have learned more about us and how I now have the right to kill you instantly." Paige whipped Thera's head quickly to the side, snapping her neck.

Thera dropped to the floor. Dead.

Paige straightened, glanced down at the knife sticking out of her, and asked, "Does someone want to help pull it out?"

CHAPTER NINE
PAIGE

The room had been cleared of maids and the dead body. When it finally happened, I wanted to smack all my men in the face and kick them in the shin. Usually I only got that feeling with Nate, and maybe sometimes Ezra. Not with all of them. Even Cedrick was being foolish.

"I think Alex should put her to sleep before we remove it," Thorn suggested again.

Cedrick nodded as he stared down at my chest. "I would agree," he murmured.

"Sounds good to me. Then it won't hurt her," Ezra added.

"Just pull the thing out quickly," Nate said. He bent and poked at where the knife was still inside me. I flinched, which caused Alex to smack him in the back of the head.

"That hurt her."

The most annoying one came from the most sensible one. Asher tapped his chin and said, "Maybe if we distract her with an orgasm—"

"Are you all serious right now?" I took the hilt of the dagger, and while they all called out for me to stop, I pulled it free with a small cry of pain. I dropped the dagger to the floor and glared at them all. "That's the last time I ask for help. Next time I have something hanging out of me, I'll deal with it myself."

"Why did that sound dirty and yet not?" Ezra asked.

I punched him in the stomach. He wheezed as I then stepped around them to go to the couch.

"Sweetheart, come on now. We didn't want to hurt you," Thorn said. I ignored him and winced a little when I sat. Already I could feel the skin knitting back together. Thorn took the seat beside me, and just as Nate was about to sit on the other side, Alex appeared out of nowhere, scaring Nate enough he cried out in surprise.

Then a scowl took over his features before he kicked at Alex's foot. "You're fucking lucky you're pretty or I'd move you."

"I know." Alex smiled.

Leaning back, I looked up, and up again, at Cedrick. My heart fluttered, remembering his naked body appearing in the room. I knew his body would be perfection, but his silky white skin, his hard muscles, his tall form, and his long, thick dick would be seared into my mind forever.

Even then I wanted to see it again. I wanted to cherish each and every inch of the man with cute pointy ears. God, those ears drove me crazy. I could stare at them, at all of him, for hours. Like all of my men.

Regret filled me, and my healed chest twisted from it.

However, I couldn't bring myself to tell him he was mine. He was made for me. He had responsibilities, and I couldn't come between him and his people.

"You know, don't you?" Cedrick asked. My body jolted, and I realized I'd been staring at him standing in front of me. It shocked me when he knelt, resting his clasped hands on his thighs. The others quieted around us and stopped trying to reason with me about why they didn't want to hurt me. I understood it, but maybe we had to stop coddling each other when it came to helping one another. Even if it hurt.

"Know what?" I asked softly and caught Kiered's pained look behind his brother.

Oh crap... was this about my mark on him?

"You're my bride," he announced as his icy eyes held mine. They told me more than his blank look. In them I could see hurt, respect, and resolve.

"Sorry, what?" No one said anything about being a bride. What did he mean? Was he expecting me to leave my lands, my people, to become a doting wife?

"Love," Asher called, then his hands were on my shoulders, his calmness rolling over me. "For elves, they call their mates brides. That is what Cedrick means."

Oh.

"Ah... okay, um, it sounds very *Bride of Chucky*, but to answer your question, I didn't know I was your bride. As far as I knew, I had marked you to be my bonded mate."

His eyes widened; then he caught himself and blanked his features.

"You've marked me?"

Alex took my hand as I blushed like a little girl who had her first crush and he was talking to her. "Yes."

Nate, from where he'd planted himself on the floor between Alex's legs, said, "We guessed it happened when we first showed. You were using your power to glamour that room?" Cedrick nodded. "Paige marks her mates when they first use their powers in front of her. Though, it seems you also marked her to be your bride."

"What do you mean?" Asher asked.

"Alex noticed it before we got interrupted. He pointed it out to me only recently and I saw it when you changed."

"What are you talking about?" I demanded.

"On the back of your shoulder is a mark, one that looks a lot like an autumn leaf."

Cedrick, with wide eyes, looked over his shoulder to his brother, who shrugged. He turned back and asked, "May I see it?"

I nodded and leaned forward for Thorn and Alex to grip my tee and lift it. Cedrick walked around the back of the couch and stopped beside Asher. Both of them leaned in. One of them traced a finger over my skin, causing me to shiver.

"I have never heard of a bride receiving a mark," Cedrick admitted. He sounded in awe. "It is beautiful."

It was *his* finger lightly grazing the mark, causing my body to react even more. My nipples hardened, my pussy pulsed, and I bit my bottom lip to stop myself from moaning. I wanted to turn around and claim his lips.

We'd marked each other.

Even though I had five mates where the marking happened nearly instantly, it still shocked me how a part of ourselves knew we were it for each other.

"Does this mean the bond is complete?" I asked, wondering if it was different for fae. When I felt Cedrick straighten, his finger dropping away, I pulled my shoulder forward enough to glance down.

A dainty sugar maple leaf, colored in browns, greens,

and ambers, sat just at the back of my right shoulder. I thinned my lips, so I didn't smile. It reminded me of when Ezra had first left his mark on my chest. His handprint. I glanced to where he stood leaning against the wall closest to the couch. He smirked down at me, as if knowing my thoughts.

I wanted Nate and Asher to fuck me and bite me again. To leave their marks deeper so they stayed permanently on me. I wanted Alex and Thorn to brand me in some way as well. We may have emotionally marked one another, but I wanted theirs to show on my body, so I could walk around proudly showing who I belonged to.

Smiling to myself, I decided I would voice what I wanted eventually because I knew they would give me it. I also knew it would be something they would love. It was just unfortunate it would have to be later.

All happiness faded and my chest ached. My smile dropped and I blinked down at my lap.

My men sensed my mood shift, and all reached out to touch me in some way. Ezra even came over to sit on the floor between Thorn's legs to be close and curled a reassuring hand around my calf.

"It doesn't have to be this way," Ezra murmured.

"What doesn't?" Cedrick asked. Obviously, his hearing was as good as the rest of ours.

I licked my dry lips. "How this won't work." It hurt to say the words; it felt like even my throat wanted to close off on the words and take them back.

"I know," he said before I could say more. I lifted my gaze to his as he walked around the couch and sat in the chair Kiered pulled up. Anguish filled his gaze, and I knew mine replicated his. It pained me even more. He smiled sadly; one corner of his mouth tilted a little. "You have your people to take care of and I have mine. Neither of us could change it. Our father wasn't the kindest ruler. I'm only just gaining the trust of my people. If I were to leave and have another elder rule—someone who went along with our father's ideas—it wouldn't be good for the people, but also for everyone outside of this realm."

"My brother's power keeps the dark fae in line and secured behind their own binding," Kiered said. "To lose him now would risk those wards, and if they were free, they would do anything they wanted to ensure chaos."

I never understood what a fae king had to deal with. In retrospect, it seemed a lot more than I ever could.

"I… um… my staying wouldn't help the matter, would it?" It wasn't like I could stay, but I still wanted to ask. However, I already knew the answer when he closed his eyes as if he'd been cut.

"No," he whispered, opening his eyes again. I wanted to crawl into his lap and comfort him, and myself. It tormented me more knowing we both knew we were each other's mates and understood we couldn't complete the bond.

We would have been better to have lived in the dark a little longer. I'd thought I could walk away if he didn't understand what we were to each other. I wasn't sure I could now.

But I had to.

Why would the Fates do this?

Why would they hurt us like this?

Walking away would no doubt break something inside

of me and Cedrick. Already, even without the connection, I could see how he suffered inside like I was.

My bottom lip trembled. I bit down on it, but Cedrick saw, and he made a pained noise in the back of his throat. He started to reach for me but stopped himself, clenching his jaw.

"The room should be cleared by now," Kiered said, seeing his brother's conflict. "Shall we rest for the night and speak of matters on the morrow?"

"No," Cedrick started, his voice sounding hard. He straightened his back. To me it looked like the king was present, gone my destined mate who I couldn't have and who couldn't have me back. "We need to speak of other matters."

It pained me to say so, but he was right. So many other things were happening. "He's right." I nodded once. "We do, and first on the agenda would be if you knew who attacked us in the room. Second would be if we need to worry about Thera's father."

He leaned forward, elbows to his knees. It wasn't a posture I would expect from him. To me, Cedrick looked regal, and I would have thought he would also act that way always. Although, maybe he was treating us to his relaxed self and the way he was behind closed doors.

He clasped his hands together and stared down at them. "We have a traitor in our palace," he announced, then looked up to meet my gaze. I would have gotten lost in his gaze, but that was news no one who ruled would want to happen.

"Rallis?" I said.

Kiered snorted. Cedrick gave me a small smile.

"You've been around him not long and you already suspect something?"

"He just seems that type of guy. No one can be that far up someone's ass without a reason. He either has a crush on you and you're lovers, or he wants to live up your butt so much so you don't suspect him of anything."

Cedrick's smile grew, while Kiered laughed loudly. "We're not lovers, and I don't believe he has a crush on me. We also think he's behind some things that have happened."

"What things?" Thorn asked.

I leaned back into Alex more and waited to hear the answer. I saw Cedrick notice my movement and was glad to see no jealousy in his expression or body.

"Little things. Mixed messages, undelivered messages. Tasks unfulfilled because he didn't agree with them. Thankfully, all have been mild where I haven't had to punish him. But lately it has been happening more frequently."

"Why haven't you confronted him?" Nate asked.

"We've been having someone follow him, hoping he will make a mistake and take us to whomever is pulling his strings."

"You don't believe he could be behind something bigger?" Ezra asked. He smirked, already knowing the answer.

"I can see you don't believe it even after questioning it. No, someone is leading him into annoying me or making me look a fool to my people."

"Maybe the two are connected," I mumbled more to myself in thought.

"What do you mean, love?" Asher asked.

I lifted my gaze and met Cedrick's. "Or maybe all of them are connected. As in Rallis, Thera and her father, then those men who were sent to attack us. They could all be following someone on the council. They're threatened by us. Trying to end the threat before it arrives, before we get into their territory. Which is also why we were set upon on the way here."

Cedrick slowly straightened. His eyes widened a little like it all clicked into place. "You're right. I hadn't seen it before because I thought nothing of the marriage arranged with Thera." I frowned. I couldn't believe he'd been set to marry that goddamn beautiful skank.

Well, she was dead now, and I smiled at the thought of it being me to kill her.

"Dove, that smile seems a little crazy. Bring it down a notch," Alex suggested. Nate snorted, Ezra chuckled, while Thorn and Asher smiled when I checked on them. Making sure my crazy wasn't scaring them, I guessed I was good since they all stayed where they were.

I looked back to Cedrick. His small smile said he'd guessed my train of thought and didn't mind.

At least, I hoped.

"As I said, I thought nothing of it because my father and hers were close friends."

"Isn't Therolidi, Thera's father, friends with someone on the council?" Kiered asked suddenly.

Cedrick stood and started pacing. "How could I have been so stupid? Yes, he is, but why would he plot to assassinate our father? It never meant he would be in power. The throne would always go to me."

"But he had Thera to try and steer you in ways he wanted," Ezra said.

"Yes, he did. But I wouldn't lead blindly. I hardly listened to her...." He froze. "Unless she was queen and I suddenly died, then everything would be in her control."

"How does Rallis play into this?" Asher asked.

Kiered laughed. "He's always been more in love with Thera than my brother."

"He's been helping them."

"Who did Thera's father, Therolidi, have involvement with on the council?" Nate asked.

"Jessica, at least I think that was the name I remembered mentioned."

Already I'd felt Alex, Nate, and Asher tense.

"She was in charge of our group when we worked for the council in their elite enforcers."

"You all worked for the council?" Cedrick asked.

Ezra rose his hand. "Not me. I was Paige's protector and teacher when she was first changed into a ghoul."

Thorn cleared his throat. "I was from the former ghoul queen's guards, sent out to meet with Paige after the queen's powers transferred to Paige."

"How is it that none of you won't go running back to the council with all this information about Paige? For all I know, one of you could be helping—"

"Don't," I clipped, cutting off Cedrick. "Before you say something you'll regret, don't say anything more against Alex, Asher, and Nate. They are bound to me. I know what they're feeling, I know they're true, and they want to take down the council with me."

"There is also the fact we became wanted men by the

council as soon as we refused to do as they'd asked," Asher stated prickly. "I would never go against my mate. Never. Even if it meant ending my own life in the process."

"Asher," I whispered, reaching up to take his hand on my shoulder. "None of that talk. No one will be ending lives, because you all know I would follow you just to kick your ass."

Asher gazed down at me, his eyes softening. "I know, love."

"Dad would also kick your ass for upsetting us," Ezra said.

"Dad?" Kiered questioned.

"Who said Asher would end up in Hell?" I demanded. My men were good men. No one got to go to Hell if I had any say in it. They deserved to walk through the pearly white gates and high-five God.

"Love, I have done many things in life that I shouldn't have. I won't be seeing upstairs in my death."

"There's nothing wrong with Hell," Ezra huffed.

I patted him absently. "You have only sinned to protect those around you, I'm sure," I told Asher.

"Love, I'll be sure to go wherever you go. Nothing nor no one will keep me back."

I hummed my approval. "Good." Then I thought. "You only said that to shut me up."

"Never, love." Asher bent and kissed my forehead with his upturned lips. The guy was playing me, but I'd let it slide until it came down to the matter where I would fight tooth and nail to get Asher where he belonged. In Heaven.

"You know she won't drop it. She'll fight with God if she has to." Thorn smiled.

Asher chuckled, as did most of my mates, before saying, "Yes, I know."

"Let's get back to why you all think Hell is such a bad place. I never suffered." Ezra glared.

I leaned down and cupped his cheeks. "No one is dismissing Hell, honey. I love you. I love that's where you come from. I just want what's best out there for my mates, and I thought Hell might not have been it. However, as long as we're all together, I don't care where we end up." I kissed his nose. "Besides, it won't be for a long time, and I'm sure if it's soon and we do end up in Hell, your dad will send us back because we'll have driven him insane."

He grinned. "You're right."

A throat cleared. I gave Ezra a quick kiss and then sat back, looking to the elves.

Actually, right then, I wanted to take a "holy shit" moment. I was in front of elves. Elves. Real-life pointy-eared, tall, sword-wielding, arrow-fighting elves.

Yes, I knew there were other supernatural creatures. I was one. But it just hit me all of a sudden. I walked through a portal into another realm, a realm full of more different species. Dark and light ones. I'd even read there were trolls, leprechauns, and merpeople there.

If I had more time, I would explore, because it did seem this place went on forever. Their kingdom wasn't the only city nestled in Airrile, but from what I'd read, I knew it was the biggest.

I'd thought the human world had enough things that

went bump in the night, but here was larger, and Cedrick had to deal with it all.

I was in awe of the elf.

I could never ask him to leave such a place for me.

Just like I knew he wouldn't ask me.

There I went, back to the sour feeling inside me because our choice to accept the bond and one another was taken out of our hands.

Then why was Cedrick chosen for me?

It didn't make sense.

"Are you saying Ezra is related to Lucifer? As in the devil? Satan?" Kiered asked. Cedrick and he stared down at us, paler than they had been.

"Yes." I grinned. "But don't worry, he won't interfere in anything unless he has to."

That didn't seem to reassure them.

"He's mellowed in age," Ezra added. "Thanks to my mom."

"That's true." I nodded.

"The devil. You know him?"

I waved a hand around. "It's a long story of sorts, and right now I know three of my mates who need to eat."

Nate grunted, and his stomach growled like it was a beast itself.

"Then come. We'll take the food back into your room and leave you to rest. I have a few people I need to speak with. They'll join the others in the dungeons, and I'll contact you when it's time for questioning."

I stood from the couch. "Sounds like a plan, and thank you for not arguing with me about going into the dungeons."

He glanced down at me as we walked out of his room side by side. His body heat warmed me all over, along with his eyes. "I don't agree, but I'm learning from watching that you would do it no matter what I say."

Laughter behind us, along with rattling of trays, sounded. I glared over my shoulder and then looked back up at Cedrick. "At least you're learning."

"One day I would like to hear the story about Lucifer though."

Butterflies took off in flight in my stomach. He'd said one day. I shouldn't have, but I did have hope.

CHAPTER TEN
PAIGE

I floated in the darkened sky, looking below to the dirt mound surrounded by woods. I watched and waited for something to happen, as if I expected a situation. And when I saw the dirt shift, little rocks and soil tumbling to the side, I knew what I was waiting for.

I knew it as well as the next breath I needed.

Dirty hands popped through the earth. They clawed out from the ground, digging their way free.

Fear clenched my stomach, despite knowing I shouldn't be scared.

The scene was surreal.

A head broke free next and tipped back. A growl shuddered through the area. Wild red eyes took in everything. It was a woman. Her light-colored hair was either blonde or white, but filthy from the muck. She pushed at the dirt and then leaped from the hole she'd been buried in. As she landed in a crouch, her eyes frantically darted this way and that. Her head tipped again, her nostrils flaring. She scented her surroundings.

Another growl rumbled from her, tore from her, the sound almost animalistic.

The dress covering her small frame was in tatters.

My stomach tightened when I saw her clutch at her

own gut as she slowly stood, as if I could feel the hunger eating away at her.

The wind brushed through the area, her hair and dress swaying in the breeze. Suddenly, she spun right and crouched again. A low, humming rumble echoed out of her mud-caked mouth and into the woods.

Again, fear bombarded me.

The woman looked crazed. Her body tensed when we heard a branch break close by. Her upper lip pulled back in a snarl, a warning, and I felt mine doing the same.

Into the small clearing stepped a....

....

Wait....

What was happening?

I blinked rapidly and shook my head. This wasn't right. This was a dream... a dream I hadn't had in a long time.

What in the fuck was happening?

My body jolted as if shaken by something, and I landed on my hands and knees on the dirt ground. I lifted my head and drew in the scents around me. It didn't smell like the outdoors. Familiar scents rushed into me, but I couldn't remember what they were.

Suddenly, I was knocked to the floor. I rolled and then sat up, flicking my hair out of my face. I glanced down and saw I wore the same nightie I had when I'd first crawled out of the ground. When I'd become a ghoul.

That was right... I was a ghoul.

I had strength. I could hear things from afar and yet... I couldn't hear anything at all.

Nothing was making a sound; it was as if I was deaf. There wasn't a sound of birds, people, or the wind rustling.

Nothing.

Fucking hell, where was I and what was going on?

I remembered… shit, what did I remember? That I was a ghoul, I dug myself out, but then nothing. Why?

I drew in another whiff. My chest ached like I had something jammed in there. I grabbed it and looked down. There wasn't anything there, or perhaps I couldn't *see* what the problem was. I screamed and dropped to my back, gripping my head at the severe stabbing pressure on my temples.

"Stop, stop, stop," I yelled.

Then it did.

Slowly, I opened my eyes and sat up. I was smart enough to know what I saw in front of me wasn't real. I wasn't actually in the woods at night. I was… after another intake of air, I sensed I was in a room. The air was clear, but stuffy.

Disoriented, I lay back on the ground. Coldness touched my back. It wasn't from dirt though, maybe concrete or metal.

Another breath in.

God, there were those scents that had me longing.

Were they people or food?

They didn't smell like food.

Pine, blood, a sweet spice like cinnamon, and—

"Roll" came from a deep, panicked voice through my mind. Only I was too shocked hearing a voice in my head I didn't listen to its warning and something invisible smashed into my face. My nose cracked, blood

gushing from it while I covered my face and yelled from the pain.

Jesus Christ, did a Mack truck hit me?

I sucked in a sharp breath as my nose healed. I lowered my hands and opened my eyes; they felt puffy, so I knew they'd swelled from the hit, whatever it had been.

How was I supposed to fight something invisible?

But that voice... it warned me. It also seemed like I'd heard it before; a part of me was telling me I had. Still, it felt new, but one I wanted to listen to. How was that possible?

Whatever was going on was fucked up.

Fear clutched my beating heart and twisted.

Something about my heart triggered my mind, but when I tried to grab that thought, it fled.

Heart, heart, heart, I chanted over and over.

Beating.

My eyes widened.

Shut the damn front door. My heart hadn't been beating when I'd crawled out of the ground. Why was it now? Did it mean I was human?

I pounded the ground with my fists in frustration.

"Move," sounded inside my mind, and that time I didn't hesitate. I was on my feet and running a couple of steps forward, spinning this way and that.

"What else?" I yelled into the still night sky. I gripped my head and whimpered as something clicked inside it, then disappeared. My heart raced at an onslaught of completeness. I felt as if a part of myself that had been missing was found. It didn't make sense, yet nothing had since I woke back in my dream.

"Paige, I'm sorry. I didn't want to complete this mind link, but I had to. You're safe now. It's time to wake up."

"Who are you?"

"What do you mean?" he demanded in a rough, sharp tone, one I sensed alarm in.

"I don't know you."

"Paige, I'm Cedrick Nelydriel, elf king to the realm Airrile."

"Sorry, buddy, it's not ringing any bells."

"What about Asher, Nate, Thorn, Alex, and Ezra?"

I had a little tingling of something, but it slipped away. *"No. Nothing. What's going on? Where am I?"*

"What surrounds you?"

"The woods where I had been buried after... wait, I don't know if I should be telling you this."

Silence, and I didn't like *not* hearing his voice. Panic twisted my insides. *"Cedrick?"* I called, twisting around in the darkened area. *"Cedrick?"* I yelled.

"I'm here, Paige."

The voice sounded so close. The sudden warmth at my back had me tensing. Slowly, I looked over my shoulder and then cried out, turning and stumbling away.

His hand grabbed mine before I fell to the ground. "Paige, relax. Please, I'm here to help you."

His touch and his voice helped me settle. It even spread nerves through my belly. He helped me stand and then slid his hand down my arm, causing me to shiver, to my hand where he held it. I lifted my gaze from our hands to see he was still staring down at them.

"Who are you?" I whispered.

He caught my eyes, and I sucked in some air at how

beautiful he was. He smiled. "I already told you. Cedrick Nelydriel, I'm the—"

"Yes, yes. Elf king of such and such." I shook my head. "Who are you to me?"

His smile upped a notch. It had me wanting to lean into him. His head tilted to the side a little as he studied me.

"God, your hair is absolutely stunning, and those ears, I want to kiss them, touch them—"

He choked.

"Fuck. I said that aloud, didn't I?"

He shook his head, and it didn't go unnoticed how the tips of his ears and cheeks were pink. He licked his lips as if they were dry, and said, "No, you said that in your mind. Only, I'm able to hear it now."

Wait, what? "I'm sorry—what?"

Since we still held each other's hands, he used his other to reach up and tuck my hair behind my ear. His finger glided down from my temple to my cheek and chin; then he cupped the side of my neck.

"How opposed would he be if I kept his hands always on me?"

His eyes widened.

"Shit." I closed my eyes and dropped my head, so I didn't look at him. "Can we stop it?"

"We can learn to stop projecting."

"You're not projecting. It's only me."

His grin grew even more. "For that I'm grateful or else you would have punched me a few times."

I laughed and glanced up at him. "Really?" It shouldn't have, but it had me feeling better.

"Yes."

"Okay. Good." I nodded. He chuckled. "Now, can you tell me who you are to me?"

"Your mate."

"My mate? As in the Australian term, like, on ya cobber, I mean, on ya, mate? Buddy? Pal?"

He threw his head back and laughed. "No. Nothing like that, though I'm not even sure what you first said. What I mean is that you're my intended wife." My eyes sprang wide. He quickly added, "A couple who were fated to be with one another forever." I jerked my head back. He groaned. "I'm not explaining it right. We're bonded mates... at least mostly bonded. We're one step closer with the mind link we now have. Meaning we're touched in some way, but there is only one way for us to complete the bond, and that would be for us to... you see, we would have to... I mean that we're to...."

I searched his face, his was once again blushing, and then a part of my mind produced an image of us naked on the ground. "If we were to sleep with each other, we would completely be bonded?"

"Yes."

"And you want to do this here and now?"

He choked again. "No, no. Christ, woman, you say whatever you think, don't you?"

I smiled. "Yes. So then you come into this place—"

"Your mind."

"What?"

"You're stuck in your mind, Paige. You won't understand it right now, but someone in my realm locked you in your mind and tried to have you forget your other bonded men."

I stepped back in shock, my hands covering my belly. "I have more?" I yelled.

He gave a laugh until I glared. He sobered and then nodded. "Yes. Asher, Thorn, Alex, Nate, and Ezra."

I leaned toward him and whispered, "Am I a slut?"

His lips thinned, and he shook his head. "No," he said darkly.

"Huh, he doesn't like me saying that about myself."

He stepped closer. "No, I don't. You're loved, cherished, and important to all of us. We've all lived a long life, Paige. Having you as our bonded mate completes us. We feel full, at peace, happy, and even loved. Not all have more than one partner. But when it comes to someone special like yourself, it's as it's meant to be. Fate put us all together for a reason. Whatever it is, I'm delighted to be a part of it. Your other men are... they're great men, and together, we're whole. A family."

I didn't know what to think or understand completely how I felt because there were so many emotions rolling around inside me. My mind spun, and my hands shook. Honestly, how he described the connection we shared sounded amazing, wonderful even. Hell, I wanted it, I did, and I knew my... mates would all be different like myself because no human could understand something like this.

"There's no jealousy among anyone?"

He blushed *again*. "No."

I narrowed my gaze. "You're leaving something out."

"It doesn't matter. You'll remember everything as soon as you're out of here."

I placed my hands on my hips. "Cedrick."

He ground his teeth together. "As far as I know, they share one another as well."

"Oh... well, that's... something I wouldn't mind seeing."

Cedrick groaned, rubbing a hand over his face.

"Wait, you said as far as you knew. Why wouldn't you know if you're mine also?" I paused at that, not liking he wasn't involved. *"God, it all sounds so weird. I have five, no six, husbands... men. Six. The sex must be outstanding."*

He snorted, coughed to cover a surprised laugh, and then shook his head. He ran a hand over the back of his neck as he sighed. "I'm new. We only met yesterday."

"And I wanted to be with you then?" I threw up my hands in the air. "Jesus, I must be—"

"Do not say anything bad about yourself," he warned, his hands clenched at his sides. "In our worlds, it's different. The Fates have a play in our lives, in our mates. Desire, need, and hope fill us once we find each other and a small connection is made. However, not all races know that what you have in front of you is an intended mate. People often mistake it for lust. Though, some do, like I did with you. From what I'd heard, you didn't know about me until I'd used my power and your ghoul side reacted to it."

"So it, *this*, the connection, means a lot."

"It means everything, which is why it pains me that we can't be together—"

"Why?" I demanded.

"You will know all of this when we're out."

Biting my bottom lip, I nodded. Even though I wanted

to know as the thought of him not wanting me swirled through my brain, but his words said the contrary. He thought highly of a mate, so there had to be a good reason why we couldn't be together.

"All right. How do we get out?"

"A kiss," he stated.

A giggle escaped. Then I cackled so much I had tears running down my cheeks. I slapped my hand to my leg as I bent over still laughing. I gasped, "A kiss." I shook my head. "How very princess-y."

"Pardon?" Cedrick asked, his face stoic.

I straightened, finally calm enough. "You know... a kiss from a prince always rescues the princess. I just never knew it would be from my own mind." I snorted out another laugh. "Why a kiss? How will that help me?"

"I'll have to drag your mind from this point in time that you're stuck in. There's a chance it will hurt. A kiss from a mate is distracting and could help with any pain you may face."

"Oh," I said quietly. I hated pain. I even considered not having a child since giving birth scared the hell out of me. I mean, I loved my niece and nephew.... Something tickled a part of my mind again. Something about my family. I lifted my gaze. "Is my family okay?"

He seemed confused, the pinch to his brows told me so, before he said, "Sorry?"

"My family... you know what, never mind. You're sure I'll remember everything once you drag me out?"

"Yes." He nodded once.

"Good. Let's do this." Only it was then I thought of

something. "Hang on, if our minds are in here, where are our bodies? Will we be waking into danger?"

Cedrick shook his head. "The men and I disposed of the danger. It's safe to leave, and our bodies should be in the old medical wing. Where we found you."

If I was safe, it meant I had time for another question, right? "What happened to me?"

He took my hand, and I eagerly held onto his. His jaw clenched suddenly. He seemed angry.

Did I want to know why?

Yes, I had to. I didn't hide.

"You may not understand everything right now, but I'll try. You and the other men were attacked. We thought it was to kill you all under the council orders. However, it seemed they were sent to drug you instead. It took some time, but you all fell asleep, and that was when they came in to get you."

The council wanted me dead? Me and my men? Why? What had we done? And what damn council?

"You're right. I don't understand a lot. So maybe it's best we do get out of here."

"Of course. Wrap your arms around my neck." I did, and he lifted me so we were eye to eye. "I'm sorry if this causes you pain."

I didn't answer right away; I got lost in his angelic features. How could one elf be so good-looking? I wanted to know everything about him, and I couldn't wait to remember my other men. Excitement had my stomach in knots.

I gave Cedrick a small smile. "I'm sure you'll be able to take my mind off it."

"It will be my honor to try, my beautiful Paige." Slowly, so the tingle in my groin intensified, he leaned in while staring into my eyes. His were warm and full of desire, and I knew mine burned for him. I couldn't wait to taste him.

He brushed his lips against mine teasingly. Feeling impatient, I growled under my breath and felt his lips pull up as he pressed them against the corner of my mouth.

"I do not like that this will be our first kiss," Cedrick admitted against my cheek.

"We'll have to make up for it then."

He let out a breath, maybe a little laugh. He nipped at my neck. "I will do my best."

I panted the words, "I have a feeling I'll like your best."

He lifted his head, and before he could say more, I pressed my lips against his. He froze for a second, probably worried about the pain, until I tightened my hold around his neck and hooked my legs around his waist. His hands slapped down on my bottom and he squeezed.

"Yes, dear God, yes."

"Cedrick will do, beautiful. I'm no God."

I pulled back quickly, swearing again. "No reading my mind, mister."

"I can't help it. You're projecting. Not that I mind at all." He smirked. "Shall we try again?"

"Yes," I answered a little too quickly.

That time he didn't smile; instead, he dipped in and claimed my lips like he owned them. The kiss was hot, heavy, and so delicious. I moaned into his mouth, opening up to his tongue that glided along my bottom lip. Hell, he tasted of cherries, chocolates, and whiskey. How was that possible?

All I knew was that I wanted more. I wanted all of him.

Until... I whimpered into his mouth. It felt as if my brain was being pulled and pushed from my head without an actual opening. My head throbbed as if someone was stabbing me over and over. I wanted to scream, to cry out, but I also didn't want to lose the connection I had with Cedrick. He kept me grounded. He kept me whole. If I let go of him, I would lose myself.

"Nearly done."

I couldn't reply because the pain intensified. I was sure my brain was on fire, sizzling away under my skull. A scream got through my block. I knew it by the way Cedrick twitched.

"I'm okay." I tried to reassure him, but even in my head I sounded weak.

The pain grew again. Like a knife being drilled into my eyes and slowly the blade was being dragged up over my forehead and skull, right to the back.

I couldn't stop it. I had to let it out.

Pulling back from the kiss, I gripped my head and screamed. I dropped back, but nothing around me registered beyond the pain.

Then it was as if a switch was turned off and the pain stopped.

I panted out unnecessary breaths. My heart was erratic in my chest. I picked up panicked voices but couldn't open my eyes.

"Paige, love. We're here. You're okay." *Asher.*

"You're out, beautiful. You're free." *Cedrick.*

"We're right here, sweetheart. We're not leaving you." *Thorn.*

"Do you feel my hand, dove? Can you feel it?" *Alex.*

"Let her relax. Let her get herself together. Paige, it's fine. Relax, angel." *Nate.*

"Yes, rest if you need to, mi corazón." *Ezra.*

My men were there. *My* men. My bonded mates.

Nate, Asher, Alex, Thorn, Ezra, and even Cedrick.

I remembered them.

God, how could I have forgotten them?

My chest constricted painfully. If I'd been stuck in my mind forever, I wouldn't have had them. I wouldn't have remembered them and wouldn't have known what I was missing out on. Or how much love I would have lost. It hurt knowing that could have happened. Although right then, it quickly switched to anger.

I cleared my healing throat. I must have screamed so much I'd hurt it. "W-Who did this?"

"Thera's father. Do you remember her? Do you remember us?" Thorn asked. He glanced to Cedrick. "We were told you didn't know who we were."

I nodded as another pang of hurt and anger twisted inside me. "I hadn't. All of you were wiped away from my mind," I whispered and then smiled. "I remember you all now though." Opening my eyes, tears filled them. I saw all of them hovered over me in different ways so they could fit as I lay on what felt like a cold metal table. I looked from one to another and then over again. My bottom lip trembled. "He took you all away from me." A sob caught, and Nate was the first to pull me into his arms and off the table. He took a couple of steps and sat us on a couch. I curled into his lap, wrapping my arms around his waist while wondering why a couch was placed in a room that looked like something out of a doctor's office, only a nightmare kind.

The room was all white and silver, but a lot of the silver on the desk, table, chairs, and cabinets had corroded with rust. I shivered from the sight and from the thought of being in there unconscious, prone on the filthy metal table.

I scented Alex at my back, rubbing a hand up and down it. Ezra was to my side, pressing into me and kissing my shoulder. Without looking, I knew Thorn, Asher, and Cedrick would be standing around us, watching, listening, and guarding.

After composing myself, I looked up and met Cedrick's gaze first. "Did he do this because of what I'd done to Thera?"

That I could understand. He took away what meant the most to me, like I had done with him by taking his daughter.

Cedrick shook his head. "Let's get somewhere comfortable and we'll explain what happened."

Nate grunted. He must have agreed because he stood with me in his arms and walked us from the room. I rested my head on his shoulder and then felt a hand on my shoulder and one on my leg. Alex and Ezra. Both needed comfort from touch as much as Nate and I did. I was sure my other men did as well, but they would be willing to wait and let Nate, Alex, and Ezra get their fill first. It reminded me again of how perfectly we worked together.

CHAPTER ELEVEN
NATE

Having her in my arms wasn't enough. My wolf and I wanted to be buried inside her, marking her with our scent all over again. The fear of waking without her in our room would live with me for a fucking long time, and it'd take a while until I could let her out of my sight. Even if it was with one of our men. My skin crawled at the thought of leaving her alone and having something happen to her.

As we walked down the hall, my mind took me back to the last few hours.

* * *

My head was knocked to the side. "Wake up" was yelled, so close to my face that the warm breath washed over my skin. Groaning, I clutched my head and sat slowly.

"Kiered?" someone asked, and I opened my eyes to see Cedrick kneeling in front of me, but he was looking over at his brother who knelt over Ezra. Asher and Thorn were helping Alex sit from his spot on the bed, while I was on the floor.

"What the fuck, man?" I asked, my throat dry and scratchy. I rubbed at my cheek; it still hurt like a bitch from his hit.

"Where is she?" Cedrick demanded.

My mind felt foggy as if it was stuffed in Jell-O. "What are you talking about?"

"Where is Paige?"

My mind spun, locked on his words, and my heart beat hard in my chest as I quickly stood in search for her. Only I stumbled a little, blinking rapidly as I sucked in a deep inhale. Her scent was in the room, but fainter than it should have been. I closed my eyes and paid more attention to my hearing. The people around me quieted as if sensing what I was doing. I could hear scuffling in the floorboards, mites or some type of bugs. Muffled sounds came from down the hall, but nothing right outside or too close.

I couldn't scent or hear her close by.

I breathed deeply through my nose and clenched my hands.

"Nate," Asher said softly. "We'll find her."

I shook my head roughly and lifted my upper lip off my teeth in a silent snarl.

"Nate, hold your shit in until we have all the damn information," Thorn demanded.

My skin rippled over my body. My teeth lengthened, as did my claws. Fur sprouted over my face. It grew longer on my body.

"Jesus, is he bigger than usual?" someone muttered.

I lifted my head back and howled into the room.

"Nate," Alex called. His scent grew close until he was right in front of me. Then Asher was there, Thorn, and Ezra. They surrounded me. They belonged to me, but our bonded female, our Paige, wasn't there.

Someone had taken her.

Someone would pay.

"Calm down. Think, talk, then hunt," Ezra said. He gripped my face in his hands and shook my head slightly. "Think, talk, then hunt," he repeated.

"Kill," we growled out harshly.

"Yes," Ezra bit out in his own growl, his eyes glowing.

I pulled the wolf back, even when he fought me for control. I dragged him back down inside me and held him tight. *Soon*, I promised him.

"We need answers now," I stated.

"And we'll find them." Asher nodded. We all looked to Cedrick.

"This is what I know. All of you came back in here to rest, and I went to speak with Therolidi regarding his daughter, but he wasn't at his home. I ran into Rallis though. He's in the dungeon with the other guards, who were rousing. We came here to get you all and found you passed out."

"How were we knocked out?" Ezra questioned. Yeah, he was kind of new, but he'd been a part of this from the start, even as his hellhound, so it was easy to be comfortable with him. Cedrick, even though I knew Paige and he were connected, they weren't bonded fully yet, so I wasn't ready to trust everything he said. Although, he looked as stricken as the rest of us with the loss of Paige.

He ran a hand through his hair and looked around the room, like he was searching for something. "It doesn't make sense."

"What?" I demanded harshly, my wolf riding my tone.

Ezra and Alex faced Cedrick, but they both reached back to lay a hand on me. Alex at my outer thigh and Ezra curled his hand around my wrist. Their contact, along with Asher's on my neck and Thorn's on my shoulder, helped ground me more.

Fuck me, but I loved my pack.

However, the most important part was missing.

We had to get her back.

A sad whimper escaped me, feeling her loss hit me once more. Our mates' fingers rubbed at my skin, calming me. We hadn't even claimed one, the hound, but he was still ours. I knew it and the wolf did also. The time would come, but it wouldn't be until Paige was back in our arms.

"How did this happen? None of you would just fall into slumber and risk your mate."

"No, we wouldn't," Asher agreed. "Especially since a lot of us need very little sleep to begin with."

"Then it happened to us without us knowing," Alex said more to himself as he stared at the floor in thought. He lifted his gaze and turned to see all of us in the room. "The food?"

I shook my head. "Not everyone ate."

"The fight," Kiered said softly. We all looked to him behind Cedrick. He stepped closer. "Look on yourself to see if you can find a mark of some type."

"Fucking hell, the fight was a setup—not to kill Paige or us, but to put us to sleep to get to her," I said while searching my body.

"There," Thorn said. His hands went to my lower back. I kept still as everyone crowded around me. Fingers ran over my skin. "It looks like a goddamn freckle, but it's not." I felt a fast, sharp prick of pain and then turned as Thorn held up what did look like a freckle.

"Motherfucker. How did they get that on me without me knowing?"

"Distraction," Asher said as he picked something off his arm near his elbow. "They used the fight to see if they could take her on their own, or if that failed, they drugged us. We wouldn't have felt it because we were getting knocked around at the time."

"Jesus Christ," I yelled. "We need to find her." I pulled Ezra around since he hadn't found his and dragged his tee from his body. I found it on his hip and pulled it free.

"Who deals with this type of magic? A magic I hadn't sensed before," Alex asked, glancing down at his in his hand.

Cedrick stepped closer to him. I grabbed Alex and Ezra and pulled them behind me, holding out my own for him to look at. I ignored Ezra's snort and Alex's grumble. Cedrick didn't say anything about my mistrust of him and held his hand above mine where the device was.

He shook his head. "Any one of my people who has the power to control earth magic. I can sense the herbs, dirt, and leaves within it myself. Used with the correct wording, which they obviously had, it all becomes a powerful sleeping spell."

"Can you do it, Alex?" Asher asked.

I caught Alex roll his eyes before looking over his shoulder to Asher. "Yes, of course."

"Do what?" Kiered asked.

"Trace where the spell was cast," Alex said as his power filled the room. His eyes closed but not before I saw them change to purple. His lips moved with his own spell. The window suddenly opened with a bang, causing a few of us to jump, and I wouldn't admit I was one. A breeze blew in and swirled around Alex.

He then smiled.

"I have a picture in my mind. A medical ward, but it looks run-down. It's dark, but a man with shoulder-length, dark brown hair and eyes cast the spell from there. It's within the walls of this castle."

"Merde," Cedrick whispered. He spun to his brother. "Right under my nose." His jaw clenched. The floor beneath us shook as his eyes glowed brighter. "Right under my nose." He looked to Alex with intense anger in his eyes. I wanted to step in front of Alex again, but I didn't. Mainly because Alex placed his hand on my arm in a warning not to. "Can you teleport?"

"Yes."

"Using that picture in your mind?"

"Yes, and with two people."

Cedrick nodded. "I'll take the wolf and hellhound."

My wolf liked being called instead of my actual fucking name; it annoyed me though.

"Let's go," Alex said, and then he disappeared with Asher and Thorn. Cedrick glided quickly to my side and swept Ezra up in one arm on the way to me. As soon as his arm wound around my waist, everything disappeared around me. My head spun for a second, and then my feet jarred when I landed on new flooring, we arrived shortly after Alex, Thorn, and Asher.

"Therolidi, step away from her," Cedrick demanded in a low, cold, and hard tone.

I lifted my gaze and growled. My wolf was already prowling close to the surface. Especially when I saw Paige unconscious on a metal table and a man standing over her with a knife to her neck.

"Where is Thera?" Therolidi asked in a mild tone and with a smirk I wanted to wipe off his face. He glanced to Ezra and me as we both growled. "Calm, beasts. I've already told the mage not to use any magic, and the vampire, if he so much as moves a hair, I'll cut her head off."

I sensed Alex, Asher, and Thorn close, but I didn't dare look toward them and take my eyes off the threat.

"Move the fuck away from her, and we'll think about letting you live," I snarled.

The motherfucker laughed. "I have a knife to her throat. None of you can tell me what to do."

"Why do you want her?"

He scoffed. "I don't. The council does, and I want her out of the way."

I felt Cedrick tense behind me. "You knew she was my bride."

"The whole kingdom knows, you foolish boy. Everyone feels the pull you have for each other."

"So you wanted her gone for your daughter to step back in?" Thorn guessed.

"My daughter would have eventually won his heart, but she wouldn't with this thing in the picture." He sneered down at Paige like she was dog shit under his foot.

My body stiffened when I felt a wave of something come off Cedrick. Christ, it warmed me. I rolled my head and then lunged when Therolidi punched Paige in the face.

"Do not move," he roared. Everyone froze. I knew the others had moved too. I could see more of them from the corner of my eyes. Asher's gaze caught mine, then moved behind me to Cedrick. I dropped my gaze to his fingers. He shifted them slightly.

Be ready, they told me.

"What does the council want her for?"

Therolidi laughed. "What does the council always want? Money, but more importantly, power. They believe they can get that from her."

Fucking stupid mongrels.

They'd never learn. As soon as we got Paige out of this and walked into their comfortable world, or what they thought was comfortable, they would soon learn they weren't safe behind their compound doors.

"Now, where's my daughter?"

"Dead," Cedrick announced, then yelled. "Now!"

Paige's body suddenly rolled. If it hadn't been for Asher flashing forward to grab her, she would have crashed to the ground. I dove over the table with Ezra at my side, but Therolidi, by Alex's magic, was lifted into the air and slammed into the roof with such force bones broke. The ground shook. Thorn shoved the table toward Asher. He placed Paige back on it and held onto her and the table as the floor, fucking *concrete* floor, split open. Ezra tackled me and we rolled out of the way.

Therolidi's scream of horror had both of us glancing up to see his arms being torn by an invisible force from his body.

"No one touches our mate," Alex clipped, his usual sweet, soft voice gone. The powerful mage stood in his place as his lips moved once more and blood poured from

Therolidi's thighs while the bottom of his legs dropped to the ground.

"What a damn sight," Ezra whispered, and I could hear the awe in his voice. Shit, pride came out of me in waves. Our Alex was not to be reckoned with. Only now wasn't the time to get a fucking hard-on over it. I snorted when I caught Ezra adjust himself.

"Alex, bury him and let him suffocate," Cedrick demanded. His hands and legs were spread wide, and I realized he'd been the one to open the floor in the room. Alex nodded. He lowered a whimpering, crying elf into the ground, and as he begged for his life, Cedrick closed the hole over him. He sealed it and set the room back to as it had been, as if nothing had happened in the first place.

"We could have questioned him some more," Thorn announced in the quiet room.

"And have him hurt her more?" Cedrick asked.

"No, I just meant after we'd captured him."

"I wasn't in the mood to have a conversation," Alex said, clenching his jaw.

I strode over to him and brought him into my arms. "She's safe now," I told him. He sighed, relaxed a little, and leaned into me. *She's safe now*, I reminded myself and my wolf. Though we weren't happy just yet, not until she was awake and yelling at us or giving us the finger for something. Still, I had the need to reassure Alex. I didn't like to see him so serious when his nature was never like that.

Ezra approached and pressed into Alex's back, nipping at his neck. "That was totally badass."

Alex let out a surprised laugh. "Don't," he said a second later.

"Well, it was."

Alex lifted his head and turned enough to kiss Ezra's cheek. "Thank you, both of you. I'm better now."

"Good," I grunted. I still rubbed my hand up and down his back as I looked to the others. "Now, why the fuck hasn't she woken yet and how did her body roll off the damn table?"

"I believe Therolidi has locked her in her mind to be able to transport her."

"Locked her in her mind?" Thorn questioned. "But she has strong mental shields. She blocks us all the time when she doesn't want us knowing what she's feeling."

"Our powers over the mind are stronger, especially when that someone is asleep and doesn't realize their mind is being messed with."

"Fuck," I barked. "Fix her," I ordered, and then added, "It still doesn't explain how she moved."

"Cedrick made a mind link with her," Kiered announced.

"And that's supposed to explain it how?" I asked.

"I reached in and spoke with her. If you wait one moment, I will do it again." He closed his eyes. I didn't like when his brows pinched or his lips thinned. He opened his eyes. "She's been locked on a loop on the night she woke from the grave she dug her way out of. She doesn't know any of you or even me."

"What the fuck?" I yelled, then curled Alex into me more when I felt him tense. Ezra moved closer into Alex's side as well.

"Can you help her?" Asher asked.

"I should be able to, but it may cause her pain."

I winced at the thought of Paige in any pain.

"If I know Paige correctly, she'll want help to remember everything," I said.

Cedrick nodded.

"But what do you mean you've made a mind link with Paige?" Ezra asked.

"Our minds will always be able to reach one another's, and we're able to speak telepathically," he said. "She's calling for me. I must go. I don't want her to worry more than she is."

"You're keeping out something." I glared.

Cedrick sighed. "It is one step closer to having our bond formed. I shouldn't have made it since we are unable to be with one another, but I had to."

"That's how she rolled out of the way," Alex said.

Cedrick nodded.

Well, crap. I couldn't dislike the guy for protecting her.

"Kiered, pull over that table," Cedrick ordered. His brother did, and Cedrick climbed on top of it. He lay back. "I will do everything in my power to bring her back with little to no pain."

Thorn rested a hand on his arm. "Thank you." Asher nodded, as did Alex, while Ezra gave him a wink.

I sucked it up, since I was grateful for his help and now the wolf and I knew he'd protected her. I rubbed at the back of my neck and said, "Yeah, thanks. You'd make a good mate for her." And he would, even if I hated admitting it. But the extra protection for her would be good. Plus, he was okay-looking, I supposed.

"Thank you. All of you," he said with a smile and then closed his eyes.

* * *

"Wait," Paige called out. She forcefully twisted in my arms so hard I had to place her on her feet. Only I didn't release her altogether; my hands went to her waist. She pointed to another room. "What's in there?" she asked Cedrick.

He glanced to his brother and then back again. "Another room."

Paige shook her head. She took a step closer and rested her hand to the door. "It... I don't know, doesn't feel right, but I feel a need to go in here."

Cedrick's eyes glowed brightly. The ground moved a little, and then he was right next to Paige, touching the door. "Yes, I feel it now that you've pointed it out. I wouldn't have if you didn't say anything."

I didn't have a fucking clue what they were talking about because I couldn't sense shit. All I knew was that I wanted to get out of this freaky hallway from the medical wing of doom.

Kiered joined in. "Someone blocked this room from anyone being able to hear or feel anything from within it."

Cedrick snarled, "More of Therolidi's tricks."

"You elf lot sure do love mind games and illusions."

Cedrick straightened and waved his hand in front of him. The door and walls wavered revealing, *oh fucking wow*, another door. Only this one was more rotten than the rest down in this dingy, stinky-as-hell place.

Kiered reached for the handle, but then his body shook violently.

"Brother," Cedrick cried.

Paige grabbed Cedrick's arm when Alex yelled, "Don't touch him." Alex stepped forward. His eyes glowed, his lips moved, and Kiered suddenly stilled and his hand dropped away. Alex floated him down to the floor. Cedrick dropped to his brother's side.

"Merde, that hurt," Kiered muttered.

"You're all right?"

"Yes, brother. I should have been more careful, but it wouldn't release me. It's lucky you have a strong mage in your bonded group."

"It is," Cedrick said. He turned and took Alex's hand, causing Alex to blush tomato red, and lay his forehead against it before kissing his skin. "Thank you."

"Ah, yeah, um, no problem," Alex mumbled.

An unease filled me. He hadn't claimed Alex and was touching him.

I wanted to rip his hand off and my wolf agreed. But a part of me, for once, held back since I knew he was meant to be in our group, but mainly because he'd helped Paige when we couldn't. Logically, we knew we needed him. It still didn't stop me from reaching out, taking Alex's wrist, and pulling his hand from Cedrick's grasp.

Kiered chuckled. "The possessive wolf comes out."

Cedrick smiled and helped his brother up from the floor.

Paige giggled. She stepped close and patted my chest. "He's just a playful puppy really."

I growled low and nipped at her. She moved back, laughing.

"Yeah, playful." Ezra snorted.

"Can we get back to the damn door issue?" I asked. Alex twisted his wrist in my hand and slid it up to hold my hand instead.

"It's unlocked now," Alex said.

"Thank you once more." Cedrick nodded. I didn't know if he realized himself, but his eyes slid over Alex in appreciation. I stopped from taking his eyeballs and let him look since he wasn't touching. Besides, Alex was easy on the eyes. Fuck it, all of them were.

Goddamn good-looking mates.

I had to reason with the wolf that we wouldn't kill everyone who looked at them like they wanted to fuck them, despite us hating it.

Cedrick, proving he was an okay guy again, trusted Alex's words and reached for the handle. He twisted and pushed, and it opened wide.

A pained noise ripped from within him and Kiered.

"Mother," Cedrick whispered.

Holy fuck.

The woman, chained to a chair with tubes running all up her arms that were hooked up to some type of machine, didn't lift her head. I wasn't even sure she was alive. Her body looked sunken in. No fat remained on any inch of her. Fuck, she looked like a skeleton.

Cedrick and Kiered raced into the room, one on each side of their mother. They reached out, pulled their hands back, and then reached out again. Kiered rested a hand to her bony shoulder while Cedrick slowly lifted their mother's head. She showed no response.

Paige moved in. I wanted to grab her and drag her back out because I didn't like the fucking feel of the room. As soon as the door had opened, my skin crawled.

"Paige," I called.

Of course the infuriating woman ignored me. Hadn't she been through enough? If this was another fucking trick, I would kill people.

I stepped in after her and felt Alex behind me. I glanced over my shoulder to see Asher, Ezra, and Thorn had also followed. We looked around the room for any type of trap or threat. When I couldn't see or sense anything, I focused back on Paige.

She had her fingers against the woman's neck. "She's alive, but her pulse is very weak."

"Fuck, Cedrick. Fuck," Kiered whispered.

"Are you sure this isn't a trick?" Asher asked.

Cedrick nodded.

"You've never mentioned her before," Thorn said. "Are you sure this is her?"

Tears pooled in his eyes and his brother's. Cedrick clenched his jaw. "Yes, it's her. God, it's her."

Asher and Thorn shared a look. I knew that look. It was one that said we weren't sure to trust this. However, the brothers were adamant that it was their mother. Kiered kept whispering into her ear that they were there and she was safe.

"Do you know what this is?" I asked.

Cedrick shook his head. "Kiered, go and get Yeno, Grandith, and Juri. They'll be able to help her."

Kiered nodded once and disappeared from the room instantly.

"Who are they?" Paige asked.

"They never confirmed it, but they were her intended."

"But your father...."

Cedrick shook his head, gazing sadly down at his mother. "Mother's parents, the former king and queen, believed it best, like my father had, to set up an arranged marriage for business purposes. Yeno, Grandith, and Juri were mother's guards."

Paige went around the chair and curled her arm around Cedrick's waist. She looked up at him, and he stared down. When Cedrick nodded, I knew they'd been having a conversation within their minds.

Why did a sudden pang of sadness for the guy hit me?

Hell, my wolf even whimpered a little.

Maybe it was because Cedrick had been through a fucking lot.

It brought up memories of my own fucked-up life before I worked with the elite force. I'd been with a drunk dad who'd changed my mother into a werewolf without her consent, and then she lived through her days stuck in half form. Not that it stopped my motherfucking father from screwing her to conceive me. She ended her life when I was five, leaving me stuck with him until I killed him.

A hand to my back had my body jolting. Growling, I spun to Paige, who stood there with a pinch to her brows. Worried for me. Christ, I didn't lock down my emotions enough.

"I'm fine," I clipped, crossing my arms over my chest.

"Okay," she whispered. She got to her tippy-toes, and even then, I had to bend a little so she could place a peck on my lips. "I don't believe you, but I'll get it out of you later."

I scoffed. She rolled her eyes and went back to Cedrick. Shit, even his eyes looked darker in concern for me. Made me feel like a dick for getting lost in my head while he was dealing with finding his mom like this. I nodded once at him, letting him know I was fine. Thankfully he turned back to his mother where Alex stood on the other side using his magic to put her in a trance while he gently removed all the shit she was hooked up with. The needles and bounds.

When the last strap was free, along with yet another needle, the woman let out a gasp. She started to droop forward, but Cedrick caught her and supported her back against the chair.

"Mother? Mother, it's Cedrick."

She moaned and shook her head.

"Mother?"

Four forms appeared behind the chair. One was Kiered, so the others must have been the men Cedrick wanted there. As soon as they appeared, they cried out and surrounded the woman, all of them speaking at once, saying different things.

All of them were also crying.

"Paige," I called. She looked over at me, her own eyes filled with tears. "Maybe we should step out?" I knew if I was them, I would want my privacy.

She nodded. Turning, I started for the door and knew the others would follow. I itched for answers, but they would wait. What I longed for most was to have my pack surrounding me.

In the hall, and once the door was closed, I ordered, "Here, please." Paige was the first in my arms. She pressed in, and I heard her letting go, crying. Alex and Ezra were on each side of her, wrapping us up at my front while Asher and Thorn curled around my back.

This was what I needed. To feel them all, to know they were safe.

I was sure I wasn't the only one needing it.

CHAPTER TWELVE
PAIGE

The door to the new room Cedrick supplied burst open, and a very pissed off Xi entered. "Did no one think to wake me from my slumber?"

Oh shit.

"He must have been drugged earlier than us for him to sleep through the fight," Asher mused. The room filled with more tension.

"Whoever did it saw him as more of a threat than us," Ezra said, sounding annoyed. "That pisses me off. I'm damned threatening."

Since he was close from where I paced, I patted his arm. "Yes, you are."

He glared at me, so I leaned in and kissed him quickly. As I pulled back, my hellhound was back to smiling.

"What is this fight? And who drugged me?" Xi demanded, pulling swords from his back. I was sure I hadn't seen the hilts there before. Were they magical?

Ezra rolled his eyes. "Relax, Grandpa, the fight is done, and the drugs have worn off. Hmm, maybe I need some of those drugs when he gets on my nerves."

"Ezra," Xi growled.

Ezra batted his eyelashes. "Yes, Xi?"

Laughing, I slapped Ezra's stomach. "Stop goading him or I'll let him eat you."

"I could eat you," he said low with a wink.

I gasped. "Oh my God, you didn't just say that."

He threw up his hands. "I can't help it. Things like that just come out with you."

It was lucky I found him cute and silly.

"Stop around anyone but us or there won't be any action at all," I warned. He used a finger and a thumb to zip his lips with an invisible zipper. Nate snorted. I whirled around. "What does *that* snort mean?"

He smirked. "Like you could hold off from having sex."

"I can and I will if that's what you want," I said with a glare and my hands on my hips. Okay, I probably couldn't when they drove me into a frenzy of desire all the time. Even just standing there eating a cookie, I wanted to jump his bones because he was damn hot. Bastard.

"Nate, shut it," Thorn scolded. Ha, at least he knew I would try to keep myself from sex and he didn't want those few days I would last to happen.

"May we please get back to what the fuck happened?" Xi roared. I'd never heard him say so much. It told me he was at the end of his leash in patience.

"Sorry, Xi," I started, and then replayed what had occurred in the last few hours or so.

At the end, Xi embedded his swords into the floor, crossed his arms, and said, "I do not like this place. It gives me the heebie-jeebies. Too many tricks and illusions. We need to leave at once."

Ezra gaped at him. "Did you just say heebie-jeebies?" He looked to Alex and asked, "Did he just say heebie-jeebies?" A smiling Alex nodded.

Xi ignored him and crossed his arms over his chest. "What is this new mess with the mother of your new mate?"

"Well, he's not my full mate just yet," I said. He stared me down blankly. "Anyway, we're not sure. They're seeing to her in another room and we're all praying she lives for their sake."

"She does seem loved," Alex said.

I nodded. "Yes, she does." It had me wondering for the millionth time what had happened. "I guess we'll get answers eventually."

"I still say we should leave," Xi said.

"I know you do, Xi, but I can't until I know everything will be okay," I told him. I wouldn't just up and leave because Xi was worried without saying anything to Cedrick. I had a feeling that even if I tried, my whole self would revolt in some way.

"At least we don't need to question the survivors," Alex said. "We know everything. They were Therolidi's minions sent to kill or drug us, and we know Therolidi wanted to hand Paige over to the council, our old boss in fact, since they were chummy. What's left for us to know?" He shrugged.

"Then we kill them," I suggested.

Nate snorted, then smirked. Asher and Alex had a small smile, while Ezra was all-out grinning. It was Thorn who approached me and said, "Yes, our little bloodthirsty mate. We'll kill them." He grinned and spun me to hug me from behind. He laid a kiss on my shoulder. "I do love how your mind works."

Hell, I wanted to preen at his compliment, but I wasn't

sure if that would look psycho since I had just mentioned murder. So I simply tilted my head to the side and puckered my lips. Chuckling, Thorn bent and pressed his mouth against mine.

Xi growled in the back of his throat, bringing my attention back to him. "Since I missed the fight, I think I have the right to kill them."

Damn. If I said no, I was sure he would get his panties in a twist. Even though I was in the mood to take some anger out on the mongrels, I would find another way to relieve some tension.

"Okay, Xi, and see if you find out anything new that we haven't told you."

He bowed, picked up his swords, and stormed from the room.

"It was a good choice, love. Xi lives by honor, and he would have struggled not being here for you."

I nodded at Asher. "I guessed as much. Plus, I didn't want a pouting Xi around."

Ezra laughed. "I second that."

"However, now I have all this energy and I don't know how I should get rid of it. I also have a need for some entertainment." I glanced over my shoulder to Thorn. "Would we have time?"

His eyes darkened as he scraped his bottom lip with his top teeth. "I'm sure we would."

I scented my other men before their heat hit me as I turned in Thorn's arms to face him.

I caught Nate as he pulled his tee over his head. "Alex, please fix the door and make the room soundproof. Plus, get everyone damn naked to save time."

Alex's power swept through the room, causing me to shiver and then moan as my clit pulsed. Then, I was gloriously naked, surrounded by my men. One was missing, but it was by our choice, and it wasn't as if I liked that choice either. I would have loved him there with us.

Something buzzed against my clit, and my body shuddered. I looked down, but no one touched me.

I glanced up and found a grinning Alex. "You were thinking. I had to distract you."

Smiling, I curled a hand around the back of his neck and pulled him closer. "Distract me again, please."

"My pleasure," he murmured against my lips, and then my clit buzzed again and again. I cried out, dropped my head back, and knew it was Nate's chest I leaned against. I made sure to keep my hand around Alex's neck when my body was lifted. Thorn picked me up easily. I wrapped my legs around his waist as he slid inside of my wet, throbbing pussy.

"Fuck, I can feel that, Alex."

Alex chuckled. "Fun isn't it, but I'll stop for now. We don't want to tire her out before we've had our fill of our mate."

"Good thinking." Ezra grinned. He squeezed in to kiss his mark on my chest, and then he claimed my mouth in a hot and heavy kiss. Pulling back, he winked and moved from my shoulder to behind Alex.

Thorn's hand on my hips tightened. He grunted, lost for words as he worked himself in and out of me, with Nate's help as he supported me from behind. Knowing my men had my weight as Asher moved in to lean down and take a nipple into his mouth, I reached down and palmed his erection. He hissed out a breath before biting down on my nipple.

"God, yes," I cried, feeling his fangs penetrate my skin. He'd only taken a sip before he licked over the puncture wounds and kissed down my body to tongue my clit even while Thorn still fucked me. Thorn slowed though, letting Asher drink me in, dipping his tongue in to take more wetness from Thorn and me.

A gasp had me prying my eyes open and smiling when I saw Alex had turned enough for Ezra to be on his knees in front of him. His head bobbed up and down on Alex's hard cock. A wave of desire from the sight had me clamping down on Thorn.

A growl rumbled up from Nate at my back. "Get the fuck off him," he snarled. Ezra didn't listen; he taunted my wolf with a wink. Alex tried to step back to calm Nate, but Ezra grabbed the back of his thighs and sucked him all the way in and swallowed around Alex. It, of course, caused Alex to curse and get lost in the sensation.

Oh shit, Nate hadn't claimed Ezra or the other way around. He wouldn't enjoy seeing them together until that happened. His emotions were all over the place when they slipped out and into the room. He was pumped full of pleasure, but angry at the same time.

Suddenly, I was lifted off Thorn. "You can have her back in a second," Nate said just as he turned me, picked me up and buried himself inside me. He was thicker than Thorn, so I threw my head back and cried out from how full I felt.

He lifted me up and down slowly on him and nuzzled his mouth into my neck, kissing, licking, and marking me.

"Had to be inside of you... fuck," Nate clipped as I clamped down around him, a surprise orgasm taking over me. I moaned and bit into his neck, trying to mark him myself. He growled low, a different sound to any other. It was the wolf telling me he liked what I was doing.

"Jesus, fuck, you always feel good."

"Hmm, so do you," I said.

"Now I got you to come, I've got to take care of something," he said into my neck.

"What?"

"Ezra."

My heart skipped a beat. I would have clapped if I'd let him go. "Um, yay," I mumbled instead. He chuckled before he slowly slid out of me and helped me stand. My legs felt like jelly, but in the best way. I glanced back to Asher and Thorn; my pulse raced. They were lip locked in a tight embrace. Their hands ran over each other's bodies while they ground their cocks against one another's.

"May I have your attention for a moment, dove?" Alex stepped up beside me.

"You can have it any time you want," I told him, taking his hand he held out to me.

He grinned, a blush coating his cheeks. God, I loved him. I loved them all so darn much. He licked his lips nervously; it was always cute to see. "Will you join me on the bed?"

I nodded. "Always." He led me around to the side where the rest of the room would be visible. He knew, while we made love, I would still want to see the other pleasure my men gave each other—especially if there was a fight about to happen.

Nate and Ezra stood apart eyeing one another. Nate glared while Ezra looked smug.

I gasped when I was pushed forward, my top half bent over, and I rested my elbows to the bed, glancing over my shoulder to see Alex with darkened eyes as they ran over my body slowly. The blush was long gone, even when he ordered, "Spread your legs more."

My nipples hardened, and my pussy throbbed. I did as I was told, because in the bedroom, I did like to be told what to do.

Alex ran his hand up and down his length while he used his other hand to reach out and run a couple of fingers through my wetness. He drew his finger up to his nose and inhaled before sucking them into his mouth.

"I love your scent, love your taste, love all of you," he whispered, and I noticed Thorn and Asher were watching him also while they jerked each other off.

"I love everything about you, Alex."

"Asher, take Thorn to the bed next to us. I want you to bury yourself inside of him while I do our Paige. It'll leave more room for Nate and Ezra to play."

A cool breeze blew over my skin as Asher flashed to our side, and then Thorn was in the same position I was, bent over the bed, his ass on view for Asher. Only Asher had a hand at the back of Alex's neck while he took his mouth in a heated kiss.

"Sweetheart," Thorn uttered. I glanced back and found him close. His lips touched mine gently once, twice, and a third time before we deepened the kiss. Wanting more, needing to touch him more, I wrapped my arm around him and scooted closer.

I could never, not ever, get enough of my men.

Alex's hands at my hips distracted me. I pulled back, panting even when I didn't need to. Thorn smiled smugly at me, knowing he was the cause because of the kiss. Only he let out a hiss and glanced over his shoulder. I looked also since I could feel the tip of Alex's cock at my needy entrance. Asher was also lined up with Thorn, and they slowly pushed inside of us. I gripped Thorn's hand, my belly already tightening with an oncoming orgasm from just the feel of Alex entering me and seeing Asher pushing into Thorn.

"Fuck us," Thorn demanded roughly.

Asher laughed low. "Are you sure you can handle it?"

"Hell yes," Thorn replied. "Paige?" he asked.

I glanced over to Alex. "Please, Alex, fuck me hard."

He sucked in a sharp breath, tightened his hold on my hips, and leaned over me a little before he did indeed fuck me hard. I got lost in the sensation, the in and out, the slapping of skin, the sounds we all made.

"Christ, I'm coming," Thorn yelled.

"Yes, come," Asher said, wrapping his arms around Thorn's shoulders and forcing him to stand up a bit. I got to see Thorn's cum shoot out over the bed, hear his cry of ecstasy. All of it had me moaning as my own release overcame me. Alex grunted. He swelled inside me, and I milked all of the cum out of him.

"Thorn," Asher clipped and then groaned as his own seed spilled into Thorn.

My mind spun as the room around me wavered. The next thing I knew, I was sitting on a clean bed between Alex's legs next to Thorn, who lay with his head resting on

Asher's thigh as Asher ran his hand over Thorn's hair, purring. I wiggled back, resting into Alex more. His arms slid around my waist, holding me close. He kissed my neck and shoulder. I smiled contently, relaxed and sated wonderfully, ready for the show about to start. As were Asher, Alex, and Thorn.

"Well, wolf, that's got me all randy. Are you ready to submit?" Ezra asked. The tip of his cock shone with precum. If it had been me watching us, then I would feel the same. Ready for my own release.

"We'll soon find out who comes out on top." Nate smirked. Then right before our eyes, his body altered, changed, and morphed into his wolf.

"He has grown," Asher commented. I nodded. It was all I could do because I was in awe whenever Nate shifted. I'd been told it hurt each transformation, but he made it look so smooth and painless. Nate barked, got down on his front legs, and growled.

I glanced to Ezra. His smile was a little wild. He clapped his hands once and then spread them wide. "Beast form, I love it." His body flew into his hellhound form. One second it was Ezra the man, and then the next his hellhound stood on all fours and let loose a deep growl, responding to Nate's.

"Oh shit, this'll be good," I said eagerly, rubbing my hands together. "The spell to block out sound is still in place?"

"Of course," Alex said. I felt his smile against my shoulder.

Nate was nearly as large as Ezra's hellhound. He had grown. How it was possible, I didn't know, but it was something to think about later. The wolf and hellhound stared each other down with their glowing eyes as they circled one another. Constant rumbles dropped from their mouths.

Ezra jumped forward then back, trying to goad Nate into action. But I knew Nate wouldn't take the bait. Ezra would have to be the one to attack. They circled some more. Ezra snarled and then lost his cool and dove at Nate, nipping at his flank, but leaving himself wide open also. Nate went to go for the top of Ezra's neck, but no doubt realized he couldn't because of the bones jutting out from his spine, so he ducked lower and bit at his neck before knocking into Ezra and taking him to the ground.

They snarled and snapped at each other as they rolled around on the floor. Neither was going to come out unscathed from this fight of dominance. I had a feeling Nate would win and hoped Ezra would just give in so they didn't hurt one another too bad.

Nate managed to get to his feet, grab Ezra by the throat, and throw him to the side. Ezra went skidding over the floor and crashed into a table, which fell on top of him. A rush of concern filled me. My blood sped through my body.

"It's fine, love," Asher said, taking my free hand since the other was already clutching Alex's. He kissed the back of my hand and then placed them down on his thigh. "They know what they're doing. Nate didn't even break his skin when he threw him, and Ezra is stronger than you think."

I nodded and relaxed again into Alex, knowing if anything did happen, my other men would fix it. Ezra stood. Wood dropped away from his body as he shook. He licked his lips, eyeing Nate and growling.

Nate took a step forward and snarled. Ezra answered it. Nate swiped at the floor, his nails easily carving into the wood. Ezra jumped at him, Nate dodged, but Ezra was there latching his jaw around the back of Nate's neck. Nate snarled. Ezra growled and shook Nate back and forth.

Nate rumbled out some more noise, but Ezra wasn't letting go and I was sure Nate knew it.

"Should we do something?" I whispered.

The men around me chuckled. Alex kissed my neck and whispered, "Look lower on them, dove."

I scanned over them and down. I spotted Nate's erection first—large, hard, with the pink tip out and leaking. He was enjoying it, and it was obvious Ezra was as well. While holding Nate in a grip around the neck, he moved over Nate more and mounted him. It was then I saw his own long, thick cock. Longer still than Nate's since his pink tip extended out further in his hellhound form.

My heart thumped so fast in my chest I was sure it would jump out of my body.

Nate snarled, glancing over his shoulder. Ezra growled back—it almost sounded smug. Ezra adjusted again. His dick was right near Nate's ass. Slowly, Ezra pushed inside. Nate stilled, dropping his head. Ezra let go of Nate's neck and licked at him. Nate lowered himself a little so Ezra got a better grip with his feet on the ground. Ezra then pumped in and out with his length. Ezra licked at Nate again. Nate grumbled but tipped his head to the side to receive the lick on the face. Still, Ezra fucked Nate hard and fast.

"Does it bother you, love?" Asher asked.

In answer, I took his hand and gently pulled it down where I spread my legs and let him feel how unbothered I was by it. Watching them, even in their shifted forms, fight and enjoy each other, love each other, got me aroused. I was close to climax already.

"Christ, you're drenched," Asher said roughly. He didn't pull his hand away, which I was grateful for. Instead, he inserted two fingers inside me, and I ground back against Alex's hardness. His arousal was proudly on display. He hissed out a breath and cupped both my breasts, rolling them around in his hands, teasing each nipple while pushing himself up against me.

"Yes," I moaned, gripping Asher's wrist while his fingers drove in and out in the same rhythm Ezra was to Nate.

Thorn twisted around in Asher's lap and took a hard Asher into his mouth, causing Asher to groan and grip the back of Thorn's head. Through hooded eyes, I caught Thorn get to his knees and run his own palm over himself.

As I rode Asher's fingers, panting drew my attention to Nate and Ezra. Nate had given up on stopping Ezra licking his face and just accepted it as Ezra pumped Nate. Nate suddenly tensed. He let out a grumble and then a sound in the back of his throat as his cum shot out his tip and landed on the floor. Asher cried out, holding Thorn down on him and came down his throat. Wetness touched my back as Alex hissed out a breath of "Yes!"

I locked Asher's hand between my thighs. As Asher fucked me with his fingers, Alex used his magic to buzz against my clit, sending me over the edge with a cry. Thorn groaned. I opened my eyes to see him pumping his hand faster over himself as he leaned up near Asher and then he shot his load onto Asher's groin.

Ezra howled as he thrust into Nate a few more times before stilling and gently slipping himself out of Nate. They both dropped to the floor in a heap around each other. Nate slowly shifted back, bones crunching and popping. When he lay there as a man, Ezra gave him one last lick before shifting back also.

"Next time, I might let you take me," Ezra teased.

Nate grunted and gave him the finger. Though, he didn't seem upset over what happened at all.

God, I loved my men.

CHAPTER THIRTEEN
PAIGE

While Nate, Ezra, and Asher rested, Alex insisted he was fine and suggested I make a call to my family. Of course I took him up on it. Seeing Yasmin glowing as she sat with Eric and Sakura standing behind them like she was their guard, helped ease more tension I didn't realize I'd been carrying. Then again, of course I was worried about my family, but they reassured me everything was fine back home.

A few hours later, I was sitting in a living room off the bedroom we'd been supplied when the door opened and Xi walked in. At least he didn't break the door.

"How did it go, Xi?" I asked as Thorn handed me a bowl of meat he'd had Alex transport him home for. It was then Asher had ordered Alex to have a rest. "Thank you." I smiled up at Thorn, which he returned.

"They are all dead," Xi announced plainly, almost as if he was bored.

"Uh, thank you," I offered. Though, I wasn't sure thanking someone for killing people was good.

He hummed under his breath and said no more.

"Xi, did you find out any new information?"

His jaw clenched. "No."

Ah, he was pissed off. Killing them for nothing had

bored him. I would hate to think what he did for fun in Hell.

"Xi, have something to eat and sit down," Ezra said from where he sat between my legs. "I'm sure we'll speak with Cedrick soon, and he'll let us know what's going on."

"Then we can leave?" Xi questioned. I was sure the heebie-jeebies wasn't the only thing Xi wanted to get away from. There was something going on with him.

"We've been here one night, Xi. We were planning to spend two nights here anyway," Asher said. He stood by the wall reading some type of papers, and Nate stood with him with his own handful of papers. They looked important, but I knew if I needed to know anything about something, they would tell me, or I'd kick their ass if I found something out too late.

"It's been two nights. It's past midnight."

I waved my hand around, not bothering to answer. If he didn't understand I wouldn't leave without seeing and knowing Cedrick was okay, then he'd figure it out, or he'd just have to learn to be patient.

Before I could even blink, Xi had a sword drawn. His arm extended to the right, the tip of the blade touching Cedrick's neck.

"Xi," I cried as I leaped over Ezra in a panicked frenzy. However, Xi was already withdrawing his sword.

"Be careful where you pop in without notice," Xi warned, then walked over to the opposite wall to Asher and Nate to lean against it. He took a rag out of what I guessed was his back pocket and started cleaning a sword.

Was Lucifer actually punishing me? Did he really think

I was too moody for his son so he sent Xi to drive me insane? I believed it could work in the end.

"Are you okay?" I asked, reaching out to place my hand on Cedrick's arm. A shiver raked over my body. His scent hit me, and I wanted to lick him, kiss him, and mark him. It felt as if I hadn't seen him in years.

He looked down at me with warmth in his eyes. "I am now, my lady." He glanced to Xi. "I apologize for appearing out of nowhere. I'll know not to do it again."

Xi didn't look at him but nodded once and kept cleaning his sword.

"How's your mom?" I asked, bringing his attention back down to me. Heat hit my cheeks because his eyes were so intense I could almost drown in them.

Was I this bad with my other men before we'd completed the bond?

It wasn't that long ago, yet it seemed eons ago because so much had happened.

He smiled. "Better. A lot better. She's been seen by a healer we trust and is already on the mend."

I grinned. "That's great." Only my gut bottomed out. It was cruel of me to think it, but knowing she was okay so soon and that Cedrick would be all right, meant we could leave.

Leave one of my mates.

Leave one of my men.

Even when we hadn't finalized the bond, the thought of leaving him behind gutted me from breastbone down to my lower stomach. It had me pressing a hand against my stomach from the ache inside me.

"Are you able to tell us what that was down there?" Asher asked.

"Never felt creeped out as much as I did walking into that room," Nate commented. He walked to the table to grab an apple. He turned, leaned against the table, and took a bite. He was always eating, well, if he could. He told me it was because shifting took a lot out of him.

"I would like to explain what we've found out. Are you all comfortable here or would you like to speak in the meeting room?"

"Here's okay, if it's all right with you?" I asked, suddenly feeling unsure of what to say, how to stand, or if I was dressed nicely enough. Hell, it felt like I was in high school and the most popular jock was speaking to me. I swore if I giggled at anything he said, I would slap myself.

Humping his leg was out of the question, right?

God, that thought seemed familiar. I was sure I'd thought it before for one or all of my other mates.

Slowly, I removed my hand and put distance between us before I jumped his bones. I went back over to the couch and sat. Ezra moved back to lean against my legs. Thorn sat on my right and Asher to my left.

"I'll go get Alex," Nate said.

"Thanks," I said, glancing everywhere but at Cedrick.

Nate grunted and disappeared into the next room.

The door to the living room opened and Kiered entered, smiling. I caught Xi straighten from the wall, but other than that, he didn't look the man's way or stop from cleaning his blade. Mentally, I rubbed my hands together. I had a feeling Kiered was why Xi wanted to up and run away fast. He was interested in him, or Kiered liked Xi and made it known to the man, and it freaked him out. Then again, it could be mutual feelings and that could also concern Xi, worried it would get between his mission to protect us. It may just need my interfering, but first I would find out how they both felt.

"Hi, everyone. Did I miss the discussion?"

"No," I told him with my own smile. "We're just waiting for Alex."

"Good." He nodded, and then moved over to the wall beside Xi. From across the room, I could see Xi tense. He shifted to the side, away from Kiered, but Kiered removed that space between them.

I got a "holy shit" moment when I saw Xi's lips twitch. I'd never seen him smile except a scary one when he was fighting.

That confirmed it.

He liked Kiered.

Thorn placed his arm around my shoulders and brought me close. "Sweetheart, don't get involved."

I gave Thorn wide eyes and pointed at my chest. "Who, me?"

He chuckled and kissed my temple. "Yes, you."

"I don't know what you're talking about." I rolled my eyes and smiled.

The door to the bedroom opened and a fresh-looking Alex walked in with Nate following. Alex moved over to sit on the floor with Ezra, between Thorn's legs, and Nate sat on the arm of the couch on Asher's side.

Cedrick took a chair opposite us. I hated the distance between us. As far as I was concerned, he should have been sitting with all of us.

He relaxed back and gave me a small smile, as if he knew what I was thinking.... Crap, he probably did. Still, I wouldn't take it back.

"Five years ago, my brother and I were out visiting close towns when the palace was attacked. When we arrived home, our father told us our mother, Queen Castilina, died in battle." His jaw clenched as he glanced to Kiered and then back to the coffee table in front of him. "We believed the story because our father was marvelous at lying. He mourned for months; tears would shine in his eyes whenever he spoke of her. He, with his army, went out in search of the survivors of the dark elves who were said to attack us and killed them all."

"It would be easy to believe," I said, hoping he'd be able to forgive himself.

He shook his head. "I shouldn't have. He'd always been a deceitful bastard. I should have made sure myself. I should have done something."

"You weren't the only one tricked, brother. There was nothing any of us could do." Kiered stepped over and laid a hand on Cedrick's shoulder as he faced us. "We never thought Father would hurt Mother. She even believed it herself. He was enchanted by her beauty and power. He'd thought the world of her, even though he knew she didn't love him. He saw her as his treasure because she brought him status. He became king after all, so he easily could turn a blind eye on the love she held for her guards. Her true grooms... mates."

Cedrick nodded. "That is why, since she thought she was safe, she sent her mates to guard us on our travels. It was the biggest mistake we all made. Our mother for believing in our father, for sending her mates away. For us and her mates listening to her pleas in the first place and giving in when she said she would die if anything happened to her children, to us." A tick started in his temple. "She didn't realize we would become nothing without her in our lives. Her mates were mere shells without their soul with them. They only stayed alive because they promised to care for us."

"The one good thing the council has done is get rid of your father," Asher said, his voice hard and rough.

Cedrick nodded. "Agreed."

"So what actually happened to her?" Ezra asked as he tilted his head to the side and rested his cheek on my knee. I reached out and ran a hand through his hair while I watched Cedrick struggle through this new development. I wished I could take away his heartache somehow.

Cedrick paled more than his fair skin already was. Kiered did too as he removed his hand from Cedrick's shoulder and sat on the armrest beside him. Like he knew when they spoke of it, he wouldn't be able to stand anymore.

"The machine you saw her hooked up to syphons her power and eventually her life source."

My pulse raced. "They were taking her life slowly."

"Yes," he snarled. "Slowly and painfully for five fucking years."

"What did they do with what they syphoned?"

The tick in Cedrick's temple intensified. He sneered, his upper lip raised as he bit out, "Our father wanted it for himself." He shook his head. "He injected himself every day. In the beginning, the power he gained was beyond any our kind should have."

"How did he get killed if he was so powerful?" Thorn asked. I glanced around at my men. All of them looked sickened by the news, as well as angered.

"Because Therolidi, his most trusted friend, killed him on behalf of the council. It was also Therolidi who told me the council had planned his death. The people we caught and questioned could have been from Therolidi since they confirmed his story of the council doing it."

"He tried double-crossing the council. Hoping you would go after them and not find him out," Alex commented.

"I can only guess that was his plan. But I know for certain it was Therolidi who killed our father because Mother heard it all. He murdered him right in front of her, then planted his body elsewhere."

"The council knew what your father was doing and got Therolidi to murder him, but didn't stop Therolidi from doing the same, draining your mother of power and life force. It doesn't make sense," Nate commented.

"Maybe Therolidi was more manageable than their father," Ezra suggested.

"It could also mean the council are doing the same, syphoning power and life source from others, and they supplied Therolidi with a taste to be able to kill your father in the first place," Asher said.

"You're correct. While our mother rested, I took two of mother's guards into the dungeons and we spoke with Rallis, who is now dead."

Ezra laughed. "*Spoke*, you make torture sound so casual."

Cedrick shrugged. "Rallis overheard our father speaking of it with Therolidi, how he stumbled upon it happening within the council's walls when he went to see them six years ago. Of course, when the council found out what our father was doing, they had to put a stop to it instantly. They didn't want their secrets going further. Therolidi and his friend on the council worked together to kill and then cover up Father's death. He would have told them of his plan for me, how he wanted to be in control."

"They would have let him go and continue as your father was doing because, like Ezra said, he was more manageable than your father. He must be sleeping with Jessica. A lot of men think with their cocks, and this would be a perfect example. He seemed stupid enough to think he'd get away with everything. Even trying to take us out for the bitch," Nate said with a scowl.

This was maddening, sickening. I wanted to scream in anger and throw up in fear and anguish knowing what the council were doing with people. But also because of what Cedrick's mother had been through.

"The more I hear about the council, the more I want to face them and kill them. This can't keep happening," I said. Ezra let out a sound, and I quickly released his hair. I hadn't even realized I'd gripped it so tightly. "Sorry," I muttered.

He turned his head and smiled big, then winked. "We can try rough play another time, mi corazón."

My face heated. An unexpected laugh fell from my lips before I could stop it, but I quickly cut if off. It wasn't the time for fun and games, though Ezra always did help settle a darker atmosphere into a lighter one.

"Anyway," I started and playfully shoved at his head, causing him to chuckle, "this must be why the council is taking other powerful members of the communities."

"I agree, love," Asher said. "At least we know they'll have advanced strength and power."

Worry creased my brows and churned my stomach. "Will we have enough power to fight them?"

"From what our mother has said, the weaker the subject, the weaker the dose. It depends on who they have and how long they've had them for."

"Since we don't know, we have to consider the worst. However, I believe we'll be strong enough to take them on. Are you still willing to give us some men to fight with us?" Thorn asked.

Cedrick nodded. He glanced up at Kiered, who smiled and nodded. Cedrick looked back to us and met my gaze. "There's one other matter with having Mother back at the palace."

"What?" I asked.

"I am no longer king."

My heart spiked. My mind spun. Could that mean…? I didn't want to jump to any conclusions; I didn't want to get my hopes up.

"W-What does that mean for you?"

"With the power I received from Father after his death, I was able to transfer it to Mother since it was rightfully hers anyway."

"Did it hurt? How was that possible?" Alex wondered. He was always after answers over many things. Ezra ruffled his hair, and Alex blushed. "Sorry, I didn't mean to pry."

"I do not mind." Cedrick smiled. "It didn't hurt as much as what Paige experienced when I pulled her from her mind. Mother and I had to reestablish the mind link a mother has with her children when they're born, and I transferred it that way. It had been suffocated with how she was locked away, cut off from the world, from us all, spelled so we couldn't trace her energy. I would have passed by that room if it hadn't been for you, Paige. It could have been too late. But with the new power boost from myself, it helped rejuvenate her quicker than anything else could have."

"I wasn't even sure how I knew, really. I just didn't want to leave before seeing in that room," I told him with a shrug, playing it off like it was nothing because he was eyeing me like it was everything. I wanted to crawl into his lap and see what he would do with me just from the way he was looking at me.

"It was everything," he said softly.

"It was," Kiered added. "Mother would love to meet with you soon if you would visit with her before leaving?"

Smiling up at him, I nodded. "I would love to meet her."

"I'll take you to her as soon as we're done speaking here," Cedrick said, bringing my attention back to him. I nodded, and he smiled in return.

"Will your mother be able to handle being queen so soon after? Is she strong enough to keep your darker brethren in check?" Asher asked.

"She is," Kiered said. "With the power transfer from

Cedrick, she would be able to take on an attack if needed. Especially since she is also reestablishing the bonds with her mates as we speak."

My face ignited. Yet I tasted regret because Cedrick and I couldn't do the same... at least, I didn't think we could. But he wasn't king anymore. Did it mean he didn't have responsibilities, or would he still have them alongside his mother?

"It means, my beautiful, that I am able to stay by your side no matter where you are."

My eyes widened. I scooted forward on the couch and felt Ezra look back at me with uncertainty. *"Are you serious?"*

His smile was the biggest I'd seen from him. *"Yes. Very serious."*

"You're mine? As in my mate, my husband. You'll be with me everywhere? At my castle? At my home?"

"Correct, and you're mine also."

My body flamed, my nipples hardened, my heart raced, and my clit throbbed. I wanted him, and now, so nothing could come between us again.

"I have a feeling we need to leave the room," Kiered said, his voice light with humor. "He's just told her he's able to become her mate fully with Mother ruling the court."

"Leaving would be a good idea," Asher answered. "I'll take the wolf out."

I couldn't seem to look away from Cedrick. I was lost in the thought of making him completely mine.

But... did he understand—

"Yes, beautiful." He said through the link. *"I'm very*

well aware I shall have to share you with five other men. I am glad you have them in your life. They help you in many ways. I've even seen it in the short amount of time with you all. However, this may seem selfish or stupid, but I have only deep need for you, my mate, my wife. I only desire for you. There may come a time when I seek pleasure from our men, but until then, I only wish to be with you. Would this be possible?"

"*Yes.*" And I knew I wasn't lying. I knew my men, my family well. They would accept his wishes, for his sake and for mine, so I could claim him as mine.

His smile turned sly. "*It does not mean I wouldn't want to watch you with them. It excites me even thinking of it, seeing the pleasure upon your face. I do not feel jealous with them touching you or having you. I know they are yours and you are theirs.*"

My body hummed. Nate drew in the scent and snarled. A breeze swept my hair over my face and then the door opened and closed. Nate's snarls lessened.

"Is he okay?" Cedrick asked.

I stood as the rest of my men did. Thorn chuckled, as did Ezra, and I caught Alex smiling before he said, "He'll be fine once you're brought into the family."

Cedrick tilted his head to the side slightly in confusion.

Alex blushed, so it was Thorn who added, "Once the bond has been finished between you two, he'll accept you as part of Paige's family. Until then, his fur is a little ruffled and he doesn't like others playing with what's his."

Cedrick nodded. "I have spoken with Paige, but I need you all to understand that, for now, I'll only have her in the bedroom. It doesn't mean I won't like watching you all together, but for now, Paige will be my focus."

Thorn grinned. "We can understand that. Maybe just watch. You don't touch any of us in front of Nate either. His wolf has claimed us all… well, almost." His eyes flashed to Ezra who looked decidedly smug, then to Asher, who smirked.

Cedrick's eyes widened.

"Unless you have the strength to dominate him and then claim him, his wolf won't like you getting too close to us guys," Ezra added.

A throat cleared. "I believe a mind link with them all could help the matter," Xi said.

Ezra clicked his fingers and pointed at Xi. "Good thinking, old man. Cedrick would then scent like us with a mind link."

"Could we all speak of this after?" I asked, then slapped a hand over my mouth. I was suddenly impatient for alone time, but I sounded rude getting what I wanted.

My men laughed. Thorn kissed my cheek. "We'll leave you to it." He started for the door and slapped Cedrick on the shoulder in passing. "Welcome to the family."

Alex kissed me on the neck and then blushed as he whispered, "Have fun." He nodded and smiled to Cedrick as he walked by him.

Ezra nipped at my bottom lip before giving me a quick peck. "I'd say enjoy yourself, but I know you will." He winked. He slapped Cedrick on the arm as he went by. He glanced back to Kiered and Xi. "Are you two going to stand there and watch? Kind of kinky there, Xi."

Xi went beet red, mumbled something about killing Ezra, and stormed from the room.

Kiered grinned and said, "Don't worry, I'll make sure your hellhound still lives." He raced after Xi, slamming the door behind himself.

I looked up at Cedrick and gulped. His eyes were darker than usual and intense again. His jaw clenched as his hands fisted.

"I have never even asked you. Would you want to be my wife?"

Was he serious?

We were made for each other.

He was mine. I could feel the rightfulness all through me.

Yet, it was charming he was asking. "It depends. Would you be happy with a ghoul as a wife? Just so you understand, I eat, um…." I glanced away, steeled myself, and looked back, jutting my chin out and up. I had to stop being self-conscious and worrying about what people thought of me eating flesh. I was a ghoul, and I was a proud one. "I eat dead people, Cedrick. If it's something you can't handle, then I know this couldn't work for us."

"I accept you for you, Paige. Being a ghoul and all. No matter what you eat."

My heart skipped a beat. "Really?" I whispered.

"Yes, beautiful."

I smiled big. "Then yes, Cedrick. I want to be your wife," I told him, and then made a run and leaped into his arms. Thankfully he caught me as he laughed. He spun me around and then pressed me close against him, wrapping his arms around my waist while I locked mine around his neck and then my legs around his waist. We both grinned at each other, which slowly disappeared as Cedrick dipped his head and for the second time—only this wasn't in my mind—he kissed me.

I moaned into his mouth over the first taste of him, and he drank the sound down. His hands slid down and cupped my ass, holding me tightly against his hardness. And God, he was big.

I pulled back enough to say, "I'm going to need you inside me, right about now."

He chuckled. "Then I shall make it happen." He placed me back on my feet and pulled his top over his head. My knees felt weak at the sight of his perfectly smooth, pale skin. I licked my lips, my mouth suddenly dry. He watched me as I looked upon him when he undid the tie to his pants. I quickly whipped off my tee and threw it to the floor, then got rid of my jeans, kicking them off to the side so I stood in front of him in panties and a bra. At least they were nice ones; they always were when Alex dressed me. This time they were black and lacy.

His pants fell to the floor and pooled around his feet. He wore no underwear, and I was grateful to see how hard he already was for me.

"You do this to me, beautiful," he told me as he stroked his hand up and down his long length.

"You've driven me crazy since arriving, so it's fair." I smiled and reached behind me to unhook my bra. Leisurely, I dragged the straps down my arms and then dropped it to the floor. Cedrick's eyes stayed glued to my chest. He swallowed hard as his hand moved faster over himself.

"The panties," he bit out as he kicked his pants off his feet. I pushed my panties down to my thighs and wiggled my hips so they slid down my legs and then stepped out of them.

"So beautiful. I've never seen anyone as exquisite as you."

I couldn't stop the snort. "Your women are the most stunning I've seen."

He shook his head and narrowed his gaze on me. "They are nothing compared to you. Let me prove how much I cherish your body, mind, and soul."

"Yes, please."

"Shall we enter the bedroom?"

"No, it's so far away, and I need you now."

He flashed his teeth in a bright smile. "It's the next room."

I nodded. "Too far away."

He took the step to pick me up in his arms. "I love how eager you are for me, beautiful."

I wrapped my legs around his waist and let out a mew when my pussy pressed against his cock.

He hissed. "Already soaked. I can feel it."

"I'm ready for you, honey." I kissed his neck. He groaned and, using his hands on my ass, pulled me against him as he walked us to the couch. I slid up and down on him with each movement, driving us crazy with desire.

He turned and sat. One of his hands slid between us so he could run two fingers over my wet folds.

"For me," he clipped.

Biting my bottom lip, I nodded. "All for you."

When he inserted two fingers inside me, I dropped my

head back and cried out. Only he gripped the back of my hair and pulled my head back up so our eyes caught. "You'll be my wife. We'll be connected forever."

"I can't wait."

His eyes brightened with a glow in them. *"Me either."* He freed his fingers from within me and brought them up to his lips. He pressed them against his mouth and then gently tugged my body forward using my hair. I knew what he wanted, so when my mouth touched his fingers on his lips, I opened and swirled my tongue over his wet fingers. His eyes glowed more as his own mouth opened and his tongue joined mine and we both tasted myself on them.

"Up," he ordered with a smack to my ass cheek. I lifted to my knees and moved closer, and while we licked his fingers, I slowly sank down onto his cock. My pussy opened up to him, but with his length and girth, he filled me snugly.

He groaned and I gasped as the bonded connection took place. He removed his fingers from between our mouths and kissed me like it was the last kiss he'd give me. Even while the fire built inside me and took over, I didn't release him.

His emotions opened up to me, his desire, his pleasure, his happiness, and even love. I knew he was feeling my own when his arms wrapped around my waist tightly and his voice swept into my mind with *"It's more than I could have fathomed. I feel you everywhere, and still I want more."*

"I know what you mean." God, did I. Having him in my mind while he was planted deep and his emotions

swirled, overwhelmed me in the best way. I wasn't sure my heart would ever settle down.

Slowly, I pushed up from his cock and then sank back down. Our hands dug into one another at the sensation.

"So tight, so wet, perfect," he murmured into my mind, kissing down my neck.

"You were made for me."

"And you me."

I nodded, closing my eyes, getting lost in the feel of him. Of Cedrick. My mate, my bonded, my husband.

When he dipped his head down, I took the chance and licked over the tip of his ear. He stilled, and next I was in the air before my back hit the couch. He made a sound in the back of his throat before he thrust back all the way inside me. His hips pistoned in and out roughly, savagely, and wonderfully. I gripped his shoulders and took it all with pleasure.

I also made a note to myself that touching his ears drove him insane.

Smiling, I nipped at his neck. He groaned and tipped his head to the side. He gripped my breast and brought a nipple to his mouth. His warm breath tickled over it. When I glided my tongue over the shell of his ear, he bit down on my nipple. I cried out and tightened my legs around his hips as he fucked me faster than even before.

"More," he demanded, and I gave it easily. I licked and nibbled on the tip of his ear. "Merde," he yelled.

My lower belly clenched and twisted in the best way. I was so close. "Harder, honey," I whispered against his ear before licking and sucking on the arch of it. He grunted and ground down onto me as he thrust harder.

"I can't hold on," he said, and it was those words, knowing he was as lost as I was, that drove me over the edge. He spoke in a language I'd never heard when my orgasm hit and my walls tightened around him even more. I gripped him to me, and he brought his mouth back to mine for a sweet but rough kiss. He pulled back and stared into my eyes. When they tightened in the corners and his mouth opened a little, I knew he was there. He swelled inside me, and his hot seed filled me as he groaned long and deep, dropping his forehead into my neck. I couldn't resist. I licked and sucked at his ear. His body shuddered over me, and he swelled even more before squirting the last of his cum into me.

His body relaxed against mine. He spoke again in a different language in between kisses over my skin.

"Thank you for accepting me." I received through my mind. I hadn't even thought he was feeling insecure over my acceptance of him being different from myself, but it was what I picked up from him at that moment.

I cupped his cheek. He lifted his gaze to mine, and I pressed a gentle kiss to his lips. *"Thank you for wanting me as your wife. I will forever hold you in my heart, soul, and mind."*

CHAPTER FOURTEEN
PAIGE

Butterflies flew in circles in my belly. My nerves were high. I glanced down at my simple dark blue dress, the only casual but nice one I'd packed, and then up to Cedrick. "Are you sure I look presentable enough?"

He smiled down at me and placed an arm around my waist. "Yes, I'm sure Mother would approve even if you wore a sack."

I slapped his stomach. "No she wouldn't."

"If I'm happy, which I am, she would."

Still, his words didn't settle my nerves. She was his mother after all.

A knock sounded on the door to the living room we stood in. "Come in," Cedrick called. The door opened and my mates walked in. All smiled, except Nate. Alex even had a blush going.

Asher dipped his head toward Cedrick and said, "Welcome to the clan."

"Thank you. I would shake your hand, but I believe a certain wolf, who is currently glaring at me, would take my head off."

Nate grunted.

Asher smirked. "He is a bit possessive. Much like our Paige, but you'll find that out."

I snorted. "You're all the same. Unless you know he's a bonded mate, then you're ready to throw me at him."

The men chuckled, except Nate. I rolled my eyes at him and his glare narrowed more.

"Only because we know he'll add to the family," Ezra said. "Otherwise we would burn the bastard alive." He shrugged, went over to the couch, and sat. His eyes darkened as he drew in a deep breath. He licked his lips. "Hmm, smells divine over here."

"Ezra," I warned. He grinned wide and winked.

"Did the others speak of what we discussed before they left?" Cedrick asked Asher.

"They did. I think the mind link is good to try. It would bring us together and be an advantage in battle."

Cedrick nodded. "Then if you all would allow me access to your minds, I would like to try. Since we are connected through Paige already, it shouldn't be that hard."

"I don't fucking like people poking around in my head," Nate clipped.

"I promise the link will only allow us to speak through our minds and connect us in a way that family is supposed to be. You can block me anytime you wish."

Nate huffed, crossed his arms over his chest, and leaned against the wall.

"That's him agreeing," Alex offered.

Cedrick smiled at him and nodded. Nate growled in the back of his throat, and I saw Cedrick quickly look away from Alex.

"Please, close your eyes."

My men did. As soon as they had, Cedrick smiled at

me and took a step back. His eyes glowed before he closed them. His body lifted off the ground, and he hovered in the air an inch or two off the floor. He spread his arms wide. I saw my men sway a little. I was glad at least some of them were sitting—Ezra and Alex. Nate stumbled to the left and then straightened, his jaw clenched, and he opened his eyes. They widened.

Together we watched Cedrick float back to the floor. The rest slowly opened their eyes; Alex even blinked rapidly a few times.

I dropped the shield in my mind.

"This is freaky. I can sense all of you in my head." Alex was the first I heard.

Nate gripped his head. *"I don't fucking like this. It feels weird having you all in my head."*

"You will get used to it," Cedrick promised.

"It could come in handy." Ezra then sent a picture that had my body quivering. It was of all of them touching, tasting and pleasuring me in some way. My men laughed, some even groaned. Cedrick was one of them.

"Not fair, Ezra." I glared over at him, and he just grinned back.

"Asher is right, though. It will be handy in battle." Thorn smiled.

Asher nodded. *"If we can communicate wherever we are, then we'll know if anyone needs help."* He looked to Cedrick. *"Thank you, Cedrick."*

Cedrick bowed his head. *"Thank you for trusting me, even those who were reluctant."* He looked to Nate with a small smile, one I wouldn't mind licking off his lips.

"Like his ears, I want to lick and suck on them or play with them."

Cedrick went bright red as I heard snickering from Ezra.

"You all heard that?"

"Yes, sweetheart," Thorn said.

"Oops."

"His ears are cute," Alex thought at us and then realized what he'd done and burned just as brightly as Cedrick had.

Cedrick coughed out a breath and shifted on his feet. He cleared his throat and said, "Shall we all go and see my mother? We leave tomorrow, correct?" My poor mate was in need of a change of subject.

Asher nodded. "Yes. However, before we leave the room, there is something we need to test first." He glanced to Nate, then Alex. "If you would, Alex."

"Me?" Alex blurted, his voice high. When no one said anything, Alex sighed. "Fine." I wasn't sure what was going on until Alex moved over to Cedrick. I glanced to Nate. His stance was tense. Alex rubbed his hands together and stuttered out, "D-Do you, ah, I-I mean, I know you don't like guys that way, but um, so we know if, um, we need to see... that is.... Blast." He ran a hand over his hot face and then let out a squeal when Cedrick hooked an arm around Alex's waist and brought him flush against Cedrick's front.

"Is this enough to tell?"

"Um..." was all Alex said as he stared flustered up at Cedrick.

I hid my smile behind my hand as I watched them.

Cedrick dipped his chin and said, "It is not that I do not like men. I do. However, Paige is my world at the moment and then eventually, when we get to know one another, I would like to explore more with you and the rest of the men."

"O-Okay?" Alex blinked slowly. "I mean, I think it's okay." He turned his eyes to me. "Is it?"

Removing my hand, I smiled wider and nodded.

"That's good," Cedrick said. He glanced over Alex's head to Nate. We all searched him out, finding him still against the wall. I didn't see any jealousy. He looked somewhat relaxed, so the mind link seemed to have helped his wolf settle.

"Let's go," he barked and opened the door before exiting.

"Is he always like this?" Cedrick asked as he released Alex from his arm. Alex stumbled back a little, but Thorn was there to steady him.

"Nate's a grumpy pain in my ass," I told him, taking his hand as we walked toward the door. "But I wouldn't have him any other way. I love the douche."

I heard Nate grunt; it was light, so I knew he liked what I'd said.

"He grows on you, like a fungus," Ezra teased and then tripped when he moved out of the room. Laughing, he shoved at Nate who'd been the one to mess his steps up. "See what I mean."

Cedrick, who was smiling, nodded. We walked down the hall, and as we did, the people moved out of our way, bowing in respect. Only one woman stepped in front of us.

She bowed so low we got a view of her ample breasts just about ready to spill out of her dress.

"My lord, it is good to see you." She straightened and smiled coyly while twisting a strand of her hair around a finger. I wanted Alex to light her hair on fire.

"Elizitenth, we're very busy at the moment. We'll speak later," Cedrick told her. We waited for her to move. She didn't. Would throwing her out of the way look bad?

Her eyes moved down to our joined hands. She raised her gaze and said, "When am I able to move back into my room beside yours, my lord? I have missed you."

"Oh fuck," Ezra muttered.

He fucked her.

She was in a room right next to Cedrick's? Wait a goddamn moment. We were put in a room next to his.

My powers rushed through me. My teeth, claws, and body grew. I dropped Cedrick's hand and spun to face him. "You put me in her room?" I snarled.

"She's in my room?" the harpy shrilled.

I snaked a hand out, grabbed her around the neck and smiled with all my teeth showing when I heard her choking. Slowly, I turned my head to her. "Shut. The fuck. Up." I shook her and looked back to Cedrick.

"I see what you mean by possessive," he commented over my head. Was that a smile on his face? I would knock it off as soon as the wiggly bitch died.

"Love, let go of her," Asher said coolly. "She isn't worth it. This is mild since you have both completed the bond. If it occurred after, the woman would be dead by now."

Cedrick's eyes flashed. He looked down at me and

cupped my cheeks. His thumb traced over my lips, ignoring the sharp teeth. He didn't look repulsed by me, how I looked, or by my actions. All I could see in his eyes was warmth.

"My beautiful Paige, she means nothing to me. She never has and never will. You are my everything from this day and until my last breath."

I dropped her and called back my powers. "You have a way with words, Cedrick." I curled my arms up around his neck and pulled him down so I could kiss him. I needed to show her he was mine.

The woman staggered to her feet, rubbing her neck and breathing hard. "D-Does she know how many women you had on that floor? One woman was never enough—" She broke off on a scream when I lunged for her.

Arms circled my waist and I was lifted off the floor and flung over a shoulder. "Let me go. She deserves to die. They all do." I kicked, punched, and yelled at whomever was carrying me. All I could focus on was the whore being shoved aside by Nate. "Punch her, Nate. I give you permission." The asshole just laughed and made his way down the hall.

A door opened as we went through. The last thing she saw was my middle finger before the door closed again.

"Put me down," I demanded. I was placed on my feet, and I glared up at Cedrick with my hands on my hips. Then I kicked him in the shin. "You put me in her room! You had many women please you!" I kicked him again.

"This was all before you captured my heart and soul, my beautiful." His hands landed on my shoulders, and he rubbed up and down my arms. "There will never be another woman in my life and bed but you."

I snorted and punched him in the stomach. "How can I satisfy you when you've had multiple women on your floor there to just jump into your bed? There's only me, Cedrick. You tied your knot to little old me, and now you're stuck. I bet you're regretting it, asshole." I threw out my hands in frustration. "Well, tough shit, you're stuck with me forever."

He grinned down at me. "I wouldn't want it any other way, Paige Alice. You're more than enough for me. In fact, I now understand why you need so many mates."

I gasped, suddenly wanting to mess with him more since it annoyed the hell out of me he'd known I was his mate and he put me in a room where his former plaything slept. "Are you saying I'm too much?"

"No!" he cried, then groaned. "Does anyone want to help me?"

My acting skills weren't the best, but I thought I would try for the moment since I wasn't ready to forgive him for being inconsiderate. "You'll all regret taking me as a mate one day. I'm an over-the-top psycho." Before anyone could see, I pinched my arm so hard it brought tears to my eyes. Then I thought I should really stop messing with him since he'd come into a relationship where I already had five partners. It wasn't fair. I had to find a new way to torture him. Though, killing all the women in their sleep could make me happy too.

"Fucking fix her. She's leaking again," Nate growled.

"She doesn't have her period anymore. She talked for hours about how grateful she was about it after she figured it out. So it can't be that," Ezra said. Now I just wanted to punch him for that comment.

A slow clap caught my attention. "She could win an Oscar for that performance," a cool, rich voice said. Spinning around, I spotted Cedrick's mother and two of her mates sitting on a couch. One of them was smiling up at me and clapping. He winked.

"What do you mean?" Cedrick demanded as he stepped up beside me.

I slapped him in the stomach. A few laughed, but I ignored them and said, "You brought me to your mom after my little reaction out there?" I glared up at him and then released the glare to gaze back to his mother. Cedrick resembled his mother a lot, only he was more masculine, of course. He even had her white-colored hair.

I bowed. I couldn't help it. She looked more queen than I would ever be. Elegant. And all she was doing was sitting on a couch. Hands landed on my waist and pulled me back up.

"I'm sorry you saw that, Your Majesty."

"Please, call me Castilina, child." She smiled. "You also have nothing to worry about. I understand your reaction, and I'm grateful to know you care for my son deeply enough to want to hurt others before you." She took her mates' hands. "I have had my moments also."

One of her men laughed. "We lost count of the people she threatened over us."

I grinned. "It's good to know I'm not the only one."

She giggled. "You're not, and my son is the same I predict. Except with your already bonded grooms."

I nodded, thinking of the guard when we'd first arrived.

"Six altogether, how lucky are you."

My chest expanded with happiness. "Very."

"May we get back to where your tears went, beautiful?" Cedrick questioned.

The one who'd clapped laughed. "She pinched herself to bring them on. She was playing you, son."

"Son. Why does he call you that?"

"He is my mother's mate. Kiered and I have spent time with all of them more than the father we had. They treated us with kindness and patience, teaching us so much. We see them all as our fathers and long ago asked them to treat us like we were their own."

I gazed up at him, taking his hand in mine and squeezing it. *"That is the sweetest thing ever. I forgive you for putting me in her room. For now."*

Cedrick laughed. He lifted my hand and kissed the back of it. "Thank you... I think." I grinned before he faced his mother again as he said, "Mother, may I formally introduce you to my wife, Paige Alice. Ghoul queen." He glanced around and added, "I would also like you to meet our bonded males, Asher Evans, Thorn Jones, Alex Smith, Ezra Morningstar, and Nate Felan. Everyone, this is Castilina, my mother."

Castilina smiled warmly. "It's a pleasure to meet you all. This is Juri." He was the clapping one. "And this is Grandith. My other mate, Yeno, is off getting more food for me, even though I'm stuffed to the brim."

"They never do listen," I teased my own men.

She laughed. "No, they don't."

Cedrick sighed. "We are standing here."

Castilina brightened. "How about you all leave us for some girl time?"

"Not happening," Yuri clipped. He glanced up at me. "No offense to you, but after everything that has happened to our mate, she will have two mates with her at all times."

Nate grunted and I caught Thorn, Asher, and Alex nodding.

"We know that feeling well," Ezra said. I couldn't say I blamed their protectiveness. I would have been the same if one of my mates disappeared for hours having God knows what done to them.

The queen frowned. "Yes, I am sorry for what Therolidi did to you."

I waved a hand in front of me. "It was nothing compared to what was done to you. I'm so very sorry." Tears filled my eyes. Now seeing her, speaking with her, even when it was a short moment, it pained me to know Castilina had been treated the way she was.

Her own eyes filled with tears. When her hand came out, I went and dropped to my knees, taking her hand in both of mine.

"We will heal from the physical and mental wounds inflicted upon us. It is why I think we've been blessed with so many mates." She gave me a wobbly smile, which I returned.

"Your people usually don't have so many mates?"

She shook her head. "No, usually we only have one. But I wouldn't want it any other way. My men complete me in different ways."

Nodding, I grinned and said, "I know exactly what you

mean." I was surprised with how comfortable I felt with Castilina. Her people must have loved her as queen before they thought she perished. However, since she was coming back from death, would it be received well or had her former husband turned people against her? If he had, could she handle the situation on her own? She could still need Cedrick's support. "You understand I have to leave here tomorrow, and Cedrick has said he will come?" She nodded. I gripped her hands tighter. "I can't have him come if I know your people will be disgruntled over your appearance and cause you trouble. You need all the support you can get if that happens."

More tears filled her eyes, and she looked up over my head. "You have been blessed with a magnificent wife, son."

"I have, Mother."

She gazed back at me. "Even though you know it will pain you to have a bonded away from you for a long period of time, you are willing to sacrifice that to help me?"

"Of course," I said instantly. I would never want Cedrick to regret coming with me, nor worry about his family every day.

She leaned forward and cupped my cheek. "You honor me, child. I assure you, my people will rejoice at my return. I shall not use his name, but he ran this kingdom down. I did what I could to stop him. My people saw this. They know I will rule strictly but fairly. Cedrick would lose himself if he is not at your side in this battle you take." She smiled. "You are a brave woman, Paige Alice. What you're about to deal with is beyond what anyone else has taken upon themselves, and you do it for your people, yes, your family also, but you show your people the strong female you are, and they will respect you always."

As I dipped my head, feeling my cheeks heat, her hand dropped away. A throat cleared, and I sensed the queen look up. "Our mate doesn't do well with compliments. As far as she's concerned, she would rather run into battle than have people say nice things about her," Asher said.

Castilina laughed. "I can see that, and again it shows me what an admirable woman you are, Paige. Now rise, child, and stand by my son please."

I did as asked. Cedrick curled his arm around my waist again. Castilina looked at us with fondness.

Sudden power surged into the room. Panic filled me until Alex called, "It's okay." Then I relaxed.

The queen's eyes glowed, much like Cedrick's had. It then extended to around her body, and she floated up to her feet with ease. Her hand shot out, and she moved it in all different directions. "I bless this union. I bless the union Paige Alice has with all of her bonded mates. I bless your travels and pray you all stay safe through your hardship."

In a blink, she was back to her normal glow. Still looking wonderful, no older than thirty, and yet she would have to be older because Cedrick seemed in his late twenties.

"I wish you all the best of luck, and I do hope you will visit when you can."

"Of course we will," I reassured her. There wasn't a chance I'd keep her son away from her.

"Thank you." She smiled, then laughed lightly. "I'll

leave my tears for the actual farewell tomorrow, which will embarrass Cedrick."

"Don't worry, I'll cry with you, and then the men will really freak out."

She snorted, then covered her mouth in surprise. "I do like you, Paige."

"Thank you. I like you too, Castilina."

A knock sounded on the door right before it came open without anyone saying anything. Kiered walked in with a bright smile upon his face. Behind him, he dragged Xi in by the arm. Xi didn't look angry, maybe nervous with his frantic eyes searching the room.

"Mother, I have wonderful news," Kiered announced. "I would like you to meet my mate, Xi Huang."

My mouth dropped open and a shocked noise fell out, which had Xi glaring my way.

Castilina clapped her hands and said, "This is a blessed day. Juri, go and collect Yeno. He needs to be here. Xi Huang, welcome to the family. It will be a pleasure to get to know our son's mate." Juri disappeared in a blink of an eye.

Xi bowed low. "Thank you for accepting me; however, it was not needed because I am not his mate."

"Say what?" I said through the link.

"Xi's being stubborn," Ezra stated.

"He's being protective," Asher said.

"I agree. He knows what we walk into, and he doesn't want Kiered to care for him or worry," Alex shared.

"But then how did they find out they were mates if Xi's not accepting it?" I put in.

"What happens when two people come together sexually?" Thorn asked.

Nate snorted. *"Bam, they find out they're bonding as mates."*

"Xi had sex?" Shock had me coughing.

My men laughed around me.

"What do you mean, Xi Huang? You do not want this bond with my son?" Castilina sounded confused and a little hurt for her son's sake.

Kiered stepped forward. "Don't worry about what he says, Mother. He wants this bond and he cares for me as I care for him." He glanced back at a scowling Xi with a warm smile and soft eyes.

Juri reappeared with Castilina's third mate. "What's this I hear of more blessed news?" he asked. He came forward to clasp Kiered's arm and then shook his hand. "Congratulations, son." He glanced to Xi. "Is this fine warrior your mate?"

"He is, Yeno."

"I am not," Xi stated.

Yeno's brows dipped. "What's going on?"

"Kiered, my dear, you cannot have a mate who isn't willing to accept you. It always turns bad for the both of you," Castilina said gently.

Kiered sighed. "He does accept me. He's just being stubborn and trying to protect me."

"Why?" Grandith demanded, now standing beside Castilina with his arms crossed while glaring at Xi.

"Because of what he is," Kiered answered.

The queen straightened. "What are you, child?"

Xi's eyes flashed with pain. He closed them quickly

and then reopened them, hardened. "I am no child, and that is another reason I cannot be with Kiered. I am over fifty thousand years old. I am a chimera, and my other half could kill Kiered instantly."

"Are you saying your other half won't accept Kiered as yours?"

Xi's jaw clenched. "He accepts him. However, it doesn't make it safe."

Nate stepped closer. "I know my beast isn't the same, but I always used to worry for my mate, if I accidently shifted in a moment of weakness and they were near, but I know my beast would do anything for our mates. He wouldn't harm one hair on their heads, unless they were being stubborn." He shot me a look, and I rolled my eyes. "Even if we were injured, we would recognize our mates and keep them safe. Have faith in your beast because they are a part of you also."

Ezra shifted closer. "I agree. Hellhounds don't have the best temper, and I know I'm only half one, but I know my beast side would never harm a mate. You can have happiness in your life, Xi. I know my father would want this for you."

"My beast is different than others. We have three minds inside of one. I cannot be certain something won't happen."

"Do you not trust my son?" Castilina asked softly.

"I...." Xi's hands fisted. He looked to the floor, but then nodded.

"Then if you do, trust that my son can take care of himself. That my son will accept you as you are, all of your beasts as well. My son will not only charm you and make you happy for the rest of your days, but he'll also have your beasts wrapped around his finger so that none of them would do him any harm because, as it's been said, you are a part of those beasts also, and you will love him with everything you have in time. Just as they will. Do not be afraid of something that could be so wonderful. I wish I hadn't listened to my parents so many years ago by putting status before love. Then again, I wouldn't have my sons, so it is as it was meant to be. Just how you two were meant for your lives to cross and find each other."

"Your mother is amazing," I sent to Cedrick.

He smiled down at me. *"She is. It's why the people love her. She leads with her heart."*

I could tell Xi was dumbfounded. He didn't know what to say or do, but he kept his eyes on the floor as no doubt thoughts ran around in his mind.

"Should we leave?" Alex asked, always the kindest out of all of us.

But I wasn't that kind. *"Heck no, this is drama I want to see. I never thought Xi could have another facial expression besides his stoic one."*

My men shifted and either looked the other way, coughed, or covered their mouths to hide their amusement.

Xi finally lifted his head and searched Kiered's face for something, but I wasn't sure he found it. Instead, he asked, "Are you certain this is what you want? I am old. I am a chimera. I am—"

"Grumpy?" Ezra offered. "Like a robot most of the time? A killer?"

Xi ground his teeth together. "I would have said colder than most people. Emotions don't come easy for me."

Kiered gave him a small smile as he stepped closer to Xi.

"Where did Xi get his name from? He looks American, but his name is from elsewhere," I asked Ezra.

"Dad said he was adopted when his real parents left him in an alley."

My heart lurched. Xi did deserve this happiness.

Kiered reached out and ran a hand down Xi's arm to his hand where he threaded their fingers together. "I will always accept you in any way or form. You're mine."

Xi's eyes shifted black and then back. He looked to Castilina and bowed. "Will you excuse us, Queen Castilina?"

She smiled wide and nodded. "Of course, and as I said before, Xi Huang, welcome to the family."

He bowed again. "You honor me." He straightened, picked Kiered up over his shoulder, and stalked from the room.

Happiness had me giddy, and I hugged Cedrick to me tightly—pleased for his brother and for Xi. "This day has been a wonderful one."

Castilina walked over and rested her hand on my arm. "Will you stay for a drink to celebrate?"

Leaning my head against Cedrick's chest, I nodded. "I would love to."

This was a future I wanted, one I would fight for. I refused to allow the council to tear this away from me.

CHAPTER FIFTEEN
ASHER

The following morning, we said our goodbyes to Castilina and her mates after they had a royal announcement of her reappearance. It was like she'd said; her people greeted her back with open arms, and I didn't have any fears about taking Cedrick from the fae. Kiered was also coming with us since he and Xi didn't want to be far from one another. But Kiered would transport back to Airrile the night before our meeting with the council to lead members of their force to the destination if they were needed.

Paige sat in the back of the vehicle reading over pages regarding the shifters. We were meeting the tiger and lion packs at the same time. Both betas were willing to greet us together. I had a feeling it was because they didn't trust anyone and hoped meeting together would help their outcome for survival. They would soon discover we weren't there to fight, but to help and give them answers, then ask if they would stand with us against the ones who needed to be taken down.

"I thought packs of different species wouldn't be seen with one another," Paige commented.

Nate grunted. "Usually no, but Asher thinks they're worried we're there to harm them. They probably thought making an alliance was the lesser of two evils and would give them enough strength to fight against us."

"Will they attack before listening?" Cedrick questioned from where he sat next to Paige. I was in the front driving, Thorn sat next to me, and in the middle seat were the rest of our clan. Nate, Alex, and then Ezra. I wasn't sure if Alex noticed he was in the middle for a reason. The other two would have done it that way to protect him. If Paige hadn't have had Cedrick next to her, I would have asked her to sit in the middle of all of us. Even on Alex's lap. However, Cedrick was fast, and he could easily move her with a thought if a threat came at us.

I wasn't sure why the men of my clan and I treated Alex as the weakest since it was the opposite. He was the strongest, yet his young features and sweet, shy manners had us fawning over him. I'd also noticed Thorn, Nate, and myself starting to do it with Ezra. Which was ridiculous because he was a hellhound for God's sake. But we couldn't help it. Our reactions were instinctive.

At least we all knew that Paige came first, above all of us, and we never took offense to it. We loved one another equally. I knew it and could feel it.

"I don't believe they will. We've told them we have some answers to their alphas' disappearances. They'll want to know first."

"Then we'll need to make sure they don't set a trap," Ezra said.

"We will. Even if they did, Cedrick and I could get us all out of there," Alex mentioned without looking away from the book he was reading.

"I won't run," Paige countered. I looked at her through the rearview mirror and caught Alex twisting in his seat to see her.

"I'm not talking about running. Just stepping away until they're not so restless."

She reached out and ran a hand down the side of his face, smiling. "I know you wouldn't run. I shouldn't have said it like that. But I think... and I'm only basing this off Nate being so prickly"—Nate huffed, and though he didn't turn, I still saw his grin—"they're scared, worried, and want to protect their people. They'll be angry and most likely act harshly. We need to keep our cool. Show them we mean no harm and have no secrets right from the start. I think what would help is if Nate and Ezra walked in there in their shifted forms."

"They could take that as a threat also."

"I have a feeling they won't. They'll have others with them, right?" She looked to me, and I nodded. "Then I'm sure they'll have some of their own people in shifted form as well. I also say we leave Xi outside the building."

"I agree," Thorn said. "If we need him, Alex or Cedrick could get him in seconds."

"I'll agree with anything as long as I'm near Paige," Cedrick said.

She snuggled into him. I waited for the jealousy, but it never came. Like with all the men in the vehicle, Paige was all of ours, and sharing her was a part of it. Besides, I enjoyed all the different parts to her she shared with each of us individually. As of now, she was still schoolgirl shy with Cedrick. She was attentive to Alex, cheeky with Ezra, snappy in a fun way with Nate, sweet with Thorn, and wild with me.

I couldn't love another woman as much as I loved Paige Alice, and I would never stop being grateful for the treasure Fate dropped into my lap with her and also with our men.

"We're here," I announced as I pulled the car into an abandoned parking lot of an old factory. Already I could feel eyes on us and knew they would be listening to everything we said. Cedrick's gift to us all came in handy. *"We're surrounded. Keep this link open, and if you need to say anything, say it in here unless we want them to hear."*

Nate grunted. *"Well shit, I guess this mind thing is good."*

"That's a thank-you from Nate," Alex told Cedrick, who smiled.

"You're welcome then."

Nate grunted once more before opening his door. I also got out, as did Thorn, who stretched and acted relaxed.

Nate tipped his head back and scented the air. Ezra did the same on the other side of the car as Alex helped Paige out of the back. Cedrick followed after her and placed his hands on her shoulders. He still looked like a king even though he wasn't now. His knee-length black shirt looked similar to what his guards wore, as if it was made out of dragon scales, but silky enough it seemed comfortable. His black pants underneath looked like cow hide, and his boots came up to the top of his calves. The rest of us wore our own combat gear, except for Paige who wore dark jeans and a long-sleeved black cotton shirt. Though she had one too many buttons undone for my liking. I had been itching to reach out and do it up for her.

"Xi," I called, needing to distract myself or I would follow through with that thought.

"Yes?"

"You and the rest of the men will wait out here. I'll send Alex out if we're in need of anything."

"I do not like that plan."

"It's not up for discussion, Xi," Paige called, her tone hard and unyielding. Xi noticed too because his body tensed, but he nodded once, even when he didn't like it.

"Kiered, wait here too," Cedrick said. Kiered saluted his brother with a smile.

"It will mean we have someone I'm able to communicate with telepathically outside," Cedrick explained telepathically.

"Very good, Cedrick," I sent him.

"Nate, Ezra," Paige said aloud, and both men removed their clothes. It was Paige's turn to stiffen.

"Couldn't you have both shifted with clothes on? Ezra, you don't even need to get naked for it. Nate, you have spare clothes in the car."

Ezra's chuckle sounded through my mind. *"But, mi corazón, there is no fun in that."*

Nate snorted but said nothing.

"I'll show you fun." Paige shot a mental image of her flogging Ezra and Nate while they lay in a bed together.

"Angel, that shit will just get me hard, and now's not the damn time." Nate growled as he shifted into his wolf form.

"Mi corazón, now you're just teasing." Ezra leaped forward, and in one swift move, he was in his hellhound form, raising his head to the sky and snarling.

"Does the mind link work in their other forms?" I asked into the link, suddenly nervous it was a bad idea. *"Ezra? Nate?"*

"It feels weird, but I'm here," Ezra answered.

"Same. It's like I'm foggy, but I still know what's going on. I still have thoughts and can help suggest to him, but he's in charge," Nate explained.

Relief had me pushing my shoulders back. *"Paige enters first with Ezra and Nate on each side. Alex is directly behind her with Cedrick and Thorn on each side. Alex, you be point to get her out if needed. I'll be at the back. Do we have it clear?"*

"Yes, boss," Alex chimed in.

Nate let out a bark, and Ezra growled. I didn't need their verbal acceptance through my mind.

"I'm ready." Cedrick nodded.

"In position," Thorn said as he stepped beside Alex who was already behind Paige.

"Have I told you lately I love how you take charge? It really turns me on." Paige sent to me.

I palmed my face and heard Alex and Cedrick stifle a groan. Thorn let drop a quick chuckle while Ezra just laughed in our minds and Nate scoffed.

"My love, any talk about being turned on or sex will not help us."

She looked over her shoulder and gave me wide eyes. *"I can't help it."*

I gave her a small smile and nodded. "Let's move," I voiced, and Paige started forward, her hands threaded through Nate's and Ezra's fur as they walked.

"Eyes everywhere," Alex said.

"I can feel movement through the ground to the left," Cedrick told us.

"Thorn, keep a look out."

"Got it."

"Right ahead," Ezra warned. A Native American man, clad in only jeans, stepped into the afternoon light from a darkened doorway. I waited for some type of reaction from Paige to see if a sudden attraction hit, but there was nothing. Her features didn't even change from the cool expression she showed. However, I did feel her concern of gaining more mates wash away, for now. She'd confided in me the previous night about her fears of traveling and the possibility of meeting more bonded mates. She didn't want any more. She loved who she had and was concerned that if more were added to the mix, she would have less time for the ones she had.

Of course, I tried to tell her that if the Fates chose her to have more, it would be for a reason that we weren't able to see yet and how it would be added protection for her. When she glared at me, I laughed and told her we would deal with it if it happened and that no matter how many men she received, we all knew she loved each of us all the same. Even if her time with us was sparse.

"Paige Alice, I presume," his deep voice called.

"You would be correct, and you are?"

"Detroit Heming, beta to the lion shifters." His eyes slid over all of us but went back to Ezra. "A hellhound. We weren't informed you had one. He'll have to stay out here."

Paige smiled. "I'm sorry. I go nowhere without my mates."

Detroit's eyes flared for a second. "He's your mate?"

"Didn't I just say that?" I asked through the link.

"Humor him, my love."

"Yes."

There was scuffling going on behind him and behind the broken windows that surrounded the parking area. More people moved closer for a better look.

"Are we having this meeting out here or in there?" Paige asked.

I shifted my gaze all around. I didn't like the number of shifters close to the openings of the building. Nate lifted his head and snarled. Ezra then did the same.

Nate growled into our minds. *The wolf is on edge. It feels like a trap.*

"My hellhound agrees."

"Do we get Paige out of here?" Cedrick asked.

"Not yet," Paige instructed.

Paige dropped her hands from Nate's and Ezra's fur and took a small step forward. She spread her arms out and asked, "What's the delay? We come in peace. We have our guards standing back near the cars. They're not infiltrating your area. We don't want to fight. We want to talk, and that's it."

He studied her. I didn't like the way his eyes ran over her and stopped on her damn breasts. I knew I should have done up that button.

"You keep looking at our mate like that, we will have a problem," I clipped.

He pulled his gaze up and over to me.

"Asher," Paige warned through the link.

"No, my love. They have to know the consequences, so they do not ogle you like they want a taste."

"It's disrespectful, dove," Alex added. *"You're queen. Remember that."*

"Detroit, let them in" was bit out from inside. The tone was male. It sounded amused and irritated at the same time.

Detroit sighed, turned, and walked back into the building. The darkness swallowed him up. Paige went to go after him until I called out, "My queen, please allow me to enter first."

She stopped, glanced to me, and showed her worry for me, but nodded anyway. She made me proud. I dipped my chin, then lifted it and started forward. I brushed my fingers over her arm as I passed.

"Be careful," she sent me.

"No one will take me from you, love," I promised, because I would do anything to make sure we all got a taste of peace after everything we had already endured.

Stepping through, I sensed movement to my right and left in the doorway. Spinning, I knocked one out and had the other pinned to the wall in seconds. "Tell me why I shouldn't take his life."

"Asher," Paige called.

"Hold," I demanded. Picking the man up by the neck, I faced the room holding the choking man in the air. Since I knew he was a shifter, I dug my claws into his flesh around his neck, ready to rip his throat out if needed.

A man stepped into the light that shined down from the window above. "They weren't supposed to be there. Detroit?"

Detroit huffed. "It was a test. We needed to see how fast you were."

"I will not bring our queen, and *mate,* in here if there are more tests around each corner. Believe I am fast.

Believe Alex is a powerful mage. That Ezra and Nate together, even separate, are vicious. That Thorn is strong, and that Cedrick is tricky. But not only that, you all need to believe we fight for everyone, not only our own people, alongside a woman, a queen, who is all that I mentioned we are, but more. She will bring about a good change to all of our communities. She is fierce but fair and so very much loved. Meaning, we will do anything to keep her safe."

"God, I love you."

"And I you, my love."

"Let him go. You can all enter in peace" came a woman's voice from a distance.

"Raquel," the unknown man clipped.

"No, Waylon. I want to hear what they have to say. Besides, they have news about our alpha, and yours, Detroit. They've proved they don't want to fight, else we would have had our asses handed to us. Let them in, you stubborn pricks."

I dropped the man to the ground as lights flicked on all around me just as the man and Detroit drew back into the room more.

I could sense them, but they all stepped out of their hidden areas and about fifty shifters moved further into the building. However, more still walked or waited throughout the rest of the building. The final number was unclear, but if they did plan anything, I knew we would be able to stop them.

"Paige," I called. Ezra entered first, growling low in warning, then Paige stepped through with Nate at her side. Ezra waited for them, and together, the three of them followed me the same way the others had gone. I ignored the footfalls and shuffles around us from the shifters moving back into hiding and kept walking through what looked like a reception area. I entered a room through double doors, and it seemed to be a large conference setting. A big round table was set right in the middle. At the opposite end from the entrance was a woman, my guess was Raquel who spoke before. Detroit, Waylon, and the woman were the only ones sitting. About ten more shifters in their animal form stood at their backs, then behind them, another ten men and women stood guard.

"Please, come in and take a seat. My name is Raquel, and I'm the beta for the tigers. Waylon is our enforcer."

"It's nice to meet you. I wish it was under different circumstances," Paige said as she sat in the chair right across from Raquel. Alex and Thorn moved the chairs out of the way so Ezra and Nate could sit on the floor next to her. I knew they were glaring down the other end at Detroit. Alex, Thorn, Cedrick, and I stood at our mate's back.

"So do I. The alpha of our pack is my mate."

Paige's pain rolled through us. She slid her hand forward on the table. "I am so sorry for your heartache and worry. We do hope to bring him back... bring them both back."

"As long as they're alive," Raquel added.

Paige smiled sadly at her and nodded. "Yes."

"So you know who has them?" Detroit demanded. His fist pounded into the table. "Who's to say this isn't some trick of your own and you have my brother yourself?"

Paige sat back in her seat more and shook her head.

"You're a fool to think I would do something like this." The lions behind him roared and hissed. Ezra and Nate stood and snarled back at them. Paige laid a hand on each of their heads. "It's okay, guys." They settled and sat back down as soon as the noise stopped at the other end. "Do you know anything about me?" Paige asked.

"We only know you're the new ghoul queen to a race we thought were extinct."

Paige nodded. "The former queen had to take our people into hiding. Over time, we also gained people of other races. They sought out our community for refuge away from the council."

"Why? As far as we know, the council has been just," Raquel said.

"So many thought that as well. Alex, Nate, and I did too, when we worked for the council as their elite enforcers," I told them.

Their shock showed from their widening eyes and how their pulses raced.

"The council is corrupt, and they are the ones who are behind your alphas' disappearances," Alex stated.

Shouts and conversations started up down the other end. Raquel's hand rose. The sound stopped immediately. "You'll need to give us more information for us to believe this story."

Alex clicked his fingers. A file dropped into his hand. He walked it down the other end and then slid it over the table to Raquel since she seemed the more sensible one. She opened it and sucked in a breath. She quickly passed some papers to Detroit. He took one look and paled.

What they were seeing were pictures Alex had found

in Councilman Gerald's computer. They were of the elite enforcers he was in charge of kidnapping both alphas after they'd beaten them senseless.

"Where did you get these?" Raquel asked, her voice thick with emotions.

"I managed to hack into a council member's computer before I was detected and found these. The people you see taking your alphas are members of the elite force."

"Why did you look into them in the first place?" Detroit questioned. I wasn't sure he bought the photos or if he still thought this was all a trick from us.

"When I came into my queen powers, I was attacked by demons. Someone sent them after me. It was lucky I had my men at my back, or I would have been taken. We found out the council was behind it."

"For what reason?" Detroit asked.

"For power," Cedrick answered. "I'm unsure if the news has been heard here as yet. In the realms of Airrile, we lost our mother five years ago. After my father was murdered, I became king." They looked upon Cedrick in a new light, with a lot more wariness. "It was only yesterday we found my mother alive. My father had made us believe she was killed when the palace was attacked. However, instead he'd locked her away to drain her of power and life force, to which he took within himself, making him stronger."

Gasps and shouts of outrage echoed around the room.

"This is what the council is doing," Paige announced. Everyone quieted once more. "Cedrick's father got the idea when he stumbled upon it in the basement at the council compound six years ago. Alex, Nate, and Asher have worked out that the cases, which seemed suspicious, could have happened for this reason."

"You think our alphas are being drained of their power and life force?" Raquel uttered, without taking her eyes from the images in front of her.

"Yes," I answered, and since they had been missing for a year, I wasn't sure about the chances of finding them alive. Yet, Castilina was down in that room for five years. However, only one person had been draining her. If all the council members were in on this, that was ten people.

We wouldn't know anything until we were in there.

"What are you asking from us?"

"To be witnesses and offer backup if needed when we go to the council."

Detroit stood. "Why would you go there?"

"Because I know my people, my family, won't be safe until something is done about them. I'm going to be the something," Paige answered.

Raquel finally lifted her head. Tears glistened in her eyes. "You have the tigers at your back. Let us know when and how you'll need us, and we'll be there."

"Raquel," Waylon pressed.

She shook her head. "No, Waylon. This is Zion we're talking about. Our alpha, my mate." She stood and turned to her people. "Who will stand with me and back Paige Alice?"

Roars erupted around in the room, but also outside of it.

Raquel turned to Detroit. "What of the lions? Will you join?"

Detroit's jaw ticked. He glanced back at his people on

his side, and I caught a woman nod. Who she was, I didn't know, but she did scent like Detroit.

He faced us. "We will be there also. Send us in, and we'll get everyone in their basement out."

Paige stood. She dipped her head a little and straightened. "Thank you."

"No, Paige," Raquel said. "It is us who should thank you. We've been doing everything to find out what happened that night, but came up empty-handed. You've given us hope, even if it's a small amount." She bowed. Her people followed suit, and then she turned and walked out of the back of the room.

Detroit nodded. "We've been in limbo not knowing. Now we have a plan of action; it gives us something to fight for."

"Something right?" Paige pressed with a small smile.

Detroit laughed, but it didn't last. "Yeah, I suppose. Call us when the time comes."

"We will," I told him, and then he, along with his people, left the building. I held up my hand until I knew there wasn't another being about, then lowered it.

"That went better than I thought it would," Thorn said.

"It did." I nodded.

"We will be able to count on them. They want revenge, but also to find out exactly where their alphas are," Cedrick commented.

"I agree. I would also like to thank you all for listening to my instructions and trusting I had everything under control," I told them with a small smile.

"It was hard, but like old times." Alex grinned.

"It's also a turn-on, like Paige said." We all looked to Ezra. Paige and Alex laughed, while Cedrick and I smiled.

Paige clapped her hands. "Now it's time for the vampires. For Asher's former lover and now friend who I hope I don't kill."

"Love" was all I said.

"Yeah, yeah, I know she's nothing to you now and all that jazz. But if she looks at you like you're her dinner, I'll be snapping the fangs right out of her mouth."

Fuck.

CHAPTER SIXTEEN
PAIGE

We drove to the airport and got on one of two private jets belonging to the former queen. Actually, they were my private jets. God, that still shocked me. Even though with all we had been through, I was sure it would take me another year or two to get used to the fact I was a queen.

On the two-hour flight, we took the time to rest, eat, and used it for alone time. Xi wasn't pleased again he couldn't get on the same plane as I was, but Kiered calmed him enough to climb onto the other one with the rest of the guards. I was looking forward to some quiet time with only my mates on board. The plane had already been stocked with the necessities, knowing in advance from Thorn what we would need. The only food we didn't have was for Asher, but that was supplied from any one of us.

I had a need to be his dinner that night.

Ezra, Alex, and Nate were all arguing over who would feed him while Cedrick sat back smiling. Thorn's laughter indicated he also found it amusing. He couldn't feed Asher since he didn't have enough blood running through him like I had with my heart working for me. Still, it didn't stop Asher from marking him with his teeth and getting a tiny nip from Thorn when he wanted. It was something Thorn enjoyed.

"Asher," I called and held out my hand.

His eyes bled green. He stood and glided over to me. In seconds I was out of my seat with him sitting in it, and I was positioned on his lap.

Asher swept my hair over my shoulder, and I shivered. The others quieted and went back to their seats. They were fine with me feeding Asher. I could tell from the way all of them watched us with either a smile or heated looks.

"You know you have nothing to worry about, love."

"I know, but I can't help worrying. She was a big part of your life, Asher."

"She was, but now you are and will always be."

I hummed under my breath. "Maybe if you keep telling me that while we're there, I won't have to hurt her."

His chuckle shook my body. "You are vicious, and I love it."

Turning to have his eyes, I smiled. "I'm glad you do." I pressed my lips to his. It was only meant to be a quick kiss, but when kissing any of my mates, it was so easy to get lost in the feeling. Which was what we did. Asher's hand threaded into my hair, and he dropped the other to my hip and up under my shirt where he gently traced the skin there, causing me to grip him closer to me.

His lips trailed over my cheek. He nipped at my ear, and I tilted my head to the side to give him better access. When he slid his tongue down over my neck, I bit my bottom lip and whimpered. He sucked on my skin before I felt him graze his fangs across it, and then he struck. It was fast and painless, but oh so very pleasurable. I grabbed hold of his arms and ground down on his lap with his first pull of my blood into his mouth. He groaned around me, and it vibrated right down to my clit. I moaned, tipped my head back, and rubbed my hands up and down his arms.

My heart was already beating hard in my chest, but on his next pull, it went haywire and my skin felt alive. "Asher," I moaned.

Another pull, I orgasmed in my jeans without a touch to my pussy. My body quivered and shook. I panted out a breath, and licked my lips just as he swiped his tongue over my neck.

"Delicious as always, love."

"Hmm" was all I could say, which made him chuckle.

"Is watching Asher feed from our mate always that intense?" I heard Cedrick ask.

Ezra laughed. "It's more sometimes, especially when we're all in a room naked together. Asher has a way of sending very pleasant vibes to the ones he's feeding on."

Cedrick made a noise in the back of his throat, and I had a feeling he was now thinking of wanting to see how it felt for himself.

"Alex, I'll need fresh clothes and a clean body," Ezra admitted, and I couldn't stop the giggle. I opened my eyes to see him staring down at the wet patch on his pants.

"I have to admit I am in need of the same," Cedrick said, and I swung my gaze to see, but his shirt covered the front of him.

"Same," Nate grunted.

"Let's just say all of us then." Alex smiled.

"Yes," Thorn said.

"Of course," Asher replied. "Our queen makes me crazed enough to act like a teen and jizz my pants."

Another giggle burst out of me, and I looked around at

all my mates smiling over at me. We needed more moments like these. Happy and carefree.

* * *

Of course the vampire's lair was an old mansion in New Orleans. Like that wasn't cliché. We'd just pulled through the huge-ass gate and stopped out front of a gothic-looking place. I climbed out after Asher and Thorn and stood out in front while thanking Fate for once that we hadn't been attacked on the way there from the airport. My nerves weren't the best in that moment after keeping an eye out the whole way there for trouble, and I knew they wouldn't settle until we got this out of the way. With Asher far away from Cynthia as soon as possible.

"We're getting the stare down from the sentries placed about," Ezra sent through the link. The mind connection had been the best asset to our family since it made communication so much easier. Yet I hoped Cedrick knew we wanted him within our fold because we cared for him, not for what he offered us.

It was something I needed to make sure he understood.

Asher nodded. *"I see them. Don't worry. Cynthia will have the place under control."*

I screwed my nose up and looked to the cobblestone ground. *"Of course, Cynthia will have the place under control. She's wonderful. She's perfect. She's dead."* Glancing up, I realized everyone was looking at me. *"Huh, I didn't block that, did I?"*

Nate, Ezra, Cedrick, Alex, and Thorn grinned, all at different watts, but still they were grinning. Asher frowned. Oh shit. Was he upset I mocked his precious Cynthia?

"You do understand I'm dead also, love?"

"What?"

"I'm of the undead. Do you have something against it?"

I placed my hands on my hips and turned to him more. *"Sorry, what?"*

"Dove, you said and I quote 'She's wonderful. She's perfect. She's dead.' Asher is concerned you have a dislike to dead beings." His lips twitched because he knew that was an idiotic thing to say. So silly. I laughed, and then laughed some more.

"Asher, you fool. I'm dead. Well, I was. I still think I am. Thorn's also dead. No, I don't have anything against dead beings. In fact, I love a few of them. I meant that she would be dead. That I would kill her fully."

Before he could say anything, our attention went to the steel doors as they slid open with a creak. A woman, who looked very similar to the younger version of Catherine Zeta-Jones, appeared. Asher had had sex with her.

I wanted to throw my hands up in the air as my insecurities took hold and told me Asher had settled for little plain old me.

"Merde," I uttered under my breath, taking on Cedrick's French swear word.

Some of my men coughed. Asher reached for my hand and took it, sending me serenity and love. I felt like dropping his hold, but I was being petty. All of my men had a past, and I had to remember it. I didn't have to like it, but I had to remember all of them were older than I was. So I would suck it up.... Well, until she pissed me off.

Like she currently was as she gazed down at Asher adoringly.

Clenching my jaw, I gripped Asher's hand tightly. Heat hit my back. Nate's scent swept over me, and then Alex's as he stepped up to my other side and took my free hand.

I touched their minds and said, "Are you guys just trying to stop me from killing someone for looking too beautiful for her own good?"

"Who, us?" Alex smiled as he stared forward, giving nothing away as we had our private conversation.

"I don't care if you kill all the exes." Nate's hands dropped to my waist.

"Really not the greatest thing to say." I could feel Ezra's humor.

"She is nothing compared to you," Cedrick said. He moved to Asher's other side and I was grateful because I hoped his steely look would get her to back off. I didn't like the smile on her as she descended the many stairs.

"I agree," Thorn added.

"As do I. Please do not kill anyone on my behalf, my love, because no matter what you do or how you act, I will love you."

Thinning my lips, I hated how he just blew my anger right out of the water.

"Asher, my darling, it is so good to see you." Cynthia made her way directly to Asher, ignoring everyone else in the process. I wasn't having it. Not only was it disrespectful to not acknowledge me as queen, but she had chosen to try and push my buttons already by making it clear she thought nothing of me, even as his bonded mate.

Unless she didn't know. A smile crossed my lips. I was more than ready to inform her. Ezra swore through the mind link when he looked at me. *"She's smiling."*

"Shit, that's not good," Nate commented.

"Not in this situation at least," Thorn said.

"Beautiful, now isn't the time to lock us from your thoughts." I sensed Cedrick look around Asher to me, but I kept my eyes on the bitch in front of us.

I wanted to roll my eyes. They were overreacting. Maybe.

Just as she started to reach for Asher, who tensed, I dropped my mates' hands and stepped in front of Asher. My smile grew. "Hello, I'm Paige Alice, ghoul queen, and bonded mate to Asher, Thorn, Nate, Cedrick, Ezra, and Alex. I don't believe we've met, and I'm sorry, I haven't heard who you are."

"Ha, she just peed all over you, Asher," Ezra teased.

"She also peed on you, Ezra, but, my love, you did it beautifully. She was disrespectful." I could sense Asher's unease. He didn't understand why Cynthia would act that way. Maybe she wasn't the upstanding vampire he thought she was after all.

Cynthia glanced over my head to Asher. "Oh, yes, my apologies, Queen. Welcome to the Barrick Clan's residence. My name is Cynthia Mirrer." She waited for some type of reaction from me, but when she didn't get it, she once again glanced to Asher. "Though, I find it strange you've never heard of me."

I tilted my head to the side in an act of confusion.

"Really, why's that?" I straightened. "I'm new to all this, sorry, but your name doesn't ring any bells."

Her jaw tightened before she was back to smiling. "Why, I helped Asher through a troubled time in his past. We became close. I thought he would have mentioned it, being your mate and all."

Oh, bitch.

"We've been very busy in such a short amount of time, Cindy. I'm sorry you haven't come up."

Nate snorted, Ezra chuckled, but my other mates hid their amusement well.

"It's Cynthia."

"Yes." I nodded. "Shall we get down to business?"

A tick started in her perfect forehead. "Of course, but do you mind if I greet Asher since we were so close?"

"Greet him all you like." I waved a hand around. She went to step around me, smiling once more, but I grabbed her wrist. "Just don't touch him. I'm very possessive of my men."

She looked down at me and must have heard the seriousness in my cold tone or seen something in my expression because she then nodded. "Yes, Queen Alice."

I nodded and released her arm. I didn't move. I stayed looking up at the ugly place when I heard, "Asher, it is lovely to see you after so long."

"A pleasure, Cynthia. However, if you disrespect my queen, my bonded mate, as you did once more, it won't be a pleasure next time."

She made a noise in the back of her throat. "I didn't think you would want to bond to something so—"

"Watch what you say here, Cynthia," Asher snarled.

"Why are you acting as such? I spoke highly of you, and this is how you pick to show yourself to my clan?"

She laughed without humor. "Your clan. Of mixed race?"

"My clan. My family, my pack, my everything. I never knew you to be prejudiced, Cynthia. What's going on with you?"

"Something's happening. The guards are moving," Nate said into the link. He pulled me close and then gently pushed me toward Alex, who slid an arm around my waist.

A rattle startled me. I glanced back and saw the gates were closing.

"Kiered just told me Xi is concerned also." Cedrick added into our minds.

For some reason, I wanted people on the other side of that gate before it closed us all in fully.

"Cedrick, can Kiered take Xi to the other side of the gate?"

"Yes, but why?"

"I don't know. I just feel like we need to."

"That's all I need to know."

"No," we heard Xi clip.

I shifted my gaze to them standing near the rear vehicle. Xi started toward me but Kiered grabbed his wrist and they disappeared for a second to reappear outside of the property, just as the gates finished shutting.

"I am sorry, Asher."

"Cynthia, what have you done?" Asher's gaze moved all around the area. Into the link he ordered, *"Gather around Paige, now!"*

My men quickly surrounded me. Thorn held his

swords out and up, ready. Nate half shifted while Alex called his powers forward, only to groan and clutch his head. He swayed and I reached out for him, crying his name as terror seized my heart and cooled my body. My hands shook as I ran them over him, searching for a wound but finding nothing. Dread twisted my insides painfully.

Ezra helped me steady him. "Alex, what is it?" he questioned with panic in his voice. Our others surrounded Ezra and me with Alex. Each trying to pay attention to what was around them and off what would be concerning them the most. Alex.

"Tell me what's happening?" Asher demanded into our minds as he stopped next to us and threw Cynthia to the ground. She rolled over and stared up at me with a tired look.

"What's wrong with Alex?" Nate's panicked tone rolled through everyone.

"Alex? Dammit, Alex, answer us," Thorn called.

"I have Kiered seeking help. We need to find out why Alex is as he is," Cedrick said.

"Alex, please, tell us what's wrong," I begged aloud, cupping his cheeks under his hands and holding his head.

Alex's weight took Ezra and me to our knees with him. His pain-filled gaze met mine. "Father" was all he said before crying out and gripping his head once more.

"What does he mean?" I yelled at Ezra.

"I don't know. I don't fucking know." I had never seen the pure fear in Ezra's features before, and I knew my own would show the same. Wide eyes, pinched brow, lips shaped in a frown or thinned.

"He means me" came a voice. Nate and Thorn parted

enough for me to see a man standing on the top of the stairs near the front doors.

"What is this?" Asher snarled. He picked Cynthia up by the throat and threw her so she sailed up the stairs to land next to the man.

The man, who I presumed was Alex's father, glanced down at Cynthia in distaste before smirking back at us.

Alex moaned. He lifted his head and sucked in a shuddering breath. He licked his dry lips and whispered, "Help me up." Ezra and I did, only we didn't dare release him to stand on his own since his body shook like it had just run a marathon. "I should have known you would be a part of this."

"You were always the slow one in the family."

"What did you do to him?" I demanded, glaring up at the short, stout man in front of us. Alex looked nothing like his father, and I could never see my Alex having that sneer of hatred on his face. How did my Alex turn out so pure, so sweet when he had a father as such? One willing to hurt his child for the council's sake.

"And you must be the pathetic ghoul queen." He looked me over, causing Ezra, Nate, and even Asher to growl under their breath. "I'd heard my son had taken up with you. Tell me something, bitch, how are you better than the one he'd been intended to? One with pure magic running through her veins? One made from a fine magical family?"

"Simple, my pussy is made of magic."

A startled laugh dropped from Alex and Ezra. Nate, of course, snorted, while my other men smiled.

The douche's face turned a dark shade of red. "You disgusting piece of rubbish."

"Watch what you say," Alex warned, his tone harsh and deadly.

"His name, Alex?" Thorn asked.

"Anthony Smith."

Anthony's gaze locked onto Alex. "You dishonor our family for this?" He waved a hand my way.

"Yes. I would do it over and over again because I never understood how I could have been born into such a cold, uncaring family. Paige has shown me love, as any mate would."

"Mate?" he yelled. Spittle flew from his mouth. "Mate?"

"Yes, mate."

"Tell me it hasn't been completed," he ordered.

Alex straightened even more, seeming to gain energy back. "It has." Alex smiled. "I am also mated to Nate. He and his wolf chose me to be one of his."

Anthony paled just before he spit to the side. "You'll never be accepted back into the family. You are dead to us."

Alex laughed, but cut it off with a snarky smile. "I have my family. I do not need any of you."

"Alex, what did he do to you before?" I asked through the link, needing to know so I could prepare if it happened again.

"Since I am of his blood, he used it against me and blasted my mind with a magical stunning spell. Families are able to cross through our barriers easier than any other."

"Can he do it again?" Asher asked.

"He's already trying. I'm managing to block him now that I'm prepared for it."

"I shall help, Alex. My mind skills are above most," Cedrick said. I reached back and squeezed his hand.

Alex looked over his shoulder to Cedrick and smiled. Tension eased from his face and body, so I knew Cedrick already helped him block his father out, no matter the family connection they had for each other. Like Alex said, we were his family now, and I would make sure none of Alex's former family wanted anything from Alex again.

Obviously, they never deserved him in their lives.

"You can't protect your mind from me forever, Alex," Anthony warned.

"I can, Father, because I have help from people who actually care about my well-being."

Anthony scoffed. "Is this about your cousin? Your tantrum took you into their arms because you couldn't handle a little heat?"

Alex's magic resurfaced; his eyes glowed brighter than they ever had. He took a step forward. Ezra's and my hands fell away from him. "A little heat? You allowed my cousin to test his spells on me while I was magically bound."

Anthony waved a hand around. "He had promise. We had to test his skills."

"If any of it killed me, would you have cared?"

"We would have missed your powers." He licked his lips as if he could imagine tasting something delicious.

It dawned on me then. "You'd offered him up to the council."

Anthony's gaze slid to me. "I didn't have to offer. The boy wanted to work for them to get away from us."

I couldn't say I blamed Alex. I would have as well if my family were mental cases.

"The council wanted to see if his powers would increase under them."

"So they had more to drain from him, you mean," Nate growled.

Anthony smiled. "Yes."

"Did they promise you his powers?" Cedrick asked.

He smiled, and it wasn't pleasant. "No, they were going to the magical members on the council."

"Then what were you getting from knowing about it and keeping your mouth shut?" Thorn questioned.

"Money and status."

"Jesus fuck, does everyone care about money and status?" I demanded loudly, frustration taking over my mouth for a moment.

"Unfortunately, most do, love," Asher answered.

Cynthia scoffed. "All you cared about was money and status back in the day. You act like you don't now, but look at you, a mate to a queen. My, you have grown."

"I learned money and status wasn't everything the moment I met Paige. In the short span of our time, she has shown me there is so much more to life. As have the men in my clan. Even if Paige hadn't been fated to be queen, I would still be with her no matter if we lived on the street because she opened my eyes to a love so consuming it's everything."

A pained expression washed over Cynthia's face, and her eyes darkened.

"She loves you."

Asher's gaze was full of surprise when it swung to me. *"No."*

I nodded and offered him a small, sad smile. "I'm sorry," I gave her. It was her turn to look at me in shock.

"What are you talking about?" I felt "fool" was left off the end of her sentence.

"Paige," Asher called.

I shook my head and stepped up beside Alex. "Asher spoke highly of you. I didn't like it, of course, because I'm a possessive woman, but he thought of you as a close friend. I'm sorry he didn't love you as you do him. I'm sorry your feelings are crushed as he stands with me. I'm sorry for your pain as you look at him, knowing you have lost him. I would never want that for another person. Especially not someone who cares for one of my mates as much as you do." I paused, letting my words sink in and watching as a few tears overflowed from her eyes. "But I can't say I'm sorry for meeting him, because my life wouldn't be the same without him in it. He helps me in so many ways. I love him with every breath, with every heartbeat, with every look, touch, and taste." I glanced to Anthony. "I love all my mates the same and will do anything in my power to make sure their future, *our* future, is one filled with harmony." I glanced back to Cynthia to find her looking at Asher longingly.

"I thought we would eventually be together. I was giving you time to love me as I love you. Maybe I shouldn't have done that. I should have told you how I felt many, many years ago because then we would have been together, and you wouldn't have found her. But I listened to your dreams of being something by working for the elite enforcers. You wanted to do good for the people. I respected you for it. I understood why, and then I let you walk out without saying anything. Since then, I thought you would see what I could have been for you. I kept waiting. I shouldn't have, and I should have stopped you from walking away from me. I should have held on to you and never let go." She looked to me and studied me for a couple of beats before looking back to Asher. "Now it's too late." She closed her eyes for a moment from whatever she saw on Asher. When she opened them, more tears dropped. She took a large gulp of air and then composed herself. "I wasn't the only sister who fell though."

"Shut up," Anthony yelled. He went to grab her, but she easily sidestepped him.

"What do you mean?" I asked.

"My sister hunts you all, not only for your powers and life source, but because she also loves a man who can never be hers."

"Shut your fucking mouth, vampire," Anthony bit out.

"Who?" Nate clipped.

"Jessica. Sister by blood, but not sire." She laughed without humor. "I asked her to take care of you since she just started out on the council when you arrived there."

"Jessica is your sister?" Asher asked.

"Yes."

"But you're nothing alike," Alex said.

"We had different mothers." She dodged Anthony's hand again. "There's something you should know—" She cried out as blood bloomed on her chest.

"Father, no!" Alex screamed. "He's shredding her heart."

Only it was too late. Whatever spell Anthony used had already taken hold, and he smiled gleefully as blood soaked more and more of her gown. I watched as Cynthia met Asher's gaze one last time and she mouthed, "I'm sorry."

"Forgiven," Asher called solemnly, just as she dropped to the ground. Completely dead.

CHAPTER SEVENTEEN
PAIGE

The area around us was silent for a moment, and then chaos reigned down upon us all. The vampire sentries appeared from nowhere, flashing into existence after their master was killed. They went for Anthony but were bounced off an invisible wall. Still, they kept trying and trying.

More mages appeared behind Anthony. Alex cursed. "My family have come to help him."

I chanced a glance away from the battle to Asher. He stared down at Cynthia's body. My heart ached for him. I pushed the thought away of Asher regretting his chosen path when he could have had one with Cynthia and concentrated for a moment on more so wanting to wrap him up in my arms and tell him he would be okay, but we didn't have time. "Cedrick, why can't Kiered and Xi get back in?"

"There's something blocking them. It's as if the house and grounds are wrapped in a protective bubble," he replied.

Alex added, "It will be linked only to those under Anthony's coven. I was cut from being a member a long time ago."

"Shit." I'd seen that before when I'd first met Alex and

the others, and I'd walked right through Alex's.... I had walked right through their protective bubble.

Could I walk people back with me?

We would have to join the fight soon, and we may need all the help we could get. I sent the plan to my men.

"I'll go and try to counter their spell to get the others through," Alex said into our minds. I grabbed him and kissed him quickly.

"Stay safe and remember you are stronger than any of them. You're amazing, Alex Smith." He nodded with a smile, and a light blush coated his cheeks. There was my mate. I looked to the others around me. *"Ezra, Thorn, and Cedrick, please help him. Cedrick, find out if you can trick them with an illusion. Ezra, see if you can frighten them. Nate, you're with me."* I took Nate's hand in mine and turned toward the gates.

"You also need to stay safe, sweetheart," Thorn called.

"I will," I said back through the mind link.

"What will you have of me?" Asher asked. His voice sounded low and full of hurt.

"Place Cynthia's body somewhere safe. She'll need a proper farewell after all this."

I stumbled when Asher blasted me with his love. I let mine wash over him more slowly as Nate straightened me and we finished the mad dash toward where Xi looked like he was about to have a heart attack as he banged on the invisible wall right in front of the outside of the entrance.

The gaps in the gates were wide enough for a small woman, like me, to slip through. But then how would I get them back over to this side? That was *if* I could get them back through. Then there was also the risk, if I did go out there and couldn't get Xi back through, he would probably keep me out there for safety.

Stopping at the gate, I said, "If I can get through and drag you back through the magic shield, are you able to break the gate wide enough for you both?"

"Yes," Xi hissed, his eyes pure black. Oh, he was angry and wanted to hurt people. Kiered stood back waiting, rolling his eyes at his mate. He was calm and collected; really they were perfect for one another.

"Promise me you won't keep me out there even if I can't get you through?"

He snarled at me, his upper lip tipped as he kept growling. Nate got closer and growled in his own way, which had Xi stopping and nodding. I wish I could speak beast; I was sure they just had a conversation.

"All right." I nodded. When I started to move closer, hands gripped my waist and I was suddenly turned in large, extra-hairy arms. Nate looked down at me in his half form. Concern bled in his eyes. Reaching up, I cupped his cheek. "I'll be fine. You just keep an eye out, okay?"

He nodded, stuck his nose into my neck, and drew in my scent. "I'll be a bigger dick if you get hurt from doing this."

Laughter bubbled out of me. I kissed his cheek and stepped back. "Then I better make sure not one hair on my head gets damaged."

He grunted.

Turning back around, I moved closer to the gates. Slowly, I put my hands up and pressed them forward, expecting to feel something stop me before I touched the metal on the gates, but there was nothing there. I pushed a hand past the poles on the gates and found that same tingle I got when I walked through Alex's shield. Quickly, I turned my body enough to slip through the tight gap between two poles. My whole body hummed from the shield.

As soon as I was through, Xi grabbed me and pulled me all the way out. Nate snarled at his roughness, but I ignored it because I knew he was worried. I was his mission. If he kept me alive, the others would do anything to stay alive, and that included Lucifer's son.

Xi's hands trailed over my body, searching for any injuries and causing Nate to growl threateningly at the man.

"Do I need to leave the two of you alone?" Kiered sniffed.

"Ew, no. He's like a father figure to me with how protective he is."

I regretted saying anything because Xi suddenly stood and his chest puffed out. His eyes, even though they were still black, seemed to soften as he took me in.

Kiered groaned. "You've touched on his fatherly instincts."

It was my turn to groan. "Now I'll never get rid of him."

Kiered moved, stepping in front of Xi. Xi's gaze moved down to his mate, his lips starting to tip up right before Kiered kissed him. "You good now? Your girl is safe, your mate is safe, can you come back to me?"

"Yes." He nodded, though his eyes didn't switch back. His beasts were close to the surface.

Kiered patted his cheek gently. "That'll do." He faced

me. "Now, how are we going to get back in there and kick some mage ass?"

"Get me through the shield and I will get us in," Xi ordered.

Nodding, I faced toward Nate, who was looking at the destruction near the house. Bodies littered the ground. My pulse raced, my insides cooled, and I prayed none of them were my mates, but I didn't want to risk checking in on them in case I was a distraction.

A hand touched to my back, and Kiered whispered into my ear, "They'll be okay. They're tough, strong, and would do anything to make sure they stay safe for you."

Smiling, I held up my hands in front of me. "Take hold of me. A hip or arm. But make sure you're touching skin. Then pray this works." Kiered placed his hand on my upper arm while Xi's cupped the back of my neck. Stepping forward, my hands were the first thing to hum. "Okay?"

"Yep," Kiered said, but his voice was rough. His hand on me tightened and I felt it shake. I glanced over my shoulder to find him clenching his jaw and his body quivering a little. It was the same with Xi. I dropped my hands.

"It's shocking the both of you?"

"Just a little," Kiered said. When I turned to him, my eyes widened in surprise. His hair looked like it had been blow-waved by a hairdresser who didn't know what they were doing. I couldn't tell with Xi since his head was shaved, but his face was tight, lips thin, and brow pinched. His hands were fisted down at his sides.

"Don't lie to me," I pleaded. "Look, I'll go through, help them, and then we'll get you both in there."

"No," Xi barked. He looked to his mate. "Stay out here."

Kiered glared, his hands slapping down on his hips. "Like hell. We're doing this together." His eyes blazed into mine. "Just be quick with it and we'll be fine."

"Xi has to break the gates. How long is that going to take while you're both being zapped?"

Xi sighed. "It won't take long. Let's do this so I can beat someone senseless."

"But—" When they both stared me down, I knew I didn't have a chance in stopping them, and now I wished I hadn't even come out to get them. Only the image of all the bodies pushed back into my mind and having Xi, hell, both of them in there would be an advantage. Sighing, I nodded once. "Fine."

Turning around again, they placed a hand on me once more. This time I didn't prepare with my hands out. I stepped right in and reached back, wrapping an arm around each man to try and help. Their bodies still convulsed, but Xi managed to grip the bars, and with a roar that shook the ground, he didn't just bend them to fit through, he broke them apart and threw the poles to the ground. Kiered stumbled forward, away from the shield, and gasped for breath. Xi, even with his body still shaking, took one step away, crouched on all fours and shifted with another roar of fury.

I took the chance to look around and noticed the mages were no longer behind their own barrier but fighting either hand to hand or magic to vampire strengths and gifts with others. They were separated at least. It could mean we had a better chance of taking them out one by one.

Xi's shifted form aimed all of his heads toward his

mate. He took a step to Kiered, who didn't look scared at all. I was even fearful of what Xi in this form could do. Kiered stood his ground as the heads leaned in and sniffed him. The snake swept out it's tongue and licked him. I took a breath when their attention moved to the fighting. It let out another roar, and I caught people stop what they were doing to look our way. What I should have been doing was paying attention to Xi still, because I then felt hot breath on the back of my neck.

I froze.

Nate grumbled out a warning, and I hoped he didn't do anything else.

I got a sniff, and then he bounded forward, his eyes set on a mage off to the left. Shaking my body out, I called my own powers forward and felt the change instantly.

"He's amazing, isn't he?" Kiered sighed with awe as he watched his mate dodge a spell right before he opened his mouth and bit the mage in half. I was sure I could still hear the mage's cry of agony as Xi chewed.

I shuddered but pushed it all to the back of my mind when I caught Anthony advancing on Alex, who had his back to him while he fought another foe.

I lifted my head and let out an ear-piercing scream, then raced right for him.

Nate, in wolf form, landed at my side as we ran with all our strength. My attention never strayed from Anthony. A need to kill him flared inside me. Nate snarled and dropped behind me. A snap of bones followed, then someone cried out in pain. Still, I stayed on track.

Just as I was closing in, Anthony turned and threw a spell out at me. My body lit with fire burning over it, only it didn't hurt, nor sting like I expected it would. I lifted my gaze to a stunned Anthony.

"How?" he breathed. His gaze shifted to his side, and Alex had turned. His lavender eyes glowed more vibrant.

"Did you not think I would protect my mate?"

"But she, you...." He shook his head. "A protection spell? I should have cut through that."

"Because you used black magic?" Alex laughed, but it wasn't his normal light one. It was sinister. His hand rose, and the fire surrounding my body evaporated, leaving me naked. With a click of his fingers, I was dressed in fighting leathers. "You underestimated me and mine, Father. Look around. It has cost you your precious coven."

"I still have people," Anthony yelled, and he was right. Ten or so mages still battled against my mates and Cynthia's vampires.

"It won't last. *Look*, look into the future you have given your coven." Cedrick appeared behind Anthony and placed his hands on the man's head. Anthony screamed over and over. He dropped to his knees even as Cedrick never took away his hands. My mate was showing him his future, even if it was an illusion.

"Paige." My name was bellowed. I twisted and dove to the ground before rolling and popping back up into a crouch. A woman stood not far away with her hands out at her sides. Her lips moved, and I knew she was conjuring another spell. Instantly, I rushed right for her. A flash of red shot out of each of her hands. That time I managed to dodge the balls of light before I jumped into the air and landed on her. In the fall, I gripped her head and twisted swiftly to the right. Her neck snapped before her back even hit the ground. Someone screamed, and then I was tackled to the ground with another woman on top of me. She slapped at my face, pulled my hair, and yelled at me. I punched up. The force behind it had my hand sailing right through her stomach. Her eyes widened above me, and blood spurted from her mouth before she collapsed dead to the side. I pushed her all the way off and lifted my gaze.

Silence.

There was utter silence for one peaceful moment.

Did it mean the fighting was done or more was to come?

I stood and looked around; my mates and our people were doing the same. We all noticed the others watching me. I straightened and said loudly, "It didn't have to come to this. All we want is to live in our world in peace." I shook my head and waved a hand toward Anthony who blankly stared up at the sky at Cedrick's feet. "Did Anthony speak for you all? Did he bring death into your lives because he worked with a corrupt council who kill and steal innocent people in their greed to be stronger and more powerful than the rest? Why can't we all live together without fearing others? Why can't we all get along and not worry if someone has an extra boost in strength or power than the others? I want a world where even those who are stronger will help those who aren't. They will stand with anyone no matter who or what they are. I'm here because the council threatened my people, my family, and I'm in need of people to stand with us to stop the killings and kidnappings."

"Who will govern us all if the council isn't around to do it?" someone called.

"I will help find the right people to do the job. Until then, I will step in along with my mates. My mates who are from different factions in this community. But I want you all to know, I'm not after anything by doing this. I want harmony between us all. I want to live with my family in happiness and not worry or fear." I threw my hands out, waving them around. "Is this how you want to go on? Fighting? For what? Money, power? It isn't every-thing in the world."

"Mages, witches, will you stand down today?" Alex called. "You have heard my mate. All we want is to find peace, and in doing so we know it isn't under people who are cruel, who kill over meaningless things."

"Who says we'll allow them to stand down?" a red-haired male vampire stepped forward. "They came into our territory to fight, to bring war by killing Cynthia, our master. They deserve to die."

"We only followed our leader here when he sent us an SOS call. For all we know, it was you vampires who started this."

"Anthony killed Cynthia," Asher snarled. "I know she wasn't an innocent body in this matter. She conspired with the mage to trap us here because they want our mate, our queen, to drain her powers and life source to extend and grow their own. This is how the council have been working for years. Cynthia made a mistake. We all knew she regretted it in the end, but it never had to come to murdering her. There is no point fighting one another when all the blame falls onto the council. They also killed your former master. We have proof to show you. Then, through Anthony, they killed Cynthia. The mage also offered up his own son, his own flesh and blood, to be drained like he was nothing. It's people like this we allow to govern us. Will you let it continue? Or are you willing to stand with us and fight who is really at fault, not each other?"

Murmurs started up around us all. We watched and waited to see what the outcome would be. I just prayed it wouldn't end in more bloodshed.

A woman moved into my view. She dipped her head just a tiny bit. "If the vampires are willing to let this go, we will leave peacefully. I will put it to the other covens and see if we will offer our own help against the council. We also offer the vampires Anthony Smith for the misunderstanding today."

She was giving up their coven leader to be tortured and killed. I respected that choice because Anthony deserved it. However, would Alex be able to live with letting it happen? I glanced to him and found him already looking at me. He gave me a small, sad smile but nodded.

Even if the choice came back to bite him in the butt, I would be there to help him get through it.

Nodding, I turned back to the woman and said, "That's all we can ask for. Please give one of my mates your details and we'll speak. But know we see the council in a week's time."

"Alex has my details."

"I do, Mother."

Mother? That was Alex's mother? She offered up her own husband without a care or tear over him? My gut burned in anger. But it wasn't because of that. No, it was the way she looked to her son, a man who was honorable, sweet, and amazing, without warmth or love. Instead, she turned and started to walk away.

"Wait," I called.

She faced me once more.

"I need you to understand it's fine if none of you stand with us. If no mage or witch comes to our aid or wishes to witness the proof the council will give when we see them. However, I will warn you to stay away, *far away* from me and what's mine. Especially Alex. If anyone causes any trouble for any of us, I will hunt you down and kill you myself."

She smirked. "And you say you want peace, yet there you are threatening us."

"I have a right to threaten the mother of my mate since it was your husband to cause all this in the first place. It was *your* husband who stood with the council in draining people, and it was *your* husband who treated my mate like he was nothing because *he* has a heart. So yes, I think I have a right to threaten you because I stand by what I say. I protect people from bullies, from people who think they're better than others."

She studied me before glaring, turning, and walking toward the gates. We all sensed the shield drop before the rest of the mages and witches followed Alex's mother out.

"Vampires, what say you?" Asher called.

The red-haired one moved closer to me until a certain wolf stomped to my side and growled. The vampire smirked but dipped his head. "I am Finnegan McGregor, now master to the clan, and I speak on behalf of my people. We stand with you, Paige Alice. You seek what we are after. From the recording today, we will contact other clans we trust and show them what has occurred, as well as the proof you have over the council murdering our former master."

I wasn't sure I liked that the whole thing had been filmed, but it could be good for us in the end. We didn't act out of turn. It showed exactly what we were about. "Thank you, Finnegan. We appreciate it. Alex will leave the files with you. However, be sure you trust the other clans completely and also that you destroy the footage after you have shown them."

"I will, Queen of ghouls." He bowed once more before ordering a man to take Anthony inside and then moving over to Alex.

"Can we leave now?" I asked, suddenly drained from everything that happened. Though I was still pissed at Alex's family. Killing Anthony over and over would be good. Maybe someone knew a necromancer and we could make that happen.

"I vote for leaving," Nate answered first, from his wolf form. *"They keep looking at Paige like they want to fuck or suck on her for hours after witnessing the way she fought."*

"I second that vote," Ezra agreed. He was now back in his human form.

"Paige isn't the only one being admired," Thorn fumed. I glanced over to see him watching a couple of vampire women approaching Asher.

Actually, it was happening everywhere. Some stood close to Thorn—not that he noticed—and others eyed Cedrick. One even reached out as if to touch his hair. I waggled my finger at him when he saw me looking.

"Can I pat your wolf?" a guy asked and then licked his lips.

I was about to tell him where he could go—straight to hell—when there was a commotion in the house. Five people appeared in the doorway. They looked crazed with their wild, frantic, glowing green eyes searching for something. They lifted their heads and drew in a deep breath.

My stomach bottomed out.

"Alex!" I yelled. *"Get Ezra out of here now,"* I ordered.

Alex disappeared from where he stood, appeared behind Ezra, and then both of them vanished out of sight.

The fledglings flashed down the stairs and sniffed the air again. A disgruntled man and woman appeared at the top of the stairs. "They broke out. Just broke out because they could smell something."

"Maybe it was all the blood," I suggested. I would have crossed my fingers for them to believe me, but I didn't want to make it obvious.

Though Finnegan knew I was full of shit since I'd yelled to Alex and then his sudden action to get Ezra out. Worry seeped into my veins. Would he question it?

I relaxed a little when he said, "Yes, must have been." He moved over to them. "Children, feel the new bond. Do you sense it?"

They hesitated, and I worried we hadn't gotten Ezra away fast enough or that the smell of his blood still lingered.

"I can't scent his blood anywhere. It must have been on him," Asher told me, as if he knew my worries already, which he probably did.

A guy, who looked no older than sixteen, finally answered Finnegan, "Yes, master."

"Good, please go back into the safe rooms. It's nearly time for your feeding." They shuffled away without another word, and I relaxed even more.

If it would come down to it, I'd think of something to say to Finnegan to explain about getting Ezra out of there. I hoped he was smart enough to leave it alone though.

"Xi, pull the guards out and have them head back to the hotel we're staying at," Asher ordered. Xi grunted but got to work with Kiered at his side. "Finnegan, we'll be in touch. However, I would like to attend the send-off for Cynthia, if you'll allow me?"

I ground my teeth together in jealousy, and then I wanted to punch myself in the face, maybe even stab myself, because feeling jealousy was so wrong. Asher lost someone he cared about. I wanted him to be able to do what he wanted and needed to, for himself and her. For closure.

"Of course, Asher. You are always welcome here. We'll have a burial for Cynthia in a few hours."

"Thank you." He nodded and walked the rest of the way to me. "We're staying close to rest for a few days as I thought this would take longer. That's where Alex would have taken Ezra."

I took his hand and we made our way to the car. "Rest sounds good, but I would like to pop home tomorrow, even if it's just for a few hours."

"I would love to see it," Cedrick said from my other side.

"And I would love to show you."

"We'll make it happen, sweetheart." Thorn smiled from where he walked beside Cedrick. Nate was on Thorn's other side, and he bumped his head into Thorn until Thorn threaded his fingers into his fur. "You big baby," Thorn teased. Nate growled low in a playful warning.

Another meeting slash battle down, where the outcome was promising. Now all we had was one more to go.

The worst one.

Or, if everything fell into place, it could be the easiest.

Please let it be the easiest.

CHAPTER EIGHTEEN
PAIGE

"I still can't believe Lucifer contacted Ezra *after* the fight to inform him that if Ezra was in his hellhound form, the fledglings wouldn't have gone crazy," I complained as we walked through my castle.

Cedrick chuckled. "I think he'll be sure to find out all information straightaway from now on, especially after your phone call to yell at him." He shook his head, smiling. "Only you would scold the devil."

I harrumphed. "He deserved it."

His smile grew. "Yes, beautiful, he did."

At least, I thought he had. Okay, maybe I had gone too far when I threatened his balls a few too many times. I rolled my eyes. "Anyway, this is my sister's suite." I pointed to the door. "Well, the kids should be here probably, with the bear shifters or their father, Eric. Yasmin is still dealing with being changed over to a vampire."

Cedrick's hands landed on my shoulders. "Relax, beautiful. From what I've seen so far, I love everything about your home. I look forward to living here once this is over."

"Really?" I asked, turning in his arms and smiling widely, as I—quite possibly looking crazy—peered up at him.

He grinned back. "Really."

Tipping my head back, I puckered my lips. He

chuckled and leaned down to claim my mouth. I curled my arms around his waist, but then slid them around his neck when he picked me up off the floor to deepen the kiss.

The door behind us opened. "Aunty Paige" was screamed by a little monster. Cedrick quickly placed me on my feet in time for Sophie to crash into the back of my legs with a tight hug. She buried her head into my hip. "You're back. I've missed you so, so, so much." She pulled back to stare up at me, but then her gaze drifted to the side. "Whoa, you're tall."

Cedrick laughed. "I am, and you must be Miss Sophie. It's a pleasure to meet you. I'm Cedrick."

"You were kissing my aunty. Does that mean you're her mate as well?"

"It does."

"Cool," she drew out. "Can I call you Uncle Cedrick?"

"I would love that." He reached out to ruffle her hair, which had her smile brightening even more.

"Do you change into anything like Uncles Nate and Ezra? Or are you really fast like Uncle Asher? Or maybe you're like my aunty or Uncle Thorn?"

"I'm different again, sweet one. I'm an elf."

She gasped and pushed me aside to get closer to Cedrick. Rolling my eyes, I crossed my arms and waited to see what she was about to say. "Are you like an elf on the shelf? Are you magical like Uncle Alex?"

I giggled but covered it with my hand. Cedrick looked confused as he looked up at me. "What is an elf on a shelf?"

Shaking my head, I smiled. "I'll explain later. Sophie,

Cedrick isn't like one of those, but he is a bit magical like Alex."

"That's so awesome."

"Sophie, you're supposed to wait by the door, not move out it," Oliver, my nephew, said as he appeared in the doorway. "Aunty Paige." He smiled and was about to step out to give me a hug when he saw Cedrick. "Who're you?"

"Prince Cedrick Nelydriel, from the fae land Airrile." Cedrick bowed. "I have heard all about you, Oliver."

"Yeah?"

"Yes, your aunt talks about you a lot."

"He's Aunty's boyfriend like Asher, and Nate, and Ezra, and Alex, and Thorn." Dear lord, did she have to list them all. "Isn't that the bestest?" she cried, and grabbed Oliver's arm waving it around. "He said I can call him Uncle and that he's an elf, but not like an elf on the shelf," Sophie informed her brother.

Oliver nodded. "That's cool."

Sophie smiled. "That's what I said." She sobered and then looked back up at Cedrick. "Wait, you said you're a prince? Like a real-life prince? Do you have a crown?"

"I am, and yes I do."

Sophie screamed, jumping up and down. It was then Leon and Jake, the bear shifters who helped guard my family, appeared with guns drawn. "What?" Leon yelled before he noticed Cedrick and me. "My queen, you're back." He bowed, as did Jake, both putting away their weapons.

"Only for a little while, guys. It's good to see you both."

"You as well, my queen." Jake smiled and Leon nodded, also grinning. Then they both looked at Cedrick.

"This is Cedrick Nelydriel, Prince of Airrile, my new bonded mate."

"Welcome, Prince Cedrick. I'm sure you'll love it here as we do now. We have such an amazing queen," Leon said with a bow, and I blushed right away.

"I'm sure I will. She is wonderful."

"Can we go now?" Oliver asked.

"Of course we can." Jake tapped Oliver on the arm with his fist. "This little guy is keen to watch the guards fight, and Miss Muppet would like to wander the stalls. She heard there may be cotton candy."

My brows dipped. "The guards are fighting?"

"In competition, yes." Leon nodded.

"What for?"

"To be on the force to protect the queen and her wonderful family."

My body jolted in shock. "People want to beat each other up so they can work for me?"

Jake laughed, and Leon grinned, showing all his teeth before saying, "Of course, it's an honor. But don't worry, it's not fighting to the death, else we wouldn't be allowed to take the children to see. Yasmin said so." He glanced down at the children. "We must be on our way. Our best wishes for the times ahead, my queen."

"Thank you, Leon and Jake. Kids, give me big hugs." I opened my arms, and they walked right into them. I wrapped them tightly and kissed the tops of their heads. "Be good, and remember, who loves you the most?"

"Ezra," Sophie shouted.

"Nate." Oliver grinned.

"No!" I cried. "I'm going to have to talk to those two. Now, who is it?"

"You," they said at the same time.

"That's right. Have fun."

Sophie turned to Cedrick. "Can I give you a hug?"

"I would love one." He bent so she could wrap her arms around his neck. She let out a squeal when he picked her up.

"It really is high up here," she commented when he straightened. Laughter rang around us all.

Leon clapped his hands and held them out for Sophie. "Come, missy, let's get you hyped up on candy so we can hand you back to your parents."

"Yay," she cheered.

They started off down the hall, but before they were out of earshot, Leon said, "Children, you know we both adore you, but we have to talk about the rules again. What's number five?"

They groaned, but recited, "Don't open the door to anyone. Only an adult can open the door."

"Yes, so what happened?"

"I'm sorry," Sophie said. "I heard Aunty's voice and got excited."

"That's okay. We all make mistakes. Just please try and remember it from now on."

"We will." Oliver nodded.

Cedrick's hand touched my waist. "They are good men."

Smiling, I leaned into him and nodded. "They are."

"You are a wonderful queen, Paige. I can see it in your

people and how much they love you."

I shrugged. "They hardly know me."

"Yet, they look at you as if you've saved them. I know with time, when they do know all there is to know, they will adore you more." He turned me toward him and looked down at me. "I'm happy to be by your side, with the other men, while it happens."

Reaching up, I traced the backs of my fingers over his smooth, pale skin on his cheek. "I'm so glad you've come into our lives."

"As am I." He pressed his lips against mine.

"All right, you two, keep it behind closed doors. Unless I can join in," Ezra teased as he and Alex walked up to us. Alex and Ezra popped back with us for the few hours, while Nate, Asher, and Thorn stayed back to go over things with Xi and the other guards.

"Did you see Sophie and Oliver? We just did," Alex said. I loved how my men all warmed to my niece and nephew as if they were their own.

"That reminds me." I looked to Ezra with a mock glare. "Are you telling them to say they love you the most when I ask them?"

"I would never.... Okay, maybe." He grinned cheekily.

I playfully slapped him on the stomach. "Come on, let's go and see Yasmin so we can get back to the others." I didn't like being away from them for long; it made my skin crawl with unease.

Since the door was still wide open, we walked in. I wasn't even sure if she, or even Eric, would be there or at Sakura's. I chanced it anyway. I started for the kitchen when I heard voices coming from the bedroom area.

"Hello?" I called.

I was sure I heard someone answer, which was why I made my way to the bedrooms. It was why I opened their door without thinking and then screamed. I covered my face with both hands and chanted, "Oh my God, oh my God."

"What's wrong?" Alex asked. I felt him move me aside and enter the room, only to yip and brush by me when he quickly exited.

"Huh, I didn't think about that move," Ezra said.

"Is now a good time to meet them?" the smart-ass Cedrick asked with humor in his tone.

"Shut the door. Shut the door!" my sister yelled.

Blindly, I reached out, grabbed the knob—not Eric's that had been dangling—and pulled the door closed with a loud bang.

Turning, I stalked back out into the living room and paced. "That was something I could have gone without seeing." I groaned and placed a hand on my stomach. "I feel sick."

"You do realize other people have sex, right?" Ezra asked with a chuckle. "It's not just you."

"Shut up," I scolded.

I stopped by Alex and rubbed his back since he was sitting on the couch with his head buried in his hands. "You could have told me they were... that all three of them... that they were...."

"Fucking, doing the tango, bumping uglies—"

"Ezra," I warned.

Ezra threw his hands up. "Our poor boy can't even say it. I was just helping him along." If only he would wipe that smirk off his face, then I may have believed him. Then again, I probably wouldn't.

"Paige, it will be fine. Don't worry," Cedrick tried.

"Fine? You saw more of my sister than I would want you to. As well as Eric and Sakura." I scrubbed a hand over my face.

I froze when I heard the door being opened and then footfalls coming our way. Was it too late to make a run for it? Save me and my mates from this embarrassing moment?

My sister came around the corner with a bathrobe on. Her hands went to her hips as she glared at me. I scowled right back.

"Don't you know about knocking?"

"I called out. I thought I heard a reply, so I came to see. Maybe you shouldn't be doing that during the day."

Ezra choked on a laugh, but when I shot him a deadly look, he stopped. I lasered Cedrick with one as well since he was smiling like a maniac.

"Like you can talk. If you're not doing your queenly duties, you're doing your men all the damn time."

"So what? I'm allowed to."

"And I'm not?" she yelled.

"Ladies, I think we all need to calm down," Eric said as he turned the corner into the living room wearing only jeans. Sakura followed him, but at least she was dressed properly in pants and a shirt.

"Calm down?" I demanded.

"Paige," Cedrick murmured into my ear as he stepped close and put his hands on my hips. "It was an accident.

Let's forget about it and move on, beautiful. I would like to meet your family."

"Oh my," Yasmin breathed. "Is he yours?"

I grinned over at my sister. "He is."

"Yasmin," Sakura clipped. As soon as my sister looked to Sakura under Eric's arm, she warmed, her eyes softened, and her body relaxed while she took in the couple she loved. It was wonderful to see. Sakura smiled shyly, her cheeks heating. "That's better."

Alex suddenly stood and blurted, "I'm sorry for seeing parts of your body I shouldn't have."

Everyone looked at his burning cheeks and laughed.

"Alex," I called and held my hand out. He walked right to me, placing his hand on mine. I tugged him close and kissed his cheek. "You're the best."

"For now," Ezra added with a wink.

"Yasmin," I called after she'd walked to Eric's other side and curled into him, taking Sakura's hand and resting it against Eric's stomach. "Eric and Sakura, I would like you to meet my mate Cedrick Nelydriel, fae prince to the land of Airrile."

"It is a pleasure to meet all of Paige's family."

"Um, sorry about what you saw, but, ah, welcome to the family," Yasmin offered.

Cedrick chuckled. "Thank you."

* * *

An hour had gone by quickly as we sat around and caught up on things. I now knew Yasmin had controlled her hunger in such a short amount of time. Though, I thought it had to do with her wanting to get back to her children. The people treated my family with kindness, and Yasmin even admitted they made her feel like a pop star. Lenora, Michael's wife, had stopped by to spend time with Yasmin, which was good to hear. I knew they would get along.

"How are things with the guards, Sakura?"

She opened her mouth to reply, but the door opened abruptly, and Alma entered. Actually, it was Virginia in her twin sister's form. I could tell when she cried, "My son." She rushed over to Ezra, raining him with lots of kisses.

"Fucking hell," Ezra complained, but I could see the soft smile he had.

"It's so good to see you." She beamed, cupping his face in her hands.

"Mom, it looks weird you being in Alma's form and so vibrant. Can you change back?" Ezra asked, pulling her hands away from his face.

"Of course." Her body shimmered, and then there stood Virginia, a woman who looked too young to have a son Ezra's age. She faced me and smiled. "I thought it good to present myself as Alma in front of your people. I didn't think they would like to deal with me as Lucifer's woman."

She would be correct.

"Good thinking, Virginia."

She wiggled her fingers at me. "Come, come, let me take a look at my daughter-in-law." I moved over to her with a smile. She was crazy—in a charming way. She gripped my wrists and studied me. "Hmm." She nodded to herself. "Very nice."

"What are you talking about?" Ezra asked.

She ignored her son and turned to Cedrick. "You must be the new mate. You are a mighty fine fae." She curled her arm around my waist and nudged my hip with hers. "You must be pleased."

"I am."

"I can see why. Would you spin for me? I do like a nice ass."

"Mom!" Ezra yelled. "If Dad heard you say that...." He shook his head.

She scoffed. "He knows I like to look, but I would never touch when I have such an outstanding man in my bed."

Ezra groaned. "I don't need to know anything about your bed."

Virginia laughed. She hugged me tighter to her side, and then her face went blank.

"Give her a moment," Ezra said with a roll of his eyes.

Virginia sucked in a deep breath and blinked rapidly. She turned me, put her hands on my shoulders, and smiled brightly. The only thing that concerned me were the tears in her eyes. "Oh my hell. This is—" She coughed on what she was about to say. Though she didn't seem too concerned about what she saw in her vision. Did I dare believe it was good news?

"This is what?" I asked. She opened her mouth and choked on her words. I thinned my lips, wishing she could say something more. "I hate that you can't say anything."

She nodded but wouldn't stop smiling. She then raced toward Cedrick and hugged him tightly. The shock on his face brought a grin to my lips. She pushed him back, patted his arm, and then moved to Alex for a hug. Alex let out a sound when she squished him to her. Finally, she was back to her son and hugging him.

"I must run and tell Lucifer."

"Is it about the council? Our meeting?" Alex asked.

Virginia opened her mouth, made a sound, and closed it. Her brows pinched in agitation. So it could be about the council.

"What is any of this about?" Cedrick questioned.

"Cedrick, I'd like you to meet my mother, Virginia Morningstar. Seer."

Cedrick's eyes widened. "You see the future?"

"Yes, it can be a blessing and a curse."

"I believe it would be."

Yasmin cleared her throat; to be honest, I'd forgotten they were in the room. "Can you at least hint at something?" Worry tightened her voice. She glanced to me and then back to Virginia, who shrugged.

"You know what?" I started. "Let's just not worry about it now. Besides, it doesn't seem too bad if you're smiling."

Virginia shrugged and then announced, "I must go, and you all should as well."

"Why?" I questioned, fear taking hold inside of me. "Is it the others? Are they okay?"

Virginia pointed at Alex. We all jumped when his phone rang. Slowly, he pulled it out of his pocket. "Nate? Right, yes. We're coming back now." He hung up. "They have news from the council. We're needed back there."

I glanced to Virginia, but she was already gone.

"I don't like this," I admitted.

"Me either," Yasmin whispered.

CHAPTER NINETEEN
PAIGE

If I could go back and hit myself for wanting to go home, I would because saying goodbye to my family was hard. Cedrick wrapped me in his arms, while Alex held Ezra close as we transported back into the motel room we'd left from. Alex also carried a container of food for Thorn and me. Apparently, Nate had ordered him to grab some before on the phone.

I had a feeling it was so Thorn and I would be at our full strength, which was possible after feeding.

My stomach was in a nervous flutter of knots though. I wasn't even sure I could eat. At least not until I knew what was going on.

Dizziness swept through me when we reappeared. Asher, Thorn, and Nate stared at us from across a table. I stepped from Cedrick's hold, as did Ezra from Alex's, and we looked back, waiting for them to tell us what was happening.

"The council have contacted us."

"How?" Alex asked.

"Somehow they knew where we were. A bellhop dropped it off."

Lifting my arms, I ran my hands through my hair from the stress taking shape in my mind. "I don't like it. They know where we are. They knew we were going to

Cedrick's. The only place they didn't show was when we saw the shifters."

"As it's been said, we believe they're doing what they suspect we would do. They've realized we aren't stupid and want people at our back if it comes to war."

"It'll come to war," Nate grumbled.

It would, we all knew it. None of us liked it, but it was certain. They wouldn't give up what they were doing and suddenly turn over a new leaf in life where killing and kidnapping were bad.

We would have to fight them.

My heart thumped harder in my chest. It all felt daunting. My hands shook from the fear I had for my mates.

"What did it say?" I whispered.

"They're moving up the date of the meeting," Thorn said, his hands clenched at his sides.

"When?" Cedrick asked, his voice cold.

"We have a couple of hours to get there," Asher bit out.

"They can't do this," I yelled, and then picked up the chair in front of me and threw it across the room. Arms circled me and brought me into a chest. Cedrick. More warmth surrounded me. I could smell Ezra, Alex, and Nate.

"Unfortunately, they can do it, sweetheart," Thorn said gently from close by.

"And if we do not abide by it, it won't look good for us," Asher added.

Fuck.

Fuckety fuck.

Nate's nose pressed into my neck. "You smell different."

I shrugged, not sure what he meant or how I smelled different than any other time. I was too concerned about what would happen soon.

"It's probably because she's been away for a while," Thorn said, and Nate hummed under his breath before sticking his nose back into my neck and sniffing.

Having them close helped my anxiety, but I still felt the turmoil floating in me. Nate kissed my neck. "They're trying to get us unprepared and without our backup. But they won't. We don't need days for it to fall into place. Kiered and Xi left as soon as we heard to speak with the vampires. Kiered will also take Xi to the shifters. We're not trusting communicating through devices just in case. They'll come. They'll assist us."

"Did my brother speak with our mother?" Cedrick asked.

"He did," Thorn answered. "She's sending your people near the council compound. We'll speak to them when we get closer."

"Love, you need to eat." Asher smiled softly. "We have an hour here, but then we need to move to make it there in time to speak with the people before going into the trap."

I snorted. "Yeah, a trap. Maybe I could go alone and—"

"No," Asher clipped.

"Like fuck," Nate bit out.

"Not a chance," Thorn told me.

"As if," Ezra said.

"We'll be by your side always, and if you try to leave, I'll have Alex place you in your own bubble, one we can move around where we want," Cedrick warned.

"I'll do it, too, if you try anything to risk yourself for any of us."

My bottom lip trembled. "You all suck, but I've never felt loved and cherished as much as I do from all of you. Bastards."

They chuckled.

Sighing, I nodded. "All right, I'll eat, and then we'll all go kick some ass."

* * *

We all stood a couple of blocks away speaking with the large number of people who showed. The lion and tiger shifters were there. Cedrick's guards had just arrived, so he was off speaking with them. Asher was by the vampires having words.

By now, they would all know what they had to do. The vampires were taking the right, and the shifters were infiltrating from below. Alex had given them the tunnel system that led right into the dungeons. The fae would be taking the left, and some of our guards would enter through the back, if possible, while my mates and I would walk right through the front door.

As I stared off down the road, my mind drifted over my time with my men. I couldn't have predicted where my life would go. No one would have thought I would become a queen. A ghoul queen at that. But I wouldn't change any of it because it took me right to my bonded mates.

I thought Fate may have screwed me over, but I was wrong. My life was better with my mates in it. All of them.

No regret lingered inside me over having my family

brought into this mess. It was meant to be. The children loved it. My sister and Eric did as well, even after everything that had happened.

All I had to do was fight for our freedom from the council so we could live peacefully without them breathing down our necks or threatening any of us. We'd be safe, our people would be safe, and the other races would be safe.

All we had to do was win.

I glanced down, fiddling with the gown Alex had dressed me in. It was large and puffy at the bottom while the top squeezed me so tight I was sure my boobs were going to burst out. Maybe Alex picked it for that reason, since the council was a formal event and I had to dress over the top for it. Not only that, but I was a queen and was supposed to look the part. I allowed it, after a few complaints and sour looks, once he promised that when, not *if*, it came down to fighting, Alex would change my outfit instantly so I could move more freely.

"We'll be okay" came from my side. Thorn smiled down at me before he took my hand in his. "Do you believe it?"

"It's scary."

"I know."

"I want to believe it, but the council has done so much damage without the people knowing. They're capable of so much."

"So are we. You've killed with your bare hands. They hide behind their minions and use them as their weapons. We can take them."

Since he said that, I realized it was true. They did use the elite force a lot, and I already knew Nate, Alex, and

Asher were confident in fighting them since they had been the top of their classes.

Confidence. That was what I needed.

Hell, I had it in my men. I just needed to have it for myself.

I nodded. "You're right. We can take them."

Thorn leaned in and kissed my temple. "There's our mate."

"We're moving out," Nate called.

I swallowed; my throat felt thick. As we moved to our vehicle, I wanted to tell my mates how much they meant to me. I wanted to tell them to be careful, to fight hard, and kill anyone they thought would be a threat. But the words didn't seem enough. Instead, I dropped my shields and let them feel everything I wanted to say.

They circled me, touching me in some way. I could feel and scent them all. My hellhound, my vampire, my mage, my shifter, my ghoul, and my fae.

Before I could let my emotions take hold and break me down in panic and fear, I straightened and nodded. "Let's get this done."

Xi and Kiered had already left in their own vehicle. They would be having their own private moment before shit hit the fan.

We rode in silence, this time in a limousine, because appearances mattered. Too soon we pulled up in the front, and out the window I took in the daunting skyscraper building. The front looked like an old church, but at the back, it branched up into something modern and ugly.

The driver opened the back door, and Thorn was the

first to climb out, then Asher, and Cedrick. It was Cedrick's hand just in the door that waited for my hand.

Closing my eyes, I took one moment to myself and prayed for the last time.

Please, whoever is listening, no matter what happens, protect my mates.

Opening my eyes, I smiled at my remaining mates and then took Cedrick's hand. He helped me slide out in this monstrosity of a dress. I stood and moved aside for Nate, Ezra, and Alex. I could see Xi and Kiered standing up near the door waiting for us.

People milled around, looking our way. Some were vampires, witches, mages, shifters, and other things I hadn't yet sensed before to recognize what they were. There were a lot of humans as well.

It seemed the people had been informed of our rescheduled visit.

Asher took my hand on my other side while Thorn and Nate stayed in front of us. Ezra and Alex were at our backs, and together, we made our way up to their doors.

Into the link, I complained, *"Alex, I see a lot of suits, even for the women. I could have worn pants. I feel over-dressed."*

"Trust me, they'll think you're a little flaky from what you wear and then, bang, when stuff goes down, you'll be in your fighting uniform."

"So it was a ruse. You should have told me that, Alex."

I didn't need to look—his voice told me he was smiling. *"But it was fun to watch you freak out over it. Plus, you do look fantastic in it."*

"Especially your breasts," Ezra added.

My face heated. *"You monsters."*

"Well, I am, not sure about magic boy."

Nate and Thorn moved aside a little when we got to the door. The two guards there bowed when they saw me and then opened the doors for us.

"Is that usual?" I asked in their minds.

"No. They're usually stationed inside the doors and at the bottom of the stairs, but not at the door to open it."

"I feel special."

"You are special, beautiful." Cedrick winked down at me.

"Thank you." We entered, and the guards followed us in, along with Xi and Kiered.

"Please sign in at the desk, Paige Alice," one guard asked.

"She will," Nate answered for me. I sent the guard a smile and a nod of thanks. His head jerked back a little, as if surprised by it, and he looked to the other guard who also seemed shocked. What had the council said about me? That I truly was a monster made from darkness?

At the desk, a young woman stepped around it and bowed. "Queen Alice, it's a pleasure to have you here at the council headquarters. My name is Kimberly, and I'll be your guide today." She waved out her arm. "If you would please sign in." Thorn stepped up to the desk and went to pick up the pen. "Oh no, it has to be the queen."

"Why?" Nate clipped.

Kimberly cringed. "The one invited must be the one to sign in."

"That rule changes here and today," Thorn said.

"Please!" Kimberly cried.

"It's a fucking trap," Thorn stated through the link.

"Alex, can you sense anything?" Asher asked.

He closed his eyes so they didn't shine. *"A binding spell, I think. Hard to tell from back here."*

"Someone wants to bind Paige to themselves to have control over her."

"Alex, are you able to diffuse it or protect me from it?" I asked.

"Yes, already doing so. I'm not leaving anyone out this time."

Ezra's love for Alex washed through the link. *"Not your fault, and it turned out better with me in my human form."*

"Thorn," I called aloud. "It's no trouble. I wouldn't want Kimberly to get into trouble from straying from protocol."

Kimberly bowed over and over as I stepped up to the desk. "Thank you," she also kept muttering.

"Shit," Nate bit out. Kimberly whimpered, but quickly stopped moving her body and mouth.

I forced a laugh. "Now, Nate, don't be so grumpy." I smiled at Kimberly. "Don't worry about him. He's all bark with no bite." I wanted her at ease around me. I wasn't who the council made me out to be. I needed as many people to see that as I could.

Her smile back was hesitant and wobbly. Her fear was obvious.

Picking up the pen, I felt a slight tingle, but other than that, nothing. I quickly signed my name and put it back down. I lifted my gaze to her and smiled again. Her eyes widened a fraction before she caught herself and turned. "Right this way, please."

It seemed she wasn't our only guide. The guards from the front door walked at each side of Kimberly. As we walked, we kept getting stared at, so I made sure to smile and wave as I went. It annoyed me most of them were as shocked as the guards had been. But some of them looked at me like I was the shit they'd just walked on.

Kimberly led us to what looked like a waiting room and said, "If you'll just wait here a moment, I'll make sure they're ready for you."

I nodded. "Of course, thank you."

She blinked slowly, nodded, and then walked through the double doors in front of us.

"Queen Alice," Kiered called, stepping close. "I just got this delivered to me as we waited outside. A gift from our mother. Yeno dropped it off." He lifted his hand, opened his palm, and inside it sat a broach in the shape of a leaf. It looked very similar to the tattoo on my shoulder.

Through the link he told us, *"It's a camera. Mother wants to show everyone what will happen behind those closed doors. She'll be broadcasting it on... I think Kiered said Youtubiler."*

Ezra coughed through his sudden laugh. *"YouTube, man."*

The guards eyed him, but one stepped forward. "I will have to check it."

"They'll look for anything magical. They don't want to be bugged," Asher said into our minds.

"Cedrick, will it pass?"

"Kiered believes so. It's very new, as in it only got

designed this morning, which is why the delivery was late."

I took it from his palm and offered it out to the guard. It was then I realized he'd been blocking us from sensing him as his power erupted when he closed both hands around the broach. His eyes glowed purple, like Alex's, but they weren't as pretty or vibrant. Since I didn't need to hold my breath, I thinned my lips, watching to see if we were found out.

He dropped his top hand and nodded before passing it back to me. "It's fine."

I took the broach, and Nate helped me pin it to my shoulder strap. We continued to wait and wait. I knew the council members were screwing with us. They were probably watching from behind those closed doors.

I stayed in the one spot and made sure to keep the smile on my face.

"I'm so fucking bored," Ezra complained.

"You're not the only one," Nate said.

"How long do you think they'll make us wait?" I asked.

"It's hard to say, my love," Asher replied.

"Sweetheart, I forgot to ask, how was the visit home?"

Thorns voice startled me because he'd been so silent. "It was great. I wish you all could have made it."

"We'll be home soon," Nate said.

"I'm looking forward to it," Cedrick added. "The time there wasn't enough for my first time, but I got to see how our mate's people love her." He smiled down at me. "She was surprised when she found out how the guards are competing against one another to win a spot in the enforcers unit."

"It's because she leads with her heart. The changes she's already made have been taken wonderfully," Asher said. "Who knew so many were living the old ways?"

"What do you mean?" the other guard asked. Not the mage.

Smiling, I asked, "What's your name?"

"William, and that's Kyle."

"Well, William, I'm new to all this, so when I was told I was queen and then presented with a castle and the people in it to take care of, it was a lot to take in, and I worried I would be too different to rule." He nodded. "However, what I saw when I first arrived was a lot of bigotry and hate among different races. My first order of business was to ensure people, no matter who they were, could love and be with who they wanted. Without hate involved. Anyone who didn't like it was offered a chance to leave because I would never want anyone to be where they didn't feel comfortable or at home in." I smiled as I watched them both take in what I'd said. William seemed to like what I said, but Kyle frowned. I shrugged. "It may have something to do with how human I still felt, but I also knew, since I have six bonded mates of different factions, that I would fight to have them at my side. Just because we are different from one another shouldn't mean we couldn't love. Do you agree?"

"William," Kyle clipped. William glanced to him and Kyle shook his head.

William rolled his eyes but then said, "It's not for me to say."

"Then do you believe that people in a position of power have the right to do what they want? Even if it means killing those weaker or kidnapping them for other purposes?"

Kyle snorted. "Who's doing those things? Point them out and the council will take care of it. They take care of everything."

I shrugged again and kept on smiling. I was sure my face would ache so damn much from all the pretending. My heart ached for him, for all the ones who were blind to what the council really were. Evil.

"So you can't say." Kyle smirked.

Ezra and Nate growled under their breath. I shook my head. "It's okay, guys. He can say whatever he wants. The truth will be told eventually."

Kyle's smirk dropped.

Moving my gaze to the doors, I said, "I only wish for peace. I don't like fighting, competing, or bullies. All I want is to live with my mates, surrounded by my people who are happy, healthy, and safe." I looked back to Kyle. "Is it too much to ask for?"

He said nothing but held my stare.

"Whose coven are you connected to?" Alex asked.

"Morrison's," Kyle answered with a glare for Alex.

Alex's lips thinned before he said into our minds, *"They're worse than my father's coven."*

"That explains the hostilities," Cedrick said.

"I see that look. But I've heard about you, Alex Smith. You were an enforcer for the council like Nate and Asher. A mixed team, a weak team. You all ran when the mission went wrong and people got killed. You all ran to be with the woman who caused over twenty deaths."

"What are you talking about?" Nate demanded, his tone harsh.

"That's what we all got told," William said.

Kyle shot him a glare. "It's what we got told and what we believe."

Were the council listening to this? Were they waiting to see how we would react?

Well, it was time to get the show started.

I took a step forward. "It may be what you heard, but I don't see everyone believing it, and good on them for being smart. Do you want to hear my side of it?"

"No," Kyle snapped.

"Yes," William answered.

I smiled warmly at William. "Then I'll explain for those who wish to know, like yourself. Then you can judge for yourself. That night—"

The doors opened and Kimberly stepped out. "The council is ready for you."

Of course they were.

CHAPTER TWENTY
PAIGE

We entered in our little group, but with Xi and Kiered walking beside Alex, and Ezra at the back. The room was something like out of Harry Potter. It was circular and you stepped down at least twenty or so stairs into the middle where the council sat on a podium, leaving room in front of them on the empty floor. I wanted to snort at the thought of them wanting to be higher than whoever they spoke to on the floor. If they wanted to look down on me, that was fine. I would take it. I didn't care, because soon they would be stopped.

We slowly descended the stairs and stopped in the middle of the floor. Thorn and Nate moved aside a little, so they all had a view of me, and I had one of them.

They ranged in people. Older, younger, and middle-aged. Four were women, six were men.

I'd seen Gregory before on footage. He was the one who'd organized the kidnapping of the alphas. It was easy to guess who Jessica was. She eyed Asher like he was her salvation, even after everything they'd been through. Bet she regretted not giving him the time off now. My men could have been back working with the council if they'd done as Asher had asked. They forced my men's hands by rejecting their request and then trying to apprehend Asher so he wouldn't go anywhere since they knew, via demons, that the ghoul queen's powers had resurfaced in the area they had been on a mission in.

"Paige Alice, I would say welcome to the council compound, but unfortunately it's under terrible circumstance. Asher Evans, Nate Felan, Alex Smith, and you are suspects in twenty murders of humans," one of the middle-aged men said from where he sat in the center of the group.

I tilted my head a little and studied him. I sensed he was a shifter, but I could be wrong. "Forgive me, you seem to know who I am, but I do not know you." I knew all their names. I'd read the written files Alex had on them. I knew how each one was involved in something disgusting and why the council needed a clean slate of members, but I hadn't put faces to their names.

His jaw clenched. He didn't like I didn't know him. I had to hold back my smile from growing. He cleared his throat. "My name is Chryston Hem, alpha to the bears." Right, no wonder Leon and his people fled from this alpha. I'd read he liked to spend time with the young women of his sleuth. He was a rapist. I blanked my features. "Beside me is vampire master Samuel Person." He drank from people without ensnaring their minds. He liked his victims to scream. "Down his side there is Aaron Jilt, mage. Stephen Kinston, troll. Jessica Frank, vampire. Fiona Gemming, Valkyrie. Along my side we have Quinton Heil, wendigo. Gregory Kelton, vampire. Desirae Hunt, witch. Sapphire Wills, fae." Aaron liked to play with young boys. Stephen raided businesses for money and supplies. Jessica… well, I just didn't like that bitch since she was my men's former boss. Fiona liked to eat people, literally, but not like I did. She did it while they were still alive. Quinton often joined Fiona and made a game out of it where they hunted the people down. Gregory sold women. Desirae and Sapphire collected men. Men who were weaker and didn't have the power or strength to stand up for themselves. They used them however they wanted. Pimped them out to others, and then killed them after years of torture because they grew bored with them. They were also in a relationship together. I wasn't sure how Alex gained all the information he had, but it was valuable, and it fueled my anger toward them. I had to remind myself that they deserved everything that would come to them.

However, Alex hadn't noted Sapphire was fae; he'd found witch on her file.

"Cedrick, do you know her?" I asked into his mind.

"She was sister to Lenora. Thought dead. Her name is different, used to be Leanna."

"Now you know our names and what we are. Can we move on?" Chryston asked with a smirk.

I waved a hand around. "Of course."

"Before we move on, Chryston. I'd like to know the mates we haven't heard of," Desirae purred as she eyed Ezra and licked her lips.

Rage surfaced inside me. I wanted to slap the bitch, rip her apart, and then spit on her.

"Ezra, *my* hellhound. Cedrick, *my* fae, and Thorn, *my* ghoul." I didn't give them their last names. I'd hoped they didn't know about the connection Ezra had to Lucifer.

"Hellhound. I thought them mindless, killing beasts," Stephen commented.

"I'm sure he's a beast in bed." Sapphire smiled and then giggled with Desirae.

Keep it together, Paige. Keep it together. They will get what's coming to them.

"All my men pleasure me in bed, but I wasn't sure you all needed to know that."

"We didn't." Chryston glared down at the sluts. "Back to the matter at hand. Will the guilty party step forward?"

"Guilty? We are not guilty of anything. You say we killed twenty humans, but where is this proof?" I demanded.

"Kimberly, bring in the only survivor," Samuel ordered.

Kimberly scuttled out a door to the side of their podium. She rushed back in, her face pale. "He's dead."

"What?" Chryston snarled. "How?"

"K-Killed himself," Kimberly stammered.

All eyes turned on us. "You've done this—"

I laughed and shook my head. "How? You've had people watch all of us since we arrived. I didn't even know you had a witness."

"Because there wasn't one, since it never happened," Alex said loudly.

"Lies," Fiona hissed.

"I would like to tell you my side of the story of what happened that night. If I may," I asked. They all looked at each other, and I was sure they communicated mentally like I could with Cedrick. I wondered if it was a gift from Sapphire.

"Very well. Speak."

I fisted my hands at my sides. I felt like barking like a

dog, but didn't. Instead, I told them, and whoever was watching through the broach, in detail everything that happened the night I became ghoul queen.

"Why would demons come after you?" Gregory questioned.

This was where I could throw them under the bus with the proof we had. However, I wasn't sure it was the time.

"It doesn't matter," Jessica said. "Asher, Nate, and Alex are under arrest for treason. No one leaves the elite enforcers without permission. No one." She clapped her hands; the door to the left of the podium opened, and enforcers streamed into the room surrounding us.

"Come peacefully and no one will get hurt."

"No!" I cried. "You cannot take them."

"Love," Asher called, his hands on my shoulders. "We'll go. It's okay."

I looked to the floor, pretending to be lost in thought, but used the link to speak with with Asher instead. *"What are you doing?"*

"Nate, Alex, and I will secure the room outside. You need to give them everything we know on them."

"Throw them under the bus," Alex clipped.

"But what happens if they do something to any of you?"

"Angel, have more faith in us. We can take these guys on with a hand tied behind our backs," Nate said.

"You had all better come back into the room in one piece."

"We will, dove. Nothing will keep us away from you."

Finally, I nodded and straightened. Asher dropped his hands and he, with Nate and Alex, were escorted from the room with half of the enforcers while the other half stayed put.

"Kiered and I believe they will attack soon. The guards who stayed behind seem to be ones who don't like our group."

I took a look around at them and noticed their distaste for us.

Thorn, Ezra, Cedrick, Xi, and Kiered moved closer to me. I lifted my chin and said, "You took some of my mates away. Haven't you already taken enough, not from me, but from others?"

Some of them laughed. "What are you talking about?" Aaron asked.

Into our link, I asked, *"Cedrick, if the guards approach, are you able to make them believe they're stuck in quicksand?"*

"Kiered and I will work together. They'll believe it."

"Fantastic. I need them held back until I've spoken, and then we can attack."

"Finally," Ezra moaned through the link, while Thorn just smiled.

Taking a step forward, I smiled sadly. "It's hard being queen. So very hard because I not only want to protect my family and my mates, but I want to protect my people. Even the people who aren't my own, but don't have a voice or a say in any matters. Since becoming queen, all I have ever wanted was peace. All I have ever wanted was to live happily knowing that no matter who you are or what you are, or what strength and power you have, that you are safe and happy against those who wish to bully you, who want to corrupt you."

"That's a nice little speech, ghoul, but what is the meaning of it?" Jessica asked, smirking at me like I was about to lose everything I held dear.

"I'm talking about change. It needs to happen, in your life, in everyone's life, but mostly in the people who govern over all of us."

More laughter filled the room. "And why do you think change is needed?" Chryston asked. Was he really so stupid to lead me into subjects that they wouldn't want people to know about? Then again, they thought they had the upper hand since we were surrounded.

"Because all of you are the worst. You're all evil, vile people, and I'm willing here and now to stand up to you all."

"Foolish bitch, you have four. We have many."

I shrugged.

"Why do you call us such things? What is it you think you know exactly?" Samuel questioned, as if he thought he was trapping me into telling them everything, where I wanted to in the first place.

"I'm talking about what you have in the lower levels of the compound. How you kidnap those who are stronger than any of you to drain their power and life source. We know for certain about the lion and tiger alphas being taken. We have footage of it from Gregory's computer before it got deleted." I pointed to one of the guards. "I was sure I saw you on there." Watching him tense told me enough. He was probably one of them involved, even when I wasn't sure myself. But he'd been glaring at us pretty hard.

Gregory coughed and choked on the water he'd inhaled.

"Preposterous." Stephen laughed. He slapped the table with his hand. "All lies."

"I haven't finished. We have proof to show the people. We have proof over all your illegal activities. No council member should be involved in killing and kidnapping people or selling and pimping out women and men. Or taking little girls and boys and using them for their sick games. We have proof of it all, and it's time the people knew exactly who they have ruling over all factors."

Chryston stood. "Even if you had something, do you think we'd allow the people to see it? You are more foolish than I'd heard about."

Jessica also stood. "We're going to destroy you and your people, Paige Alice. I look forward to breaking the bond you have on Asher and claiming him as mine." She made her way to the doorway my men had gone through. "In fact, I might go and try now."

"May I eat her?" Xi asked.

I ignored his question and slowly leaked my power into the room. My claws grew inch by inch, my teeth lengthened, and I knew my eyes glowed.

"You'll not have him. You'll not harm what's mine. And I will protect anyone who wishes for it. This is the last day of the pain and destruction you've delivered on people. As of right now, my allies are infiltrating the compound."

Chryston roared. He pointed to Fiona and Samuel. "Go." He gestured to a guard. "Contact the others. Bring them here."

The guards tried. He called them on their two-way radio, but no one replied. When Fiona and Samuel opened the door we'd entered, we heard the chaos happening on the outside.

"The room must have been spelled silent," Ezra commented and chuckled when they started to look panicked. Fiona and Samuel disappeared out the door. Two gone, now eight to go and the guards.

"What have you done?" screamed Desirae.

"I've brought people with me who have seen the proof, who know just what type of people you all are, and now they're willing to help put a stop to it."

Jessica started for me, and I welcomed it. I was ready to rip off her head. But Desirae appeared in front of me. Her glowing hand pressed against my chest. I cried out at the sudden onslaught of pain. My mates swung to me, but Ezra was taken to the ground by Quinton. Thorn was thrown up into the air by Aaron, and Cedrick, along with his brother, were busy using their magic against the guards while Xi had shifted and was currently eating the screaming elite enforcers.

I was on my own, and I didn't mind at all.

I grabbed her wrists, and using my strength, I snapped them. She howled in agony and fell to the floor. I spun to Ezra, who was in his hellhound form, just as the wendigo sank its fangs into Ezra's hide. I sprinted over, grabbed the thing around the waist, and held on while it screeched and fought to loosen my grip.

Something hit me in the back of the head. I stumbled forward, dropping Quinton in the process. I glanced at

Sapphire. She stood there holding one of the seats in her hands, breathing hard.

"Stop!" Chryston bellowed. "Fellow council members, please come back. Take a seat. We shouldn't have to lift a finger to take down something like her." They moved quickly, all smiling, like they knew what Chryston had planned, which they probably did. "Aaron, if you will."

"My pleasure." Aaron's power choked the room. It wasn't like Alex's. It was smooth and sweet. It stunk and I wanted to get away from it.

"Blood magic," Ezra warned.

A portal opened, and a tall, smiling man stepped through.

"Fuck, that's the demon who worked with Grace. Rebellious," Thorn told us.

Shit just got real.

Rebellious smiled at Thorn. "Ah, the ghoul I was promised. Where is my mage I was also promised?" he asked.

"Capture them all first and we'll give you who you're after," Chryston ordered.

Rebellious glowered at the man. Chryston was smart enough to take a seat. Rebellious sniffed the air. "I want the girl too."

"No," Aaron said. "I am your master. I called you here. You will do as we ask."

Rebellious turned and stared him down, but Aaron looked right back. Xi stalked closer to the demon. I wanted to call him off. I didn't want him hurt. He was a pain, but a part of our family.

Xi leaped. Rebellious turned, grabbed Xi's snake head that was going in for a strike, and ripped it right off.

"Xi," Kiered cried. Cedrick quickly grabbed his brother.

"No, stop," I yelled. Xi dropped to the ground, and Rebellious kicked him hard enough his body went sailing across the floor, slamming into the seats. Xi tried to climb to his feet, but he fell back down.

Rebellious laughed. "Really, Xi. We've fought before, and you've failed. I know your tricks, beast, so don't bother."

Cedrick let Kiered go. He raced over to Xi and knelt over him, whispering things over and over.

Rebellious scoffed. "Pathetic." He turned back to Aaron. "Now, let's get back to business. The girl is mine."

"She's ours. You take the ghoul and the mage."

"You promised me riches and power like I wouldn't believe. You said I would be stronger than the devil himself. The girl's life will give me the boost I need. I'm taking her."

"I'm the one who controls the portal. I can send you back, and you'll never grace Earth again, neither will your minions."

Rebellious dropped his head back and laughed heartily. In a blink, he was right in front of Aaron with his hand over Aaron's face. Aaron screamed, and we all watched as his body shrank in on itself. Rebellious had drained him of his power in seconds.

"Now I control the portal. Come," he called, and demons crawled, flew, and raced out of the portal. Rebellious faced the other council members. "Shall we talk about a new deal?"

Desirae stood, her hands alight with her powers. "I can still send you back to Hell, demon."

Didn't they know when to shut up and let him think he was getting his own way?

"Alex, Asher, Nate?" I called, using our link.

"We heard, angel," Nate answered. *"We're trying to get back in there."*

That was all I could ask for. I knew they would be dealing with a lot outside those doors.

"You are not strong enough, witch." He waved her off as if she were nothing. To him, I supposed she was. He turned to me, and my heart dropped to my feet. He smiled. "You smell delicious. I have a feeling I could drain your power again and again and you'd just get more back. I'm going to have fun with you."

"You'll not have her," Cedrick said. He moved in front of me. Thorn also stepped in front of me, and then Ezra, back in his human form.

Rebellious paused. He glared at Ezra. "Why do you look familiar?" He drew in a breath. "You smell of home. Who are you?"

"Paige, break the broach," Ezra said through our link, and it was the first time I'd heard him so serious.

Still, I asked, *"What?"*

"Break the broach. Cut off the video, now." His tone scared me.

"Cedrick, can you make yourself look like a guard and grab me?" I asked. *"I don't want people to think I cut off the connection to the live feed."*

"Done."

I could still see Cedrick as himself, but I felt his powers around him. He grabbed the top of my dress, tore off the broach and held it up. "What is this sorcery?" He dropped it and stomped on it. His acting skills could do with some work, but it wasn't too bad.

"Answer me," Rebellious roared. He still hadn't looked away from Ezra. "Who are you?"

I took a step forward. "You don't need to know."

Rebellious's eyes swung to me, and he smiled. "Maybe I don't. You come to me, and I'll forget all about him, little queeny."

"No," all of my mates roared into my mind.

Movement caught my attention. I glanced to the council members who were currently trying to sneak away. "If any of you take another step, you'll be dealing with my mates."

Ezra snarled and shifted his attention their way. I could tell he didn't want to. He wanted to focus on the bigger threat, the demon. *"Don't go near him, Paige,"* Ezra sent me.

I couldn't promise that because I didn't like the demon's attention on Ezra, so I said nothing.

The council members froze; their faces drained.

"I have them," Cedrick said, his voice tight and hard. *"Please be careful, beautiful."*

"I'll keep an eye on the demons," Thorn said.

Pride filled my chest. I knew my mates hated the thought of me in danger, but they still showed me trust by leaving me to deal with the dickhead demon.

However, since Cedrick had the others under an illusion, Ezra shifted his attention back to the demon and me. Now it was my turn to trust him, even when it scared me stupid at the thought of something happening to him again.

"Little queeny," Rebellious sang. I glanced at him and discovered his hand stretched my way, wiggling his fingers.

"Do you really think you'll get away with taking me?"

He laughed. "Who will stop me?"

A form dropped from the roof onto Rebellious. The demon made a grab for Asher, but it was as if Asher was a spider as he crawled over the demon's body. Anywhere my mate touched, blood welled.

Rebellious screamed in anger before he closed his eyes and stilled.

My heart was in my throat; I didn't like it at all. I made a dash forward. A scream built inside of me when I saw Rebellious's eyes flash open. He smiled as his hand whipped out and clamped around Asher's throat.

"Fast little fucker," he growled, and then Asher's neck snapped. His body dropped to the floor, and he was kicked to the side.

I stopped.

I couldn't move.

I couldn't comprehend.

Then it all hit me—the rage, the fury, and the pain of seeing Asher staring up at the roof with no life in his eyes. Even though in the deep crevices of my mind I knew he would heal, I let in all the anguish and used it to fuel myself.

I locked my mind from my mates, shut down the link,

and slowly, I pulled my gaze from Asher's body to drill into Rebellious.

The demons around him yelled and cheered. Ezra snarled back.

I pushed them all away from my mind and focused on Rebellious.

Lifting my upper lip, I bit out harshly, "You shouldn't have done that."

Rebellious scoffed, his smile telling me he was amused by me. It was time to show him he shouldn't be.

A growl filled my chest and spilled from my mouth as my teeth grew longer than ever before and my claws extended even more. My body felt thicker, taller. "Asher is mine. You harmed him."

I rolled my head and stopped, my eyes on him again. He opened his mouth to say something, but he paused when I advanced faster than I ever had. In seconds, I was in front of him with my fist jabbed into his gut. He roared in my face when I looked all the way up at him.

He grabbed my arm and tried to pull it free. His eyes widened for the first time, and I saw panic. "You can't be this strong."

"You fucking touched what's *mine*," I yelled up at him.

Chaos descended around us. I could hear fighting, but I didn't move my gaze away from the one in front of me. The one who would pay the most.

Sluggishly, I twisted my hand up in his tight grip and moved my hand upward toward his heart. His body healed as I went, and I grinned, knowing I would be able to inflict more pain since his body repaired itself.

"No," he clipped. His hands around my arm smoked

black. It grew upward on my body. His eyes narrowed. Was he trying to work a spell and it wasn't happening? "What are you?"

"I'm Paige fucking Alice, goddamn ghoul queen." I ripped my hand free and easily slashed down through his head. I stepped back and watched him heal.

I laughed. Once he was back to somewhat normal, I asked, "Are you ready for more?"

He said nothing, so I picked for him. I flashed forward, burying my teeth into his shoulder while I grabbed one of his wrists and forced my other hand between his legs. I tore off his balls. Flesh and fabric filled my grip. He screamed and thrashed, but I didn't let go. My teeth stayed in his flesh, my one hand on his wrist as I dropped his balls to the floor. When I pulled my mouth back and moved away once more, shredded skin came with me. I wiped at my face with the back of my arm as I looked at the black smoke circling me.

"Why won't my power work on you?" he puffed out, his voice full of fear and pain chasing his words.

"I'm protected by my mates," I guessed, because I wasn't exactly sure why either.

His hands lifted in front of him. More black smoke poured out and made its way toward me. I stood still and felt its cold touch brush over my skin. I watched it for a moment and then grinned up at Rebellious.

"You fool. She's a ghoul. She can't be controlled or killed by darkness. She's made of it. But our queen is also right. She's protected because of her mates. You didn't think about that, about the other ghoul for her mate, about her vampire, and you didn't know about me," Ezra said from behind me. *"Mi corazón, you've had your fun, but there's only so much your mates can take. He will be dealt with. Come. Step back more."*

"No. He has to pay."

"He will." Ezra's words whispered through my mind.

"Love, I need you." Asher said.

I searched out my vampire to find him propped up leaning against Nate, with Alex at his side also. My heart ached. He was there, gazing back at me with his love shining through.

Rebellious roared. "Who are you?" he asked Ezra once more.

"He's from my own loins, Rebellious" came a voice I knew too well.

"Did he have to say it like that?" Ezra growled through the link.

The other demons all screeched and went straight back into the portal. Back into Hell. I shook my head in shock, not realizing Lucifer was that scary. I just found him annoying.

Lucifer appeared right beside me, causing me to jump. He winked down at me, and I glared up at him. He chuckled and slung an arm over my shoulder. "I'll have to watch myself around you, my dear. Taking his balls was a little harsh, darling."

"Not harsh enough. I would have made him eat them."

"And I believe you, but you have better things to do." He smiled and looked at Rebellious. "You've really fucked up this time, Rebellious. If you had stayed away, this battle would be over. But then you showed your face. Did I hear you want to steal my daughter-in-law?" He shook me slightly at his side.

"Daughter-in-law?"

Lucifer clicked his fingers and pointed at Rebellious. "You got it. Sweet but temperamental, which I'm sure you've noticed by now. Paige Alice is mated to my son, Ezra. Do you want to run right back through that portal and let it be known to any demon who fucks with my family they'll be turned to ashes instantly?"

Rebellious stayed still.

"No? Pity. I'll have someone else spread the word then." Lucifer sighed. "I guess it's time I take care of you, Rebellious."

"Please no, master. I beg you. Please let me live, and I will do anything you want. Anything."

Lucifer straightened. His calm exterior faded and, in its place, stood a hard man who nearly had me fleeing from the look in his eyes.

"It's too late. You harmed my loyal guard. You threatened my family." In a flash, Lucifer was in front of Rebellious. His body glowed red. The heat coming off him swept out around the room. Lucifer wrapped a hand around Rebellious's neck as his body grew brighter and brighter. It traveled up his arm and down over Rebellious, who bellowed in agony. His skin peeled away, revealing flesh, then bones, then nothing.

Lucifer sighed. The heat withdrew with the glow of fire. He walked over to Xi, who was in his human form, leaning against Kiered's chest. He crouched beside them. "See you've found your mate, Xi. Lucky bastard. I guess you're staying with them then?"

Xi nodded.

Lucifer reached out and placed one hand on Kiered's shoulder, the other on Xi's. "I wish you both the best of luck."

The doors behind us opened, and a group of vampires, as well as lion and tiger shifters, entered in a rush.

They all paused.

Lucifer walked back over. He ruffled Ezra's hair on the way. "Always good to see you, kid." Ezra complained under his breath and shoved him away.

"Dear Paige. Do you want me to take these imbeciles to Hell with me?" He gestured to the council members who didn't seem to be under Cedrick's illusion any longer, but all stared at me as if they saw something scary.

Cedrick's mind touched mine before I heard, *"They witnessed what a fierce, strong, and amazing queen you are, beautiful."*

Pleased they'd witnessed me at my worst—or perhaps my best depending on how you looked at it—it meant they might be more compliant with what I had in mind. *"Thank you, honey."*

I returned my attention to Lucifer, who waited for my response. "No, thank you, Lucifer. They need to stand trial for the people and be punished."

He bopped me on the nose. "Right then, I'm off. See you soon." He vanished right in front of me.

"T-That was the devil," Detroit stammered as he stomped down the stairs.

"Yes, it was."

He whistled. "You are a badass." He made his way over to the remaining council members. "Move and we'll kill you right now in defense." None of them did. I kind of hoped Jessica had. I would have loved to see her dead, and now. Though, it would come.

"Take them all to lockup," I said. "I meant what I said. We'll make it public—their trial and their execution."

"Asher, please. Asher, Nate. I never meant any of it. They forced me into it," Jessica begged.

Waylon stepped into her path and pushed her. "Move, bitch."

Raquel approached me, along with a man who looked like he was on his death bed at her side. It seemed she held him up. "Paige, thank you."

I smiled. "You found your mate. Was Detroit's brother there?"

Raquel nodded, and I could see, even with the unshed tears, she was happy. The alpha cleared his throat. "I have heard wonderful things about you, Queen Alice. The tigers are in your debt."

"As are the lions," Detroit called.

"No need." I waved them off. "I'm just happy it's over."

"We still have a few things to deal with though, love. Before we can leave," Asher called.

I groaned as I made my way over to him. People laughed. Finnegan was in front of me in seconds. He bowed. "If you will, we will take care of everything here while you all rest."

"That would be amazing, Finnegan. Thank you." He bowed again and then flashed away. Others started out the doors as well.

"Come to me, please," I said as I dropped to my knees

beside Asher and took his face in my hands. I studied him, my heart only easing a little seeing him alive. Tears brimmed and blurred my vision. I leaned in and kissed him. Suddenly I was surrounded by all my men in a huddle on the floor.

"We've done it," Thorn said, smiling.

"We have." I grinned, letting Thorn's words sink in.

Finally, the fear evaporated from my body. We actually had a future I looked forward to.

EPILOGUE
PAIGE

"Dearly beloved, we are gathered here in the sight of God —" A throat cleared, and the minister blanched. "—and Lucifer." He nodded. "In the presence of family and friends to join together these men and this woman in holy —" A throat cleared again. The minister wiped at his sweaty brow while I looked over my shoulder and glared at the devil. "—in holy *and* unholy matrimony. Who here gives this bride away?"

"I do," Xi answered and glared at everyone.

"It should have been me," I heard from Lucifer. Thankfully Virginia shushed him.

The minister tipped his head at Xi. "Thank you. You may take a seat now."

"No," Xi clipped.

The minister's head jerked back. "No?"

"I'm staying here."

"Xi, I swear I will cut off Kiered's—" Before I could finish my threat, he backed away.

"See what I mean about her temper?" Lucifer whispered, not quiet enough though, of course.

"We should have eloped," I told my mates.

"Relax, sweetheart, it's nearly done." Thorn smiled from around Asher, who was at my side.

"Then we can get to the good part," Ezra commented,

causing laughter from the crowd. His father was the loudest.

"Everyone shut the fuck up so we can get married," Nate yelled.

"Nate, really?" Alex snarked.

I glanced up at Cedrick on my other side. "Your mother must think we're all crazy." I was too scared to even glance at Castilina to see her expression, worried it would be a scowl of disgust.

He grinned down at me. "My mother loves you too much to be worried about any of this."

I hoped that was true and stayed that way because I was close to killing Satan.

"Love, it's fine. Now pay attention so we can have you as our wife."

A grin swept over me. I beamed up at Asher. "Okay."

The minister went on, and I was grateful Lucifer didn't open his mouth again. I still couldn't believe my men agreed to do this for me. When I'd brought up the idea of marking them in some way, it hadn't even crossed my mind about having them wear my ring from marriage. When my sister suggested it, I fell in love with the idea but wasn't sure the guys would go for it.

I was wrong. They loved the idea.

Which was how, one month after the battle with the council, after their trials and executions, which all factions could view, we were finally home and getting married. It had taken us what seemed like forever to figure out who would make good council members. People we trusted, people we knew wouldn't lead anyone astray or become corrupted by power and money.

Until Alex suggested the people we already knew.

Aggie, Clyde, and Felnick all moved to the council building. They would be missed dearly, but I knew they were going to do amazing as they worked alongside Raquel, Detroit, and William. They still had two more positions to fill, but there was no rush, and my mates and I were willing to lend a helping hand when needed. Though, from what we'd heard, everyone was happy with the choices, and those who didn't agree either kept silent or lived the way they wanted. Unless it was a way we didn't agree with; then we'd send the enforcers to their doorstep.

Already men and women were coming out of nowhere with complaints of their master, coven leader, or alpha and how they'd been treated poorly. Each case was looked at more thoroughly. We wouldn't blindly believe people until we had hard evidence in our hands.

It would be a long road to a world of peace between all communities, but it would be worth it in the end.

I was just grateful we were finally home. It was amazing to see my family again and it felt like the kids had grown too much since we'd been gone.

Since everyone had viewed what really went on in the meeting room with the council, I had the mages take down the shield protecting us from outsiders. We'd gained more people, even while we'd been away, but I'd made sure to meet them all when I got back. They'd been scared but hopeful for the same future my mates and I were after. Of peace.

The minister broke through my thoughts and said, "I ask you each now to repeat after me."

My men each took their time and repeated the vows. I

teared up over each and every one because they said them with such honesty, such conviction, I knew they meant every word.

Then it was my turn. "I, Paige Alice, take you Asher Evans, Nate Felan, Thorn Jones, Alex Smith, Cedrick Nelydriel, and Ezra Morningstar for my wedded husbands. To love and cherish. For better or worse, that means you Nate and Ezra, for richer or poorer. In sickness and in health. From this day and for the rest of our existence."

The minister smiled and nodded. "May the Lord and Underlord—" He winked at Lucifer. "—bless these rings, which you give to each other as your sign of love, devotion, and ever-lasting peace."

"Also a warning," I added.

"I'm sorry, child?" the minister asked.

"The rings are a warning to those who try and touch what's mine."

The minister cleared his throat and tugged at the neck of his outfit. "Yes, of course. As you place these rings on your partners' fingers, I ask that you repeat these words. This ring is my sacred gift to you. A symbol of my love. A sign that from this day forward, and always, my love will surround you. With this ring, I thee wed." As soon as we were all done, the minister announced, "I now pronounce you, ah, men and wife." He shrugged. "All of you may now kiss your wife."

My men surrounded me, each taking their time kissing the daylights out of me. Where if I breathed, I would be panting at the end. Hell, I still was.

We faced the room and the cheers of congratulations were deafening.

Ezra stepped forward with his hands out and pushed them toward the ground. The room quieted. "Thank you, everyone. Please enjoy the drinks and snacks in the throne room. Right now, we have somewhere to be."

I let out a squeal when I was picked up over a shoulder. Asher flashed us out of the room, but I still heard the laughter ringing out behind us.

As soon as he had me in our bedroom and the other men joined us, with Thorn closing the door after him, I turned and ordered, "Help me with this dress."

Alex had a better idea, of course. He clicked his fingers and all that was left on my body were my black lacy bra and panties.

"Are you sure about this, angel?" Nate asked as he stalked toward me already naked. My stomach swirled in delight.

"Yes. Double yes, triple yes, forever yes."

A few chuckles went around the room, then Thorn said, "She sounds sure."

"All right, angel. Anything for you." He lunged. His arms wound around my waist and we were airborne for a moment, while I felt Nate shift into his half form, before we dropped to the bed. He was getting faster and faster at shifting; it amazed me. He pulled back enough that I saw his snout, the extra hair, and his sharp teeth. He licked at my neck before he latched his teeth into my flesh and bit down hard. I wrapped my legs around his waist and gripped his shoulders, holding him tightly against me.

He growled against my skin when he realized my panties were in the way and he couldn't push inside me.

"Alex," I moaned and felt the bed dip. He was beside

us as Nate let out another growl of frustration. Alex clicked his fingers and I felt the cool breeze over my most heated part.

"He's more wolf at the moment," Alex said. I could tell since he wasn't already inside me like Nate, if he was in his human form, would have been. Instead, he was holding me while using his hips to try and find where he desperately needed to go.

Alex reached between us and gripped Nate's length, but Nate didn't want to be pushed back to line up at my entrance; he kept trying to find it himself.

"Asher," Alex called. I caught Asher behind Nate, his eyes glowing green with desire as he stared down at me over Nate's shoulder. He assisted Alex by pulling back Nate's hips. Alex lined Nate up and Nate thrust right inside, ripping a cry from me.

"Paige?" Cedrick called.

"I'm okay. He feels good."

Nate fucked me hard and fast while his teeth stayed embedded into my flesh. The pain and pleasure hissed through me, driving me wild. All I could do was hold on and enjoy the ride.

Nate paused. I opened my eyes and blinked lazily up at Asher where he remained behind Nate. It was then I noticed he was gloriously naked as well.

"I'm going to fuck him and drink from you, love."

"Yes, please." I nodded.

Nate let out a whimper when Asher slid into him. It took a moment to gain the rhythm back, but Nate soon fucked himself on Asher while he entered in and out of me.

"Wrist," Asher demanded. His pinched brows told me he wasn't going to last long. I loved how my men got so aroused by watching me with the others. I lifted my wrist over Nate's back and gasped when Asher sank his fangs into my skin.

My body reacted as well. I moaned long and loudly when my stomach ignited with that sweet swirl before shooting down to my pussy. My orgasm had me seeing stars behind my closed lids. Nate lifted his head and roared into the room as he shot his cum inside me. Asher hissed out a breath, leaned into Nate's back, still with his mouth around my wrist, and groaned through his own release.

Asher dropped to the bed, gently taking Nate with him. His chest rumbled with a purr.

"Alex," he ordered.

"Right here. Turn your head a little, dove." I did and felt Alex's magic fill the room. He laid a hand over Nate's bite and his other hand pressed down on my wrist where Asher had taken from me. It burned, but I gritted my teeth through the pain.

Asher's purr grew closer. I opened my eyes to see Nate had moved and gently rested his head on my stomach while Asher curled into Nate and leaned up to reach me. A finger traced my lips; then he bent and pressed his mouth against mine. I could drink down the purr he continued with when our mouths opened and we deepened the kiss. It helped me take my mind away from the pain, and excitement and lust surfaced once more inside me.

A loud groan had me breaking the kiss, but it didn't stop Asher from kissing, licking, and nipping at my shoulder, while I looked across the room to see Cedrick sitting naked on a couch and an equally naked Ezra between his legs.

My stomach clenched in the best of ways while my clit throbbed. My gaze stayed transfixed on Ezra's head bobbing up and down on Cedrick's erection. I dragged my gaze up to meet his stunning shining eyes.

"I couldn't resist a bit of play while watching you," Cedrick said.

"Play all you like, honey. I like watching you all as well."

"Merde," dropped from Cedrick's parted lips. "He's so fucking good at this."

Nate snorted. Through the pain, I could now feel him tracing his fingers over and around my stomach. *"I'm better."*

"You wish, wolf," Ezra said, only he never stopped sucking Cedrick's cock.

"Christ, you might want to back off. I'm about to—" Cedrick dropped his head back to the couch as he gripped Ezra's hair and held him still while he lifted his hips and finished coming while fucking Ezra's mouth.

I was soaked, and not just from Nate's cum but from seeing that.

Ezra suddenly stood. He pressed a hand to the back of the couch beside Cedrick's head and I knew, even though I couldn't see, his other hand would be stroking himself.

"Can I come on you?" he asked, his voice rough and low.

"Merde, yes." Cedrick ran his hands up and down Ezra's sides. We heard a sharp hissed breath, and then Ezra grunted out his release all over Cedrick's pale, perfect skin.

Alex sat back beside me, drawing my attention away from Cedrick and Ezra. He clicked his fingers, and I heard Cedrick say, "Thank you." Alex must have cleaned him. I grinned up at him before quickly glancing over to see Ezra resting his back against Cedrick's side while Cedrick had his arm wrapped around Ezra's shoulders, holding him close.

The sight thickened my throat. I loved how comfortable my men were with one another. Hell, if I wasn't me, I would be completely jealous of myself. I was a lucky, lucky woman.

"Is it our turn, Alex?" Thorn asked. I turned to find him naked, erect, and leaning against the wall on the other side of the bed, his eyes dark and hooded.

"I believe it is," Alex said. He moved up the bed and laid on his back. "Paige, come here," Alex ordered. Nate lifted off me and Asher moved back. I rolled over and climbed up the bed on my hands and knees.

"Slowly," Thorn demanded. I moved as if I was a lazy cat toward Alex, who was up on his elbows watching me, his cock hard, ready and waiting for me. "Suck Alex." Thorn's hard voice came from beside the bed. He'd moved without my noticing.

When I got to Alex's hips, I kept my ass in the air and bent forward. I cupped Alex's balls and gently rolled them around while I licked up his length slowly, causing him to suck in a shuddering breath.

"Changed my mind. Straddle Alex's hips," Thorn said.

He stood there running his hand up and down himself while watching. "Make sure you sink onto him."

"Gladly," I whispered.

"Please," Alex said just as quietly.

I shifted up, lifted a leg over Alex, and leaned forward as I gripped his cock and lined it up. I teased my opening for a little while, until Alex's hands gripped my hips tightly and he pushed me down onto him. We both sighed in pleasure as soon as I was fully embedded on Alex's length.

"We're going to fill you up, sweetheart." Thorn's hand traced down over my back as he climbed onto the bed behind me. His hand stopped at my ass, where he gave my cheek a light tap.

"Yes, God, yes." I nodded.

Thorn kissed my shoulder. "Give me your mouth first," he demanded. I rocked against Alex gently. He moaned under me as he looked over my shoulder. Thorn kissed me hard and yet so damn sweetly, it had my heart racing faster.

He nipped at my lower lip. "Lean down for me, sweetheart. Present your gorgeous ass to me." I did. I leaned down and captured Alex's mouth in a hot, slow kiss as Thorn prepared me for his hardness.

By the time Thorn removed his fingers, I was grinding down on Alex so hard we were lost in the motion, of the feeling of a close release. Then Thorn edged nearer. He pressed a hand to my lower back and I stilled enough for him to push into me slowly.

I was full, absolutely full, but it was wonderful. Thorn, with his hands over Alex's on my waist, controlled our movements. He pulled me back and I withdrew from Alex, only to thrust back into me and I slid back down on Alex.

I rested a hand on Alex's chest and one back on Thorn's hip, all of us slick with sweat. I let myself enjoy the sensation of being thoroughly fucked by two of my mates.

"I'm close," Alex warned.

"Me too," I said.

"Then let's do it now," Thorn clipped, and I felt his power fill the room and mix with Alex's power. His hands on my hips grew claws, but only one scraped across my skin over and over. Alex's hand slid up to under my breast where his power caressed my body, and too soon, I was climaxing. "Alex, Thorn," I screamed their names. Both men swelled inside me, and their cum implanted into me at the same time.

I collapsed against Alex's chest and felt Thorn back gently out of me. He helped Alex roll me over, and then Alex was there, using his powers on my hip and under my breast again. The same burning had me whimpering.

"Nearly done," Alex promised. I nodded, but kept my eyes closed. "There."

Opening my eyes, I glanced down my body. Alex handed me a mirror he conjured out of thin air. First I looked at Nate's bite mark on my neck. My pulse sped up. I dropped the mirror and drew my wrist up to see the two puncture marks there from Asher's fangs. A smile crept onto my lips. I skimmed my eyes over Ezra's mark while I sat up on the bed. I flattened my breast a little and caught sight of Alex's mark—it was of a purple flower. I bit my bottom lip and tears welled in my eyes. I kept looking and found Thorn's claw marks on my hip. I traced my fingers over them as I sniffed. My heart burst with so much love.

Not only had they been willing to wear my rings so everyone knew they were taken, but they'd agreed to mark my body in their own special way. Alex then used his magic to make sure those marks would always stay on my skin like Cedrick's and Ezra's did.

Lifting my head, I sniffed again. "I love them. I love you all. This is the best day of my life."

I first tackled Alex and hugged him tightly as I cried my happy tears. Thorn was next, taking my embrace with a chuckle. When I got to Nate, he groaned and complained about me leaking again. Asher swept me up into his arms and stood from the bed, hugging me just as close as I did him. He took me to the men on the couch and planted me on Cedrick's lap. I twisted and wrapped my arms around Cedrick and Ezra. "Thank you. Thank all of you for giving me this day." I sobbed into them.

"Beautiful, we would give you anything."

"He's right, mi corazón. Anything."

"What's that?" Alex asked. We all looked to him as Cedrick moved me around and tucked me into his chest while I held Ezra's hand. He stared at something on the floor near the door. He started to get up, but Nate held him back.

"I'll get it," he stated. Alex rolled his eyes, and we all watched as Nate went to the door, bent and picked up the piece of paper. He unfolded it, read it, and then his eyes became so wide I got scared. His heart also took off in a crazy beat.

"What is it?" Asher demanded. He flashed over to Nate

just as Nate's eyes rolled in the back of his head and he dropped to the floor. I cried out his name and rushed over there. Crouching over him, I checked his body for something, anything.

Asher laughed. I looked up glaring, but his radiant smile wiped that glare away.

"He fainted. He actually fainted."

"Why?" Alex asked. I realized all of my mates stood around us. My men had sleep pants on, while Alex had placed me in a thin teddy.

Asher straightened out the note and read from it. "To my lovely family, this is Virginia, Ezra's amazing mom. As a wedding gift, I am now able to tell you all something. Congratulations, you'll all be parents. Paige is nearly two months pregnant with a little ghoul or elf."

I froze. My body turned to stone. Cedrick dropped to his knees beside me. His eyes welled with tears as he dragged me against him and held me while Asher went on. "I've done my research, and I learned elves have healing powers. While Paige's heart beats, it didn't fix her reproductive system. Cedrick did when they bonded. Paige, darling, your body is now in working order. Of course, there is still some advantages to being different, you still won't menstruate or use the bathroom, but you'll be able to reproduce."

I lowered my hands from my throat and pressed them against my belly. I had a baby in there. A little blob of a baby. I'd thought I'd lost that chance. I was going to be a mother. My men, its fathers.

Asher cleared his throat, and I looked up to see Cedrick wasn't the only one with tears in his eyes; they all had them. We were all overwhelmed with happiness from the news. Asher scrubbed at his face and went on, "Congratulations to you all again. You'll make wonderful parents. I just know it. And Paige, if you think they're protective now, you haven't seen anything yet. I wish you luck because now they know their treasure carries another new treasure."

"Pick her up. Carry her slowly to the bed," Thorn ordered.

"Yes!" Alex cried. "I need to check her over. I wish Virginia told us before I used my magic on her."

Cedrick had me in his arms and did as Thorn said. He took me to the bed but sat on it with his back to the headboard and me between his legs. His hands splayed over my belly protectively.

Ezra paced the floor. "Did you guys fuck her too hard? Did we injure the baby? Fucking hell. Fucking motherfucking hell." He ran his hands over his head.

"Stop!" Asher clipped loudly. I was grateful for it. I knew he would be calmer than the rest. "Thorn, run and get a doctor. Alex, look between her legs. Ezra, go get some warm towels." They all raced into action.

Groaning, I thumped my head back against Cedrick's chest.

"Paige, my love, what is it? Are you in pain? Is the baby okay?" Asher cradled my hand in both of his.

Cedrick hummed under his breath. "Please, beautiful, talk to us. Tell us everything is okay."

When Alex tried to pry my legs apart, I'd had enough. It was my turn to yell, "Stop! Just stop." I held up my hand and waited for the others to come back. Ezra ran into the room from the bathroom and threw the towels at us. Thorn rushed into the room with the poor doctor over his shoulder. "See to her," he bit out and pointed at me. Nate then moaned and slowly stood, almost swaying on his feet until Thorn reached out to steady him. Nate sucked in a sharp breath, looked to me, and his eyes warmed in a way I had never seen. But then he shifted, causing the doctor to jump back. Wolf Nate trotted to the bed, hopped on it, and stood over me. He sat on my lap and snarled back at the doctor, the only person he didn't really know in the room.

"My queen, are you ill?" the doctor asked, ignoring the vicious-sounding wolf. She had balls. Good, she would need them when it came to dealing with my men and this pregnancy, it seemed.

Rolling my eyes, I shook my head. "Sorry to bother you. They're overreacting. We just found out I'm expecting."

The sweet older lady, whose name I couldn't remember for the life of me, clapped her hands and gushed, "Oh my goodness, this is wonderful news."

"Thank you, but please don't let anyone know yet."

"My lips are sealed. Please come and see me soon and we'll do some tests."

"I will. Thanks again."

She bowed and backed out of the room, closing the door behind her.

"Now," I started. "As you've seen, I don't need a doctor right now." Nate growled. I smacked his rump. He shifted off me, curled into my side, and rested his head on my belly. I melted. It was the sweetest thing to see. All of them were. It may piss me off, but I knew they were doing it out of devotion and love. However, I still had to say, "I'm not hurt. The baby isn't either. The baby and I can't get hurt if we have sex, so don't think any of you are taking that away from me."

"We will try our best not to hover too much," Thorn said, with a small shrug. He almost seemed chastised, but the way his eyes kept flicking from my face to my belly, I knew it would take time for him, for all of them, to understand. Maybe with a few kicks to their shins, they'd get it. Thorn leaned down and kissed me. He pulled back and smiled. "You're having a baby."

Giddiness rushed through me. I grinned back. "I am." Each mate then took their time to kiss me and then my belly. Although Nate stayed in his wolf form, he still lifted to lick me and then drop his head back to rest on my belly. It was going to be tough, but it was a hurdle I would love to jump through because this wasn't dangerous—this was one made from love.

My life couldn't get any better. I had everything my heart desired.

I guessed the Fates weren't bitches after all.

ACKNOWLEDGMENTS

The biggest thanks and appreciation goes to *Jay* at Covers by Juan. His outstanding talent for the cover work on the trilogy has blown me away. He's been an absolute pleasure to work with and I look forward to working with him again in the future!!

Becky, Donna, and *V,* from Hot Tree Editing, thank you all so much for your love and support on this endeavour.

Lee Ching, thank you for formatting these books and making them look beautiful!

To *all readers,* thank you for taking a chance on my work. Not only do I appreciate it, but Paige, Asher, Thorn, Cedrick, Ezra, Nate, and Alex do as well. If it hadn't been for you reading and falling in love with their stories, I wouldn't have had the strength to keep going because it takes a big leap for an author to try something different and believe it could work out. I'm so bloody grateful to you all for boosting my confidence with this series.

Lindsey, Rachel, Amanda, Susan, and *Sarez,* thank you for reading it early and helping me believe ghouls can find love… and a lot of it!

MORE BOOKS
Titles under L.Rose

<u>Hidden Kingdom Trilogy</u>
A Torn Paige
A Lost Paige
A Final Paige

MORE BOOKS
Titles under Lila Rose

Romance
<u>Hawks MC: Ballarat Charter</u>
Holding Out (FREE)
Climbing Out
Finding Out (novella)
Black Out
No Way Out
Coming Out (m/m novella)
(They're also available in box sets in KU)

<u>Hawks MC: Caroline Springs Charter</u>
The Secret's Out

Hiding Out
Down and Out
Living Without
Walkout (novella)
Hear Me Out (m/m)
Breakout (novella)
Fallout

<u>Romantic Comedies</u>
Making Changes
Making Sense

Fumbled Love

Paranormal
In The Dark (standalone)